Legal
Reserves

JAMES ROSENBERG

Legal Reserves

Copyright © 2018 by James Rosenberg

ISBN 978-1-7327612-0-9

Legal
Reserves

Prologue

July 16, 2017—Five Years after Graduation from Law School

BRIGHT LIGHTS ILLUMINATED the fourteen leather chairs surrounding the gleaming mahogany table. A video screen dropped into view with a faint mechanical hum. Once he received the signal from the nattily dressed man seated at the table, Jack Rogers dimmed the lights and as he started the video said, "I hope you are pleased with what you are about to see."

The man did not react, sitting motionless, staring at the images on the screen. The presentation lasted less than five minutes and when it was over the man leaned back in his chair, resting his hands behind his head. "That was tremendous," he said. "It should help our case significantly."

Jack let out a scarcely audible sigh having received the blessing of his mentor. "Ed, do you think they're going to be pissed when they see this?"

"Does a bear crap in the woods?"

Jack laughed as if this were the first time he had heard his mentor ask that question, his black hair thrown back slightly as his head nodded. "Speaking of the woods, that little scene where we caught them doing it behind the trees was entertaining, wasn't it? Do you think we should send them this video and give them something to think about?"

The man thought for a moment and responded, "No, if they really want to take this case to trial, you can shove the video up your buddy's ass during cross-examination. What we just watched will seal the deal if a jury ever sees it. We'll save it as our little insurance policy." He looked over at Jack with a wry smile on his face. "You finally seem to have this case under control."

Jack felt his pulse slow for the first time in weeks.

———

Mike Reigert glared at his clients, his clenched fist pounding the table. "I can't believe what my investigator reported. Can you explain it to me?" The middle-aged couple sitting in the fake leather chairs lifted their eyes from the copies of the seven-page report Mike had given to them at the beginning of their meeting.

The couple stared at Mike without responding. Rubbing his hands through his light-red hair, Mike's heart rate accelerated and he felt a trickle of sweat under his arms. He looked squarely at the woman dressed in an unflattering pantsuit. "Martha, I thought you spent all day in your bedroom. My investigator has you leaving your house by yourself three times in a week. Doesn't sound like you are so hurt to me."

The beefy man in the ratty sports coat sitting next to Martha put a hand on her arm to indicate he would respond. "Mike, this doesn't seem so bad to me. This means she didn't leave the house four days during that week."

"Mr. Gebbert, you don't get it, do you? Close is not good enough. You have to be perfect. If Martha is injured, then she has to act like she's hurt. Understand? The report has her going to the grocery store and then over to a friend's house. Think about what their lawyer would do with that information if he had it. You testified she couldn't leave the house. That can't be true if she is running all over town. If for some reason she absolutely has to leave home, like if she has to go to her shrink or to come here, you are holding onto her as if she is the most fragile thing on Earth."

Paul Gebbert stood from his chair and looked directly into Mike's eyes. "We understand what you are saying. She will do better. I will make sure you can trust her."

Martha stood and weakly grabbed her attorney's hand to say goodbye. Mike watched his clients leave the conference room and wondered what curveball his case would throw him next.

———

The peeling paint and stained carpet didn't bother Jeri Richards. She looked at the seal of the Commonwealth of Pennsylvania mounted behind the desk and felt a surge of pride. "Mom, can you believe this is mine?"

The well-attired woman with Jeri shook her head at the dilapidated state of the office. "Oh Jeri, look at this desk," she said as she pulled her hand away from the grime coating the top of the desk. "This is a mess."

"I know, Mom, but this is easy to fix. Judge Wecksel didn't care much about decorating. His bigger problem was he liked to use this office for non-legal acitivites. It's going to be different now." Jeri folded her arms across her chest and stood tall.

Sandy Richards stepped towards her daughter and embraced her. "I'm sorry to focus on the unimportant stuff. I'm so proud of you. I can't believe you are a judge."

Jeri beamed and allowed the hug to linger. The corrugated paper box her mother had put on the leather armchair in front of the desk diverted her attention. "What surprises have you brought for me?"

Sandy pulled back and cleared her throat. "It's some of your dad's stuff. I thought you might want it."

Jeri opened the box and grabbed a picture frame sitting on top. Her eyes immediately welled-up. "He was so handsome, wasn't he?" she said pulling her mom over to look at the picture. "I always thought he looked so strong in his dress whites."

Sandy put her head on Jeri's shoulder. "He was so good looking. At least you got his beautiful dark skin and not my pasty white coloring."

They paused for a moment, staring at the picture before Jeri said, "What else is in the box?"

"Just a few of his things I thought you might like to have. You can do whatever you want with them."

Jeri hesitated, sensing that digging deeper into the box might rip open old wounds. She slowly pulled out her father's police academy graduation certificate, followed by his badge and then some ribbons and other commendations. She gasped when she extracted the last item from the box.

"No way! Mom, how did you get this past security?" Jeri asked as she held up a sleek patrolman's sidearm.

Sandy blushed. "The nice security guard downstairs helped me with the box. I think he just took it to the other side of the scanner without sending it through. I guess I didn't look terribly threatening."

Jeri laughed, but kept her focus on the gun while she felt its weight in her hands.

"He never shot it. Twenty-two years on the squad and he never drew his weapon." her mom said. "Kind of ironic, isn't it? He was killed by that drug dealer, but never unholstered his gun."

Jeri sat into the chair behind the desk as her mother stood motionless on the other side, their gazes fixed on the gleam of the revolver.

Chapter 1

August 27, 2010–First Year of Law School

NINETY PEOPLE ATTEMPTED to enter the empty room at once. An excess of energy filled the space as the new students struggled to locate their seats, even though the chairs had name tags on them. The class swiftly realized they were to sit in alphabetical order and found their proper locations. The fresh-eyed students squirreled their backpacks underneath their seats and set their laptops before them on the tables. Some engaged in nervous conversation and made brief introductions, but most concentrated on the small door at the bottom of the lecture hall.

At exactly 9 a.m., the door opened and a tall, youthful man with one file folder under his arm entered. Dressed in a stylish suit and appearing in his early thirties, he contradicted every expectation they held of what a law professor should look like. The room fell silent as the instructor stepped to the lectern.

"Happy Monday everyone. I am Professor Norden. Welcome to Torts class." He immediately addressed a nervous young man in the first row without even looking at his seating chart. "Mr. Cashman, can you tell me what a tort is?" The distressed student cleared his throat and read out loud from the notes on his computer: "A tort is a wrongful act, not like a breach of contract, resulting in injury to another person, property, or reputation."

"Excellent, Mr. Cashman. You have passed your first test in law school. You may now breathe." The hall filled with laughter, dissipating a bit of the tension in the room.

Continuing his lecture, Professor Norden addressed the class. "The study of torts is fascinating. You will learn whether you are liable if you touch your friend, when you owe a duty to help a stranger in times of need, how words can injure and how to dissect the concept that in order to recover for a tort, the wrongful action must cause harm. This course will cover your entire first year of law school.

"You will be required to read numerous cases and discuss them intelligently in front of the class. We use the Socratic method, which allows me to call on anybody at any time, whether or not you want to be called on. I will ask you about each case to determine not only if you understood the opinion, but also how the court's ruling affected the development of the law. Not seeing any questions, let's start with our first case."

The energy level in the room spiked as the students accessed their computers to find their notes about the first day's assignments. In the third from the last row, a tall, rugged student shifted uncomfortably in his seat. "Did he assign work for this class?" he whispered to his neighbor.

Not wanting to draw attention to their conversation, in a hushed voice the woman responded, "Yes, didn't you receive the email about the assignments for the first week?"

"Shit, never got it."

From the front of the lecture hall, Professor Norden detected the conversation and zeroed in on the participants. "Mr. Rogers, please tell everyone what the case of *Vaughn versus Menlove* is about."

Jack Rogers fumbled with his laptop, hoping the opinion would magically appear on his screen and he wouldn't suffer the embarrassment of being the first person to implode in class. Realizing he couldn't bluff his way through, Jack considered admitting failure, but noticed the computer to his left shift towards him, allowing him to view the writing on the screen.

"Professor, *Vaughn versus Menlove* is the seminal English case that introduced the idea of the reasonable person to the law," Jack said, surreptitiously reading from his neighbor's laptop.

"Correct, Mr. Rogers. Can you give us the facts?"

"Sure. A landowner built a haystack somewhere near to the boundary of his property. He constructed the haystack with a chimney he believed would prevent the haystack from setting itself on fire," Jack said, now reading directly from his classmate's computer. "People living near to the defendant, the guy who constructed the haystack, warned him he had designed the chimney improperly, but he didn't do anything. The haystack caught on fire, burning down several of the adjacent property's buildings."

"Outstanding. Tell us more about what happened."

"At the trial where one of the neighbors sued the guy who built the haystack for destroying his property, the judge instructed the jury they should consider whether the person who fabricated the haystack had proceeded 'with such reasonable caution as a prudent man would exercise under the circumstances.'

Jack paused as the woman next to him handed him a note under the table. He placed the paper on his computer and read from it. "The man who built the haystack lost at trial and on appeal argued the court should have instructed the jury to consider whether he had acted with his best judgment. The appellate court rejected the argument, saying a better rule is to hold people to the standard of what an ordinary man would do in those circumstances."

"Well put, Mr. Rogers. You got the facts correct and also stated the holding of the court accurately. What is the significance of the case?"

Sounding more confident and no longer looking at information he received from his neighbors, Jack continued. "It means it's not an excuse to say 'this is the best I can do.' Courts will hold all people to the same standard–that of what a reasonable person would do."

"Well done, Mr. Rogers," said Professor Norden, turning his inquiry to other students. Jack let out a sigh. He leaned toward his neighbor and patted him on his back. "Thanks man, you saved my ass. Jack Rogers," he said in a hushed voice.

"Mike Reigert," whispered his new friend. "You did an amazing job appearing like you had a clue what you were talking about." They both nodded and laughed to themselves. Jack turned to the woman. "You also came through in the clutch." He gently touched her shoulder. She smiled at him and responded, "Jeri Richards, at your service."

In the hallway outside the lecture hall, the woman joined the two young males. "That was kind of fun. Think anyone knew that Jack here was completely faking it?" she said, while pointing at Jack, who was tall and trim with a flop of black hair highlighting his lean face. Almost laughing, Jack said, "anytime either of you need anything, ask. I will take care of it for you. You saved my law career."

Mike flushed red while Jeri put her hand on his shoulder. She said, "guys, if we continue to perform this well in class we are looking forward to an exciting year." Mike took a small bow and responded, "I think the three of us are going to work well together."

Jeri, wearing a t-shirt reading 'No Government is Better than Big Government,' said, "I can't believe Professor Norden didn't bust us today. We need to come up with some plans for how we are going to attack law school. Plus, if I ever forget to read an opinion for class, you boys are going to help me. Let's go get something to eat and talk about our futures." The three fledgling law students headed to the stairwell leading to the cafeteria, beginning a tradition that would last until they graduated law school.

Chapter 2

December 1, 2011–Second Year of Law School

THE NORMAL BUZZ of the school had waned hours before, leaving three figures sitting at one of the square tables in the basement lounge. Papers they had strewn about while studying lay on the floor beneath them as they gathered their belongings and began placing them into their backpacks. A few other dedicated students studied at distant tables.

"Good session, boys. Two weeks until finals and I think we are starting to have this under control," said Jeri to her two companions.

"Thanks for the pep talk. Keep it positive, even though we still haven't touched Labor Law or Administrative Law."

"Hey Jack-ass," Jeri responded, deploying her favorite nickname for her taller friend, "this technique worked pretty well for us first year. I think we're going to do even better this year." Jeri stood, ready to leave, when she felt her other friend's hand on her shoulder.

"Hey, I'm feeling a little horny tonight. You think we can have a quick one in the bathroom?"

"I would Mike, but from what the other women in our class tell me, it wouldn't be worth the three minutes it would take."

Jumping in between his two friends, Jack waved his hand in front of Jeri, compelling the slender woman to high-five him. Jack suddenly stopped and looked seriously at Jeri. He put his face directly in front of hers. "I've never realized how hot you really are. You have those beautiful, narrow eyes and that jet-black, perfectly straight hair. Let's dump this loser and do it in my apartment."

"Idiot," Mike said to Jack, "that's my apartment too."

"Good point," Jack responded. "Jeri, I guess we're going to your place."

"Not tonight Jack, I've got some laundry to fold."

Jeri put her arms around both of her friends. "Maybe tomorrow both of you will come to my place and I can do both of you."

Jack and Mike looked at each other and shouted, "Nasty!" They walked towards the staircase where Mike said to Jack, "Jeri would never touch either one of us before. It always seemed like she thought she was too good for us. As far as I can remember, nobody has gotten anywhere with Jeri. Maybe she's just a prude."

Jeri blushed and turned away from her friends, gently rubbing a small scar under her eye. Jack saw Jeri's reaction and said, "Sorry Jeri, we know you'll hook up with someone once the right guy, or girl, comes into your life."

Jeri yelped at Jack's semi-apology and jumped on his back. Mike smacked Jeri's butt, the sound echoing throughout the nearly empty space.

Responding to the commotion, sitting at a far table by himself, a silhouetted male looked up and *shooshed* the group. The three friends immediately stopped, directing their attention to the figure. Jack and Mike walked towards the table, smirking.

"Hey, Catulla, studying with all of your friends?" Jack called, loud enough to get the attention of the few other remaining students.

"Shut up Jack. I'm just trying to finish for the night."

Jack and Mike stood over Catulla, who held his law treatise in both of his hands. Mike joined in. "John, give it up. Law school's probably not for you."

Jack laughed at Catulla's evident discomfort. "Maybe you should quit and go to nursing school."

"You're an ass, Jack."

"Good one, John. Unfortunately, you can't back it up, can you?" Catulla slowly stood, looking up at the two boys, both whom were at least five inches taller than him. "You both think you are royalty and can do anything you want. "

Mike was enjoying watching Catulla get annoyed and responded, "We can, because everyone at the law school likes us. I can't say the same about you."

"Screw both of you," he exclaimed.

Jack immediately gave Catulla a two-handed shove, hard enough to push him back a couple of steps. Mike laughed and then patted Catulla on top of his head. "It's okay John, I'm sure if you study hard you might find a paralegal job after law school."

"You two think you're so tough, but you're just posers. You've both been given everything."

Jeri saw that the exchange was becoming heated and approached. "Boys, play nice. Let's get out of here."

"But we were just having fun with our friend John," Mike said. "He wants to join us when we go out tonight."

"Yeah, John's getting a beer with us, aren't you John?"

Jeri stood in between the boys. "I'm sure John already has plans. Let's just leave and let him finish his studying."

Jack and Mike looked at each other, straightened up, and then headed off towards the staircase. Once they were outside, Jeri gave her friends a stern look. "You guys have to stop doing stuff like that."

"We were just having fun," Jack replied.

"C'mon boys, it's actually time that you grow up."

They walked down the sidewalk towards their apartment building in silence.

Chapter 3

May 8, 2014–One year after graduation from law school

THE COURTROOM WAS teeming with activity. In the front rows, families huddled in clusters waiting for their loved ones to face the charges the government pursued. Off to the sides, two groups of attorneys, all dressed in suits, held stacks of papers and waited patiently. A few solitary individuals sat alone in the back rows.

Picking up a file from the pile on the table in front of the judge, the tipstaff called out a case. A young assistant district attorney appeared from the group of attorneys to prosecute the case. A public defender approached with his client from the back of the courtroom. The judge took the file and after a moment's review instructed the DA to begin.

Jeri watched the proceedings with detached interest from among the assistant district attorneys. She thumbed through the file for her next case, waiting for it to be called.

"Hey good looking," said a pleasant voice, momentarily startling her. "You checking out your boyfriend?"

"Oh, hi Cara. What the hell are you talking about?" Jeri asked.

"Mahon, I think our judge has a little crush on you."

Jeri laughed, closed her file and turned her attention to her co-worker. "And what would make you come to such a conclusion?"

"Everybody's saying it. You never lose in front of him. He's captivated by you. He sees you and bam, the defendant is guilty."

"Cara, none of us lose in front of Mahon. He's a prosecutor's dream. He doesn't worry much about burden of proof. If he doesn't like the way the defendant looks, he's going to rule against him."

"I don't know Jeri, I do fine in front of him, but you've never lost one case with him as judge." Cara lowered her head to look over her glasses into Jeri's eyes. Jeri turned away.

"Cara, I'm doing the DUI's. Any monkey can win those cases. All I have to do is show that the defendant was driving, get the officer to testify about the blood alcohol test, and I've proven my case. Not real hard."

"Did you see that article in the *Post-Gazette* yesterday about Mahon?"

Jeri shook her head, allowing Cara to continue. "Ninety-eight percent of people who go to trial in front of Mahon he finds guilty. Minorities make up a disproportionate number of the defendants. None of them have any money, so they all have to use the public defenders. They are good attorneys, they have a ton of principle, but they are so overworked they can't represent their clients properly."

"Plus," Jeri added, "a lot of their clients are actually guilty."

Cara nodded in agreement. "Some PD was quoted saying that Mahon doesn't even get the concept of presumption of innocence. In his courtroom, everyone is assumed to be guilty unless they are proven innocent. Mahon's not going to like that. That PD better hope Mahon doesn't find out who said it."

"He may be tough on defendants, but the people of the county seem to love him. He won his last retention election by the biggest margin ever."

"I know. He's going to be on the bench for a long time."

Cara stopped talking for a moment, checking out Jeri from head to toe. "I don't know girl, looking at you it looks like you are dressing for someone. Nice tight, but professional skirt. Blouse absolutely wrinkle-free. Even your hair looks better today–I don't think I've ever seen a bun that tight. Are you sure you aren't trying to impress our hot judge?"

"Yes, Cara, I'm sure. Generally, I don't go for fat, balding, middle-aged men with little to no personality." Jeri stopped and began to whisper even more quietly. "Didn't you hear? Corcoran's supposedly coming to the courtroom to check us out."

"No shit, I didn't know that. Are you sure?"

"I hope so. I need to move divisions. It's getting a little old prosecuting DUI's day after day. I want to move up and start working on the real crimes. Get some of that scum off of the street. Do I look appropriate?"

Cara leaned closer to Jeri. "Absolutely, you look perfect. You know he's always looking for talent and he's good at spotting it. I heard he once fired some young DA after seeing him ask just two questions of a witness."

"Damn, that's rough. Now I'm worried. I better look at this file a little closer so I make sure I can impress him."

Jeri picked up and opened the file. It took her about a minute to determine the facts of a file and to place it within the rubric she utilized to try her cases. In this one, like many of her other DUI's, the patrolling officer had witnessed the defendant driving erratically. The officer administered a field sobriety test, which the defendant failed. Later a blood alcohol test revealed an alcohol level well over the legally allowable limit.

Just as Jeri finished her review, the bailiff announced, "*Commonwealth v. Anderson,* all persons having an interest in this matter, please approach."

Jeri walked to the designated area in front of the judge to deliver her opening statement. "Your Honor, the Commonwealth will prove Mr. Anderson knowingly drove his vehicle while intoxicated. We will demonstrate his blood alcohol exceeded the legal limit by a significant amount. We will seek the maximum penalty for Mr. Anderson."

Judge Mahon didn't bother making eye contact with either of the attorneys. "Does the defense care to give an opening statement at this time?"

The public defender, a freshly minted lawyer who looked like he should be studying for his freshman calculus exam, had arrived at the table where Mr. Anderson sat only moments before the trial began. They hadn't met before. The PD, nameless to his client, fumbled with the file, attempting to review it as Jeri gave her opening statement.

"Your Honor, the defense will reserve its opening until after the Commonwealth completes its case."

"Very well, the prosecution may proceed."

"Thank you. The State calls Officer Yan Gomez." The patrolman took the witness stand next to the judge and was sworn in. Jeri jumped right in.

"Officer, please tell the court what happened on the evening of May sixth."

The police officer held his report close to his face to review it, and stated, "My partner and I were on routine patrol in the Sheridan area. We were situated off the side of the road when we noticed Mr. Anderson's vehicle being driven in an erratic manner. We eased into traffic and began to follow. The car proceeded to drive over the center line on three occasions. I turned on my flashing lights and pulled the vehicle over. When I approached, Mr. Anderson was in the driver's seat. When he responded to my questions, he slurred his words. I noticed his eyes were glassy and I smelled alcohol on his breath. I asked him if he had been drinking, He responded, 'yes'."

"Please continue officer," Jeri instructed.

"I got him out of the vehicle and administered a field sobriety test. He couldn't touch his finger to his nose, he stumbled when I asked him to stand on one foot, and he couldn't walk on the white line painted on the side of the road. I placed him in handcuffs, read him his *Miranda* rights and drove him to the station. Another officer administered a blood alcohol test which reported an alcohol level of point zero one three percent."

"Thank you, patrolman, I have no further questions." Jeri turned the cop over for cross-examination, having completed her examination by asking only one question and adding one "please continue."

While cross-examining the officer, the young public defender attempted to confuse him on his identification of the driver of the vehicle and on the record keeping for the blood alcohol testing. Gomez had testified for dozens of DUI arrests and understood the potential pitfalls. The PD was unable to alter the officer's testimony.

Jeri rested her case, assuming Mahon would convict the young man. In her brief experience, nothing more of significance would occur, as the defendant and his attorney recognized the looming conviction. The young public defender, after giving a brief opening statement claiming he would prove the defendant's innocence, surprised Jeri and called the defendant to take the stand.

The defendant sat in the witness box next to and slightly lower than the judge's imposing seat, his appearance suggesting a mixture of cocky and overwhelmed. In response to his attorney's questions, Anderson admitted to driving impaired, but claimed he chose to do it only because his friend was more drunk. He also said he knew he would arrive safely because he had previous experience operating his vehicle while intoxicated. Finally, he testified that the office lied on the stand and never offered him his Miranda warning, nor did the officer give him a field sobriety test.

Judge Mahon did not pay much attention or listen to Anderson's excuses as he testified. Jeri, however, saw the rare chance to cross-examine a defendant and wanted to demonstrate her skills.

She began, "Mr. Anderson, you knew you were drunk when you got into the car, didn't you?"

"Probably, but I was worried about my friend."

"Did you give one thought to anyone else on the road?"

"I guess not."

"Did you think about the elderly woman who might be crossing the street?"

"No," he said, avoiding eye contact.

"Did you think about the mom pushing her baby in a stroller?"

"No, I didn't."

"You didn't think about anything but getting home, did you? You didn't think of taking an Uber?" Jeri's voice increased in volume.

"I am sorry, I didn't."

"Sir, you admit you have driven many times before while impaired?"

"Not really," Anderson stammered, trying to make eye contact with Jeri, but unable to hold her gaze.

"You said during your direct examination you knew you could drive home safely because you did it before."

"I didn't mean I did that a lot."

"Yet you attempt to impugn the reputation of patrolman Gomez. Are you aware he is a distinguished police officer doing his job?"

"No," Anderson said, steadily shrinking in his seat.

"Sir, how many times have you driven drunk before?"

Judge Mahon finally started to take an interest in the courtroom proceedings, interrupting before Anderson answered. "Ms. Richards, why are you getting into that area of questioning?"

Mahon pointed at the public defender, not able to remember his name. "Please object to these questions. We are on the verge of creating appeal issues and that's the last thing we want to happen." He sneered and pointed at Jeri. "Ms. Richards, do you have any more for this witness?"

Jeri, recognizing she had gone too far, stepped back. "Nothing further, Your Honor."

Judge Mahon did not delay issuing his ruling. "Upon review of the evidence, the court finds Mr. Anderson guilty of DUI. Sentence to be imposed at a future date."

Jeri returned to the group of assistant district attorneys to await her next case. A tall man with short, jet-black hair, olive skin and an impeccably tailored suit walked deliberately over to her wearing a concerned expression.

"Jeri, can I have a word with you?

"Sure Alan, what's up?" Jeri responded nervously. "Did you like my cross-examination?"

Alan Corcoran stared directly into Jeri's dark eyes. Jeri found it difficult to hold his gaze.

Corcoran kept his eyes locked on Jeri. "You might want your convictions, but remember you represent the people of the Commonwealth also. You had your case won, and there was no reason to cross-examine the defendant in the manner you did. You almost lost the conviction by going too far."

"The defendant took the stand and I took the opportunity to question him," Jeri said.

"Listen, my job for the DA is to find talent to prosecute the real cases. The DUI's are crimes, but as far as I am concerned they are training for the nastier criminals who rape and murder. Remember, you represent all the people of the Commonwealth. Even if someone is accused of a crime, don't trample him. Everybody, even those who violate the law, deserve respect. Don't go too far."

A familiar tingling under Jeri's left eye reappeared. Corcoran's criticism shocked her. "I am trying to convict people."

"I understand. You have tremendous talent as a prosecutor, but you need to learn balance. Save the anger for the right cases. I've seen you now a couple of times let anger overcome you while questioning a witness. You need to maintain control and not let your personal issues get in the way. There are enough scumbags for you to go after. Guys like your last defendant aren't in the same category. He made a mistake. Go for the conviction, but use it as an opportunity to educate rather than to demonstrate your superiority."

Jeri recognized the merit of her superior's argument. "I understand, Alan. I will think about it."

"I have my eye on you Jeri. You have a ton of potential. I don't want whatever unresolved feelings roiling around inside of you to squash it. You can go far. Trust me."

Corcoran turned away to speak with another assistant DA. Jeri stood with one hand in her pocket, happy some decent people were looking out for her.

Chapter 4

May 16, 2013–Third Year of Law School

A **SENSE OF JUBILATION** consumed the law school students as they poured out of the last scheduled final examinations. For the first-year students, this marked the first time in nine months the overwhelming pressure subsided. For the students taking finals in their third year, this was the last time they would have to cram for exams, creating a sense of completion and an expectant look to the future.

Mike Reigert sat on the bench outside of the classroom stuffing his books into his backpack. He fidgeted until he spied Jeri leaving the exam, the last student out of the room. Jeri sauntered over to him, a huge smile on her face.

"We're done," she announced.

Mike looked at her with a weak grin. "Why so glum?" Jeri asked. "No more finals. Ever."

Mike took a moment to react, wiping some imaginary smudge from his pants. "I liked law school. I knew where I had to be. I had you to take care of me. I had Jack to raise hell with. Now I'm going to have to take care of myself."

"Dude, you know exactly where you are going to be. Geneva. Fighting international crime. Right?"

"It's not so certain anymore."

"What are you saying?"

Mike paused, organizing his thoughts. "Let's put it this way: things are evolving. You knew you wanted to be an assistant district attorney pretty much starting in second year. You interned there, you met the right people, and you got that job."

Jeri nodded and added, "Of course, I want to get scum off the street, but what does that have to do with you?"

"I don't know...you and Jack always had a plan. Jack made Law Review and told everyone that he was going to work for a big firm and make lots of money, which is exactly what he's going to do." Mike stood with his backpack and motioned for Jeri to follow him outside.

The two friends started walking down the street, leaving the law school behind. Mike continued talking. "I would love to make lots of money like Jack, but I didn't make Law Review and the big firms never seemed too interested in me. The job in Geneva would be great, but now something else has come up."

Jeri stopped and turned to Mike. "What's come up Mike?"

"You remember my Uncle Stan?"

Jeri smiled. "Of course, he took us out drinking first year. He's been to your apartment a few times. He's kind of cute, for an older guy."

"That's gross Jeri. He's old enough to be your father." Jeri smiled to signal Mike she wasn't interested in his uncle. Mike continued. "My aunt died before we started law school and he called me last week to tell me that his law partner just died. He says he has a bunch of cases going to trial and he needs some help. He asked me to come and work with him."

"What are you going to do?"

"I don't know. Uncle Stan has always been there for me when I needed him. When my parents split up, he made sure that we were okay. I want to help him, but that would mean missing out on Geneva."

Jeri pondered the problem for a moment and asked, "Is there anything positive about going to work with him?"

"Well, he lives close to here, so I will get to see you more. I certainly would get more experience handling files myself and would probably get into court a lot more often. Plus, I would be helping him out."

"How well will he pay you?"

"That's open for discussion, but it wouldn't be close to what Jack will make at Carlton and Sanders in Chicago. I think Jack's going to have to take us to dinner when he comes to visit."

"Jack will enjoy knowing he's making more than the two of us combined," Jeri added.

The two friends walked slowly towards the setting sun.

Chapter 5

July 9, 2014—One Year after Graduation from Law School

THE GRASS WAVED in the wind and the birds flew lazily above as the blue sky painted a soothing backdrop behind the two people ambling towards the house at the end of the field. The older man, dressed in jeans and a sport coat, carried a folder while talking to his younger companion, who was dressed similarly in jeans and a darker jacket.

"Mikey, we did good today. Got the delivery company to come to the table and we got a reasonable settlement for our client," the man said. "Mrs. Middlebaum should be happy. She never wanted to take her case to trial and now she will receive some compensation to pay her son's medical bills."

The man paused to look down at his feet and then turned to his colleague. "Mike, you helped a lot working up the file. Without you, the company might not have offered as much money. I am not sure if I've told you this, but having you here is a huge help. If you had decided not to come and assist me after Tom died, I would have been in trouble. You gave up so much to be here. I will take you to Geneva someday for the greatest vacation of your life. I wanted you to understand how much I appreciate what you have done for me."

"Uncle Stan, stop. You've told me. I'm enjoying learning how to become a lawyer with you. This is different than my original plans, but I like what I am doing. Would I meet someone like Mrs. Middlebaum if I lived in Geneva?"

"Probably not," said Stan, lean and trim, his salt and pepper hair moving with the gentle breeze, with a glance up to the heavens.

"I enjoy helping you with your files, but I want to handle more on my own and try cases in court. After working with you for the last year, I think I am ready to run with some files without you constantly looking over my shoulder."

Stan stopped and again turned towards his nephew. "Funny you should ask. I wanted to talk to you about this while we grabbed some lunch at the house. I am handling an arbitration hearing next week for an old client of mine, Mrs. Samson. The air conditioning company apparently charged her a little too much when she scheduled them to fix her cooling system. Overbilled her for a few things she says they never did. I'd like you to go visit her this afternoon to prepare her for the arbitration. She's a smart old woman."

Mike hesitated for a moment before asking how much was at stake.

"About two hundred and seventy dollars," Stan answered, avoiding eye contact.

"Wow, I better open up my calendar and make sure I have enough time to handle this massive case."

As they approached the front steps to the house, Stan said, "Listen Mike, I am lucky with my practice. I can take whatever I want and don't worry about how much I get paid. I try to represent solid people and if they need something, I assist them. From your perspective, I would suggest the dollar amount of the case doesn't matter. You want fair results and to gain some experience."

"I want to learn, Uncle Stan, but two hundred and seventy dollars, are you kidding?"

"Go talk to Mrs. Samson and help her."

"I'll go this afternoon."

A week later, Mike walked into the office Stan kept in the back of his house. Stan was reviewing deposition transcripts, but peeked over his bifocals when Mike entered. "So how did your first arbitration hearing go?"

Mike, dressed for court in a dark grey suit, crisp white shirt, and a steel-red tie knotted and hanging to his belt buckle, smiled sardonically. His combed hair framed his face and highlighted his piercing blue eyes. Mike eased into the wooden chair in front of his uncle's desk. "What's the difference? We fought over two hundred and sixty-three dollars."

Stan dropped the deposition and pursed his lips. "Let me ask you a couple of questions. Did you give an opening statement?"

Mike leaned back in his chair and contemplated the question. "Yes, I told them in thirty seconds how Mrs. Samson asked the air conditioning company to fix her thermostat, but the company charged her for an inspection of the air conditioner unit and repairs to the unit which they never did."

"Excellent, did you do any direct examinations?"

"Yes, I questioned Mrs. Samson about what she asked the company to do and what they billed her. I got her to explain how the company never did anything but replace her thermostat. We got into evidence the bill showing they invoiced her for more things than simply replacing the device."

"Perfect." Stan returned Mike's stare with his hands clasped behind his head smiling. "Did you cross-examine anyone?"

"Yes, I cross-examined the owner of the air conditioning company and got him to admit all Mrs. Samson requested was a repair to her thermostat and he admitted he had no documents indicating she agreed to anything other than purchasing a new one."

"Sounds right. What else did you do?"

"I objected on hearsay grounds when the owner tried to say his employee told him Mrs. Samson wanted additional services and gave a brief closing argument summarizing the evidence, discussing the relevant points from contract law and asking the arbitrators to award her the appropriate amount of damages."

"Wow, sounds like a productive morning. You gave an opening statement, directed a witness, objected, cross-examined another witness, and gave a closing argument. That's an awful lot for one day." Stan glanced at Mike in earnest. "Mike, those are the things you have to learn to do to become a trial attorney. Anytime you can do any of those, you do it to gain the experience. It doesn't matter how much the claim is worth, you need to develop those skills. If you can do those things in a two-hundred-dollar case, the skills are the same in a two-million-dollar case. You just don't want the big dollar one to be your first time."

"Okay, I understand, Uncle Stan. Thanks for the opportunity," Mike said failing to hide his sarcasm.

"Do you want to look-up the result?"

"Sure."

Mike walked behind Stan's desk to view the computer screen. Stan pulled up the court's website to check the arbitrators' award.

"Well lookie here, you won. The arbitrators entered an award in favor of Mrs. Samson for two hundred and sixty-three dollars, plus interest. You got everything you asked for. Congratulations."

"Thanks Uncle Stan, perhaps in my next case we can win six hundred dollars for my client."

"If you are lucky," Stan chortled while printing off a copy of the docket evidencing Mike's first victory. Mike grabbed the sheet of paper out of Stan's hands and stuck it deep in his file cabinet.

Chapter 6

April 19, 2013—Third Year of Law School

JERI, JACK, AND Mike entered the basement gathering area of the law school like they had hundreds of times during their three years of study, but the transformation of the lounge from earlier in the afternoon held them transfixed. Since classes ended, twenty round top tables, each covered with white linen, ivory colored plates, and shimmering silver utensils, replaced the scattered Formica slabs which usually occupied the space.

Like the room itself, the three friends had undergone a transformation, changing out of their casual class attire into suits and a flowing dress for Jeri. The room was filled with other students, faculty, and local attorneys attending the dinner. Jeri, Jack, and Mike had been so busy taking pictures earlier, that when they arrived everyone was already taking their pre-assigned seats. The three friends found their table, nodding to the classmates seated near them.

The lights immediately dimmed and Professor Norden appeared at the dais at the front of the room. Dressed in a tuxedo, Norden smiled at the audience and waited for quiet.

"Each year," he began, "we turn our venerable lounge area into a fancy gathering space to honor the students who have worked hard, achieved academically, and served as leaders in our small community. I want to welcome all of our distinguished guests and colleagues and remind everyone to eat quickly because we have lots of nominees in the various categories. So, enjoy the fine food and I will rejoin you afterwards to announce the winners of this year's law school awards."

A surge of applause rolled over the room as Professor Norden left the stage. Twelve members of the faculty outfitted in elegant server outfits emerged from the hallway carrying trays and began to serve the appreciative audience.

Jack, Jeri, and Mike quickly attacked the salads their Labor Law professor placed before them. They talked, forgetting the others at the table. John Catulla, sitting on Jack's left, leaned forward to interrupt. "Good luck to the three of you on your nomination for the leadership award. I'm sure you will get it."

Jeri opened her mouth to thank John for his kind wishes, but Jack spoke first. "Not sure we need luck, there isn't much competition."

Jack winced in pain when Jeri elbowed him in the side. "John, I think you and Steve have an excellent chance to win. I thought the retreat to the Supreme Court in D.C. you planned sounded amazing."

Jack rolled his eyes and made no attempt to hide his sarcasm. "The trip was *awesome*. At least four people signed up."

Catulla sat back, looking wounded. Mike leaned in to join the conversation. "Jack don't be an ass. A lot of work went into planning their event and I heard it was a success."

Catulla nodded at Mike and offered, "Everyone knows you three are going to win. You started the project to help victims of crime and I see so much action at your table every morning. I think half of the law school is involved."

"It's sweet of you to say John, perhaps you should also join us," Jeri suggested.

Jack rolled his eyes and spat out, "I'm not sure John wants to be a member. Plus, I'm not sure we are looking for his kind." He turned to Jeri and said, "Look at him, with that haircut and the clothes he wears to class. Wouldn't that be embarrassing?" Jeri immediately turned beat red and stared at Jack. "Jack-ass, now would be a good time to apologize and then shut up."

This time Catulla lashed out at Jack. "What the hell is that supposed to mean, Jack?" Jack refused to respond and looked straight ahead, smiling. "C'mon Jack, what are you saying? You think you're better than the rest of us?"

Jack continued to ignore Catulla. Enraged, Catulla set upon Jack. "You are such an ass, Jack. The project the three of you started is wonderful, but everyone knows you had nothing to do with how well it's going. It was Jeri's idea. She got the ball rolling and Mike does most of the work getting people involved. You Jack—you don't do anything but hang around collecting underserved glory and using it as a resume builder. They do everything and you take the credit. Jack, you're nothing but a fraud."

The commotion at their table was attracting the attention of others. Mike walked over to Jack's seat and placed himself between Jack and Catulla. He spoke to them softly. "Guys, this is a wonderful event. Everyone worked hard to get invited here, so let's sit back and finish our meals before we all get thrown out." He stood there for a few moments, waiting for his two classmates to calm down, and when he saw the tension level at their table dissipating, he returned to his chair. Jeri gently grabbed Mike's arm to thank him for handling the crisis. With her other hand, she touched the scar under her eye.

When dinner was over, Professor Norden began his announcements of the year's winners. For each award, he made the nominees stand, waited a moment to build tension and then identified the winner, who received an engraved plaque.

Norden announced the nominees for the Student Leader of the Year as one of the last awards. Jack and John Catulla stood next to each other without sharing a glance. Catulla did not respond when Jack nudged him with an elbow. After a suspenseful moment, Norden announced Jeri, Jack, and Mike had won the award.

When the three friends returned to the table with their plaques, Catulla enthusiastically shook Mike's hand and offered sincere congratulations to Jeri. He turned to Jack and under his breath said, "You're a poser Jack, and you always will be."

Chapter 7

August 20, 2014—One Year after Graduation from Law School

FIVE HEADS POKED from the tops of the hastily set up cubicles in the dusty storage facility. The smell of sawdust permeated the air and the lights swayed overhead emitting a pulsating, fluorescent glow. A computer sat on the desk in each work area, with piles of documents strewn about. Hundreds of boxes stacked floor to ceiling along the long bare wall of the barnlike structure remained untouched.

The five attorneys, who had each been present at the facility for months, entered the building daily at precisely 8 a.m., and left each evening at 7:30. Each day, without reflection, they ate the same sandwiches for lunch and pasta for dinner, dutifully returning to their cubicles to review additional documents to determine if they were relevant to the claims in the litigation or whether any contained privileged attorney communications.

Interrupting the sound of rustling papers, a male voice came floating out from one of the workstations: "Can anyone tell me what this case is about?"

"Not me," piped up a female voice from a different cubicle. "Doesn't matter either. All I want is to review my share of documents and go home."

"Like we did yesterday," echoed a third voice, "and the day before and the day before...." Laughter broke out among the lawyers in their stations, which quickly subsided, allowing them to return their attention to their computer screens.

A few minutes later, another voice rang out, "This case might be worth billions of dollars, but these documents are borrrrrrring."

"Why don't the partners in Chicago come here and help us review some of the documents?" asked another.

"Because we are the grunts of Carlton and Sanders, and it doesn't really matter if we understand what this case is actually about."

"Shut up guys," a deep male voice interjected. "I am reviewing a thirty-six-page contract right now. I think it may be the key document in this case." The voice paused for a moment, then continued, "Nope, it's just for cable television service. I'm going to mark it as 'significant' anyway because our client's cable service somehow might be relevant to some issue in this case."

Laughter again rose up from the cubes. The female spoke: "Guys, let's hold it down. I need to keep my billable hours up so I can get my bonus later in the year. Hopefully I will get it before the partners realize that I miscoded a bunch of significant documents."

For the lawyers, each day at the facility was indistinguishable from any other. An imposing neon clock hung on the wall near the entrance, its glowing numbers keeping digital track of the passing seconds, and serving as a reminder of everything they were missing outside of the trailer.

Late in the afternoon, Jack Rogers stretched out his long, lanky legs and tilted his head up towards the ceiling. "Who is going to the NOB tonight to let loose?"

Another voice responded, "I don't know. I heard there is a Shakespeare festival tonight in the park. Of course, only after they move the trailer homes will there be enough space so that the citizens of Chadron can attend."

Jack chimed in, "Since there is nothing to do in this backwards town, we will for the seventeenth night in a row be drinking beer and eating stale pretzels at what we call affectionately, Nebraska's Only Bar. Drafts will again be on special at two dirty glasses for a dollar. Can't wait to see you all there."

"With three million more documents to review, I'm not so sure I can go. I promised we would finish them by the end of the day," Vy Bock yelled from his cubicle at the back of the trailer.

"Not a problem," Peggy Gamble called out, "we can mark everything as significant and nobody will be the wiser. I do that anyway. I'm too scared to determine something is insignificant." Peggy made a small guttural sound. "Somebody please tell me what this case is about. If one of the partners sat us down and explained what the causes of action and defenses were, I might be a little more confident understanding how all of these documents fit together."

"You understand everything you need to understand," Jack said to the group, which he couldn't see from his cubicle. "We all know that smaller energy companies filed a class action lawsuit after they purchased electricity and resulting tax credits from our client and claim our company. . . ." Jack paused, waiting for the rest to call back. . .

". . . improperly billed them for the past six years," they yelled in unison.

"I find it funny," echoed Bill Pycheck's voice, "we can all quote from the one memo we got about the litigation, but none of us knows what we are doing or how any of this has any impact on the case."

The group of lawyers rose from their seats and assembled in Jack's cubicle. They were there unsupervised and frequently congregated to analyze the events of the day.

"I think I would be so much more effective coding these documents if I understood what the case was about, but nobody will tell us so I've been guessing since I got here," Peggy complained. "We're a pretty smart group. We were the elite at our respective law schools. We thought we would be at the center of significant cases, but every day we are stuck here."

Bill Pycheck eased his head into the center of the group and said, "The partners don't care if we understand. They think they have the litigation under control. Their primary concern is whether we are here billing away. Do you guys recognize the staggering amount of money the firm makes every day while we sit in this trailer?"

Pycheck ran over to Jack's cubicle and grabbed a yellow pad off the desk. After jotting down the numbers, he said to the other lawyers, "Five of us are here at all times. Each one of us is billing about eleven hours per day. Most of us don't go home on weekends and so we bill more. Conservatively, we all bill two hundred and fifty hours per month to our client; one thousand two hundred and fifty hours for all of us each month. Our hourly rate for this job I believe is three hundred and fifty dollars. Every month we are here, the firm is receiving over four hundred and thirty-seven thousand dollars."

Carl Shineen stood back from the group, dumbfounded by the amount they generated for the firm. "At least they are paying us decently."

"Decently?" Jack said mockingly. "We're each getting four grand in salary each week. I suppose we're doing okay, but think about it. Our salaries total eighty thousand every month, but that leaves over three hundred and fifty thousand. Where is all of the money going? Right into the partners' pockets as we do the work and they sit in their well-appointed offices back home counting the cash."

The group pondered Jack's conclusion. Carl Shineen gestured to the untouched boxes still stacked against the wall and said, "If we keep bullshitting like this, we may be stuck in Nebraska through the winter. I would like to sleep in my own bed someday, so let's finish some more boxes."

The group retreated from their conversation and straggled back to their cubicles to continue the review of the endless supply of documents. Two hours passed before they gathered their belongings and left the trailer. After a quick change into attire more appropriate for a bar, the group of five reconvened at the NOB and took their usual spot near the window. A few regulars sat on the vinyl stools aligning both sides of the bar. A barkeep wearily refilled the patrons' glasses. A gigantic moose head with a full set of antlers hung on the wall above the jukebox, stuffed and staring lifelessly over the small crowd, who were drinking whatever beer was on special. After ordering a round, the lawyers sat back to relax. The alcohol and conversation helped to diffuse the tedium of their routine.

"Another day, another four hundred twenty-seven documents reviewed," said Bill Pycheck, the only one in the group who ever said anything positive thing about their project and the time spent in Nebraska.

"I stopped worrying about how many I logged a long time ago," said Peggy Gamble, overweight, blonde, and the top student at her law school in North Carolina. "I realize now that I'm not where I thought I would be, but I do my work and by the end of the day, I've earned another eight hundred dollars—only thing getting me through those documents."

"They are starting to run together. Half the time I reflexively code them as 'significant,' so I won't worry I missed anything," said Vy Bock, a Romanian immigrant, with likely the highest IQ out of the lawyers present.

Jack wanted the group to understand his point. "This has to end soon. We've been here four months and if we are here four more it will interfere with my plans."

"What plans?" Bill asked.

Jack took a sip of beer and made sure everyone was paying attention. Staring Peggy in the eye, he pushed up the sleeves of his blue oxford jersey. "I am doing this because the partners told us we had no choice, but this is the last time I do their crap work again. This is for the bottom feeders, not for me."

"Where are you going to be the next time one of our clients tells us to review six million documents in Alaska?" Peggy retorted.

"I'm going to be the one who sends you to the frozen tundra while I'm back at the office having lunch with the client and making money off your work. They pay us decently, but the partners aren't doing any of the hard work, yet they extract a little bit of money from every hour we are working here. In a couple of years, I will send drones like you guys to review thousands of boxes of documents and I will take a little crumb from every minute you bill."

"You started at the firm about a year ago. How can you be so sure?" asked Carl Shinen, who was scruffy at the end of every day, with a tuft of chest hair peeking through the top of his shirt. At 26 years old, his head retained only a small portion of his curly hair. "Me, I'm not so sure of anything anymore. I thought working for a big law firm the women would come crawling after me. It's hard to test that thesis when every woman at the NOB is over forty."

Jack ignored Carl's personal complaint and responded to his original question. "Because I thought this through and understand how the game is played. My dad taught me a long time ago: it is not *what* you know, but *who* you know. I have spent a lot of time getting in with the people who are making decisions at the firm. Take Tyler Glass, the head of the transactional department. I had lunch with him and asked him to include me on any new mergers. He appeared receptive. Ed Wagner, the guy who got the huge verdict in the Gulf Oil matter twenty years ago, called me to his office a number of times. He says he wants to play golf with me. While you guys are reviewing documents, or researching the law for some memorandum you will spend three weeks writing that will be put at the bottom of a file and never read, I am making time with the decision makers at the firm."

The four other members of the group took in Jack's statement with astonished silence.

"Guys," Jack began again, "I intend to make partner and make real money. I am not going to bill three thousand hours every year and only drive a Beemer. The mega-dollars are the only reason why we should be doing this crap. I'm meeting the partners. They will introduce me to their clients and in ten years the associates who are performing document review are going to be drinking a beer and talking about how they want to spend more time with me. It's the circle of life, baby."

The others stared at Jack blankly. Jack held up his beer and his co-workers tentatively raised their glasses to clink. Their glasses touched, and Jack made them all say together, "Circle of life."

Chapter 8

May 26, 2011–First Year of Law School

THE SUN BLAZED down on the law school, the dark windows glistening with reflective heat. Nearly every member of the first-year class huddled outside the lecture hall where they had first met nine months earlier. Nervous chatter again rose through the room, but all eyes focused on the closed entrance doors. Every sound coming from inside the auditorium caused them to inch closer, but the doors remained unyielding.

"Dammit, this is so nerve-racking," Jeri said to Mike as they hung on the periphery of the masses. "Open the doors already."

Mike nodded and put a hand on Jeri's arm. "This is nothing compared to finals. We've done all the hard work. We can't change anything now. Although it might be fairer to everyone if they just mailed us our grades rather than putting us through this torture."

"Just one more way of testing us. It's tradition. They post all of the grades in one room. Force everyone to come in at once to find their grades. We will have to listen to people like Selma Weingard crow about how great her marks are or watch others slink out the side door so they don't have to talk about it. It's just humiliating. Our first year wasn't bad enough and now they put us through this just so we can find out how we did."

As they were commiserating, Maggie Conti, short and intense, approached with a nervous scowl on her face. "Where's your third wheel? I thought the three of you were joined at the hip."

Mike flashed a dirty look. "Jack will be here any minute. He went for a run to let off some steam. Said he wanted to just show up and walk right in the room. By the way, what did you think of that Con Law final?"

Maggie looked up to the ceiling and threw her hands in the air. "A complete ball buster is what it was. That last question—I typed for almost an hour. I spotted every possible issue in the fact scenario, or so I thought. Then I spoke with some people and they pointed out about six others I never considered. I suspect their analysis was crap, but they spotted more issues, so they win. I think I'm failing that one."

"I doubt it," Mike responded. "Those tests are like marathons. It's survival of the fittest."

"I'm sure you were just like us," Jeri said to Maggie. "We had our study group. We spent weeks developing our outlines and quizzing each other. Mikey here was our expert in contracts. But we all had to take five finals in the span of two weeks. It's just not humane. They treat us like animals."

"Yes, and waiting in this cattle call is our reward for doing such a good job," Maggie said as she walked away to join another group of friends.

Jeri and Mike stood in silence, but saw no sign that the doors were about to open. "It was so nice what you did for Jack," Jeri said.

Mike stared quizzically at Jeri without responding.

"The contracts final. You know what I'm talking about."

Mike didn't say a word.

"Come on. That night before the Contracts and Con Law finals—you were so ready for Contracts. At the study session, you led the discussion on adequate consideration and the measure of damages when a party breaches a contract. You said you needed to make one last push for Con Law. You wanted someone to help you study the proper scope of search and seizure and the limits of the Second Amendment's right to bear arms. But Jack asked you for a last quick review of adequate consideration for contracts and the applicability of the Uniform Commercial Code. You agreed to help Jack and, four hours later, you and Jack left my apartment. You never got to do a Con Law refresher."

"I know, but it helped me to go over the contracts material again."

"I don't think you needed it."

"We'll see. I just hope I did well enough. My dad probably doesn't think I will do particularly well, but I guess after my performance in college, he might have reason to doubt me."

"You're going to do just fine."

Mike suddenly flew forward a couple of steps after being pushed by Jack who had appeared from nowhere. Jack laughed. "Oops, I slipped." Mike ran his hand quickly through his hair and tried to appear as if nothing happened.

Jack smiled broadly. "I see they haven't opened up the doors to Oz yet. How's the tension level?"

"Pretty high," said Jeri. "I think they are keeping the windows locked."

"I'm looking forward to getting my grades and my invitation to Law Review."

"Pretty cocky Jack," said Jeri. "You know only the top ten percent get invited to join the Review."

"Yup. I'm better than top ten percent."

Mike smacked Jack on the back of his head. "What an arrogant ass."

"I need to be on the Law Review so the big firms will want to interview me."

"You know there are other jobs in the legal field than just working for some big firm?"

"There are? That's news to me." Jack preened for his friends, who turned their backs on his gesticulations.

As Jack was finishing his performance, the imposing metal doors at the bottom of the lecture hall swung open and a petite woman emerged. "Hey, it's your buddy, Ms. Andrews, the friendly neighborhood registrar," Mike whispered to Jack. She raised her hand and waited for the crowd to calm.

Once everyone quieted, she spoke. "Your scores for all of your classes are posted next to your student identification number. I placed a list at the far end of the lecture hall by the ID number of those who will receive automatic invitations to join the Law Review. Please take your time and please respect the feelings of your fellow classmates."

She stepped aside before thirty students pushed and shoved their way through the small door. The rest waited until a little space opened up before entering. Loud cheers and an occasional moan emanated from inside the classroom.

After waiting a few minutes, Jeri, Mike, and Jack entered, but split up, allowing each other to gather their individual grades without having to display false sensitivity in reacting to the scores their friends received. They met again in the hallway after viewing their grades.

Jack spoke first: "We don't need to compare if you don't want to, but sooner or later we'll find out what everyone got. I'd rather you guys found out from me than from the grapevine."

"I agree," Jeri said, "I'll go first." She glanced down at her notes and informed the two others she'd received A's in Torts and Civil Procedure, a B plus in Criminal Law and B's in Con Law and Contracts.

"You did so well," Mike said, trying to be supportive, yet overcome with a tinge of guilt, knowing his grades were higher.

Jeri looked at Mike. "Play your cards, big guy,"

"I got A's in Torts, Contracts and Criminal Law. An A minus in Civ Pro and a B plus in Con Law." Mike accepted Jeri's congratulations after she embraced him. He turned to his other friend. "Okay, Jack your turn."

Jack triumphantly pulled out his notes and announced he'd received A's in Contracts, Torts and Con law, an A minus in Civil Procedure and a B plus in Criminal Law. "We got the same grades," he said, grinning at Mike, "three A's, an A minus, and a B plus. Not bad, I must say."

A small wave of heat spread over Mike's face as he realized Jack's statement was inaccurate. "We got the same grades, but in different courses." He squinted as he tried to make the calculation. "Your worst grade was in Criminal Law, which is a four-credit course; mine was in Con Law, a six-credit course. If I am correct, your scores are a little bit better."

Jeri patted Mike on the back. "Guys, you did amazingly. Did either of you check if you made Law Review?"

Mike and Jack considered each other self-consciously and shrugged their shoulders.

"Go, you morons. I'll wait here and when you return we can celebrate how smart both of you are."

A few minutes later, the boys returned with Mike draping an arm around Jack's neck. Mike spoke first. "Amazing news, Jack made Law Review."

Jeri grabbed Mike's wrist. "And what about you?"

Mike's eyes couldn't hide his disappointment. "I wasn't on the list." Jeri put her arms around Mike as he sunk his head onto her shoulder. Jack excused himself to go to the bathroom. When they were alone, Jeri expressed her frustration.

"Damn, Mike, that sucks. He must have been the last person who made it and you missed by percentage points. I'm so sorry."

Mike hung his head momentarily, upset because he viewed making the Law Review as validation of all of his hard work. To be so close unexpectedly hurt.

Jeri turned to him again. "I feel so bad for you. You helped Jack so much in Contracts, I bet you raised his grade from a B to an A. I wonder if you got the chance to make that last Con Law push if it would have made any difference."

Mike let the question hang, because the same issue was bouncing around in his head.

After a few moments, Mike's spirits lifted. He turned to Jeri. "I'm fine. I did a lot better than I expected. Certainly better than my dad thought I would do. I still have next year to get onto Law Review."

Chapter 9

May 26, 2011, First Year of Law School

AFTER GETTING THEIR scores, Jeri, Jack, and Mike hurried out of the law school into the fading sunlight. The intolerable stress of first year, building for nine months, vanished with the knowledge they would ultimately become lawyers. Not muddle their way through, but actually do well in their classes, with a chance of having successful legal careers.

"They can't break us. We made it," Jeri yelled as she skipped backwards down the sidewalk, facing her two friends.

Mike felt the fading sunlight on his face and responded, "No more Socratic Method this summer. I can start thinking like a human again and not analyze every situation from every angle."

Jack smacked Mike on the back of his head and ran further ahead. "They may have broken us down, but we survived. We're going to Loopers and celebrate."

They entered the bar and spied a few of their classmates at tables in the back, but wanted to avoid them. They grabbed a table away from the crowd. Throwing their backpacks under the high-top table, Jack motioned to a waitress and ordered them a pitcher of beer. None of them cared what type they drank as long as it was cold and kept coming.

The coolness of the mug in his hand relaxed Mike. "Congratulations to us. We made it through our first year of law school." They clinked their mugs and laughed as froth sloshed over the rim of their glasses onto the table.

Taking a generous swig and gagging slightly, Jeri announced she was still unable to drink beer, especially in the quantities of her two friends. She put her mug down and glared intently at Jack and Mike. "I love hanging with the two of you. You made our first year bearable and I will always be grateful." Again they raised their mugs.

"It was an amazing year, guys. I enjoyed spending time with you much more than I would have with the other bastards in our class," Jack said, tossing his head over his shoulder towards the others in the bar. Jack gave a sly smile. "I was actually waiting for the two of you to thank me for getting you through all of your classes."

He sat back, looking smug, enjoying his joke, but Jeri flashed annoyance and said, "C'mon Jack, you may be joking, but I don't find it funny. We all helped each other. The entire year we had each other's backs through those horrible times when we had to spend all night briefing cases and thinking we were going to die. Don't make fun of it. We needed each other."

Jack looked wounded, but Jeri continued. "You're pissing me off. I expect more out of my friends. I assume you do too." She stared at Jack. "Don't be a shithead. Mike babied you through Contracts and got you an 'A.' You never could have done it by yourself. Do you realize he never really got a chance to study Con Law? You ended up with better grades than him—by the tiniest amount—but you did it only because he helped you. You make Law Review and he barely misses it. You need to acknowledge what he did for you and not make jokes."

"Jeri stop, it's not a big deal," Mike interjected. Turning to Jack he said, "You don't have to say anything, I'm okay with how things turned out. Now you will do all of that extra work on Law Review and I'll enjoy so much more free time."

Jack started to make a joke, but stopped. "Mike, Jeri is right. I never would have gotten through Contracts without you. Thanks. I mean it."

Jeri beamed with everything now out in the open. She looked at her two friends. They would never think the way she did, which was probably why she loved them so much. She reached out and placed a hand on each of them. "Not many of the women in our class wanted to hang with me. I'm glad I have the two of you. Peace is now restored, so I won't feel bad getting out of here. I'm going to visit a friend of mine from college who's in town. She's staying on the other side of Oakland. I'm supposed to be at her place in fifteen minutes. Later guys, hopefully I will see you tomorrow before you leave me here alone for the summer."

She grabbed her jacket and breezed towards the door. A gust of wind blew her hair back as she walked into the darkness that enveloped the city. Through the window, the boys witnessed Jeri hustle determinedly down the street.

Chapter 10

May 26, 2011, First Year of Law School

J ACK AND MIKE downed a couple more beers and offered their farewells to their remaining classmates. They left the bar to stroll the three blocks back to their apartment.

"I haven't enjoyed a beer that much in a long time," Mike said.

"Probably because for the first time in nine months we haven't had some professor breathing down our necks, telling us we had to brief six cases for the next class," Jack responded.

When they got to their apartment they grabbed beers out of the refrigerator and flicked on the television. "I'm so glad we found this place. It was awesome Jeri got a place downstairs. Certainly made our study sessions easier," Mike said.

Jack was already reclining on the couch. "I am going to sleep well tonight. Maybe my mind will finally turn off and I won't worry about the next final or have some fact scenario from Torts playing in my head. It will be nice to get more than three hours of sleep."

Mike was trying to listen to Jack while the baseball game on t.v., played in the background, but exhaustion was beginning to take control.

He mumbled, "I know, I keep dreaming about Professor Konos asking me some question about Contracts and I answer but I have no clothes on. Everyone is laughing." Mike's voice faded as he was nearly asleep.

A short time later, when the game was approaching the seventh-inning stretch, both boys snored contently, their bodies finding stasis for the first time in weeks.

Mike startled when a buzz in his pocket signaled a call. Jeri's hysterical crying on the other end caused him to bolt upright. He tried to understand what was happening, but she was nearly incoherent and unable to form sentences. Before she hung up, he only learned she had been hurt and was in the hospital.

The boys darted out of their apartment, sprinting the five blocks to the hospital.

After they entered the emergency department they were directed to a treatment room where Jeri was attended to by a nurse. They were stunned when they saw Jeri's bruised and battered face. Her right arm rested in a sling. They approached her cautiously. She raised her head and immediately began to cry.

Mike and Jack gently sat by her on the bed as the nurse left the room. They waited for Jeri to speak. A small vibration emitting from a medical device on the wall was the only sound in the room.

"I can't believe it. I was so stupid." Tears rolled down her cheeks, her swollen lips garbling the words. "I was walking to my friend's apartment. I was close to her place and this guy asked me for directions to the Arena. I stopped and began conversing with him. He was young, nice looking. As I was talking, he suddenly grabbed me and pulled me down this staircase. He smacked me and punched me and said for me to be quiet. He grabbed my pants and tried to yank them off.... Oh my god." Jeri paused, burying her face in her hands. Her body heaved.

"I pushed him and he punched me again, right in my face. I got up and clawed his face with my nails. I ripped this one completely off." She held out her hand to show them the bloody remnant of her third fingernail. "I managed to push by him and started running up the stairs screaming. Three guys came right away and pinned him down until the police got there."

The boys listened to Jeri's story, taking in the extent of her physical injuries. A series of stitches held together a long, jagged wound below her left eye, which was swollen shut. She told them her arm had been x-rayed and was broken in two places. The doctors were coming to place it in a cast.

Mike gingerly placed his hand on Jeri's shoulder not sure if she would welcome the contact, but Jeri melted and leaned her head onto Mike. She again sobbed filling the room with her wails.

"He was going to rape me. He got so close. Oh my god, it almost happened to me." Jeri's body heaved.

The doctor told Jeri her mom was already on her way from Detroit. Jeri appeared relieved and crossed her arms on her chest, causing her to grimace in pain.

"In a little bit, when you feel better, perhaps you can talk to someone about this," Mike said.

Jeri jerked upwards. "No, I am ready to put this behind me now. I'm not going to let that slimebag affect my life." She paused and softened, reaching out her uninjured arm and signaling she wanted some personal contact. "Thank you for getting here so quickly. I needed you with me, but please, don't tell a soul. I don't want anyone to think I am weak. I can deal with this." The boys protested, but Jeri remained firm—no one was to talk about this outside of their group.

Jack and Mike recognized they would not change Jeri's mind. The silence enveloped the room and they waited until Jeri's eyes slowly closed and her rhythmic breathing signaled she was asleep.

Chapter 11

March 9, 2011–First Year of Law School

MIKE ENTERED HIS apartment and was not surprised to see Jeri sitting on the couch. She waved and asked a question that Mike couldn't quite hear. He said, "Everything is fine. How about you?"

Jeri smiled as that was not what she had asked, but didn't correct him. "I'm good. Just hanging here for a little until I can drag myself down to my apartment."

"Stay as long as you like. It's pretty much your apartment anyway. I'm going to bed soon. Just spent three hours in the library. I'm toast."

"Don't burn yourself out yet, we still have six weeks until finals. Plus, we have a study group meeting tomorrow. First year finals are just around the corner."

"You don't have to worry. I'm ready for tomorrow. My Contracts outline is shaping up." Mike held a black binder. "People will be willing to pay serious cash for a copy of this."

"Not me, I get a free copy."

"Me too," came Jack's voice as he entered the room. "Hey Mike, back from studying already. It's only one in the morning."

"I have to work hard to keep up with naturals like you and Jeri."

Jack sat down on the couch next to Jeri. He pointed to a couple of pieces of mail on the cheap wooden coffee table. "You got something today."

Mike picked up an envelope and inspected it. He ripped it open and started to read the handwritten letter inside. The message was short, but as Mike was reading it he yelled, "Fuck you, you bastard."

Jeri and Jack stared at Mike, waiting for him to finish reading the letter. Jeri looked empathetically at Mike.

"It's nothing. Don't worry," Mike said, still looking at the letter.

Jeri stood, walked over to Mike, and placed an arm around him. "It's pretty clearly something. Can we help?"

Clenching his teeth, Mike sat on the fabric chair that faced the couch. "I don't know what to say. It's my dad. He wants to visit."

Jack flipping through a magazine, casually offered, "What's the problem with that?"

"Nothing, if I wanted to see him."

"You've never mentioned your dad," Jeri added.

Mike looked at Jeri and tilted his head. "For good reason."

Jeri leaned forward. "What's the reason?"

"I'm tired," Mike said, turning away. "I don't feel like dealing with this now."

"Oh Mike, none of us like dealing with our parental issues, but it helps to talk about it. I think it took me like five minutes from the time I met you guys to start talking about what happened to my dad."

"Yes, we all know the story," Mike said. "It's horrible. But not everyone is an open book like you."

Jeri looked disapprovingly at Mike. "I'm not an open book with everyone. Just my friends. Nobody else in school knows anything about my dad."

Mike threw the letter on the coffee table and sank into the couch. "You really want to know? It's not that exciting."

Jeri smiled. "We're listening. Aren't we Jack?"

Jack placed the magazine on the table. "Yup. I'm all ears."

Mike leaned back, looked up at the ceiling and said, "Fine, it's not that great of a story. When I was six, my dad left my mom. One day he wasn't there anymore. My mom told my brother and me that he was moving to another town. I didn't see him much after that. Got an occasional card. Talked to him every now and then. After a while, I stopped caring. The problem was that every time I heard from him I ended up feeling like shit. Somehow with a card for my birthday or if he just called I would end up feeling worthless."

"How did that happen?" Jeri asked.

"I don't know. It was a special skill he had. It was usually just a comment, like, 'Well, not everyone can be the smartest one in class.' It's just that I never felt like he thought much of me. When I graduated high school, he wrote a note that said, 'Congratulations. If you studied just a little harder, you would have made it into a really good school.' My first couple of years at college were tough. I never could quite figure out how to manage my life. I tried calling him once for advice, but he didn't have anything helpful to say to me...," Mike's voice trailed off.

"Damn, dude, that's some deep-seated stuff you're digging through," Jack offered.

They sat in silence for a few moments. Jeri looked at Mike, who stared off into the distance.

"Have you talked to him since you've been in law school?" she asked.

"Nope, this is the first I've heard from him. My mom must have sent my address. I don't think he even has my email address."

"What are you going to do?"

Mike thought for a second. "Probably nothing. Law school is tough enough without adding a lot of familial drama to it. I want to feel good about myself and if I talk to him I'm pretty sure I will end up feeling like I'm still not good enough."

Mike rose and walked towards his bedroom.

Chapter 12

September 7, 2015—Two Years after Graduation from Law School

ON THE LOWER floors of the office, where the young associates toil at Carlton and Sanders, there is no wood paneling. The pungent wood odor that permeates the upper floors where the partners sit in their well-appointed offices is replaced by a musky dankness reminiscent of a neglected jail cell. Jack loved the offices on the higher floors and how they exuded power and money. On his floor, a sense of desperation lingered, especially late in the evenings when the lawyers labored in their small offices, unwilling to allow others to appear to be working harder.

Jack walked with purpose and turned into a small office at the back section of the floor. "Hey good looking, your desk makes you look like an elf."

"You're still an ass, Rogers," Peggy Gamble replied, looking up from a stack of documents. "I can't help it if I haven't gotten a real desk and I am left to sit behind something that belongs in a fifth-grade classroom. Someday I hope to be like you and get a real desk. But remember, you are still on this floor and haven't really gotten anywhere. Come on in and sit. What can I do for you?"

"Wagner summoned me. I have to be there in ten minutes. He wants me to do a presentation on the hedge trimmer case."

Peggy winced in the same way everyone did when they thought of what happened in that case. "What kind of presentation?"

"I think he wants me to be able to do a summary for the client. Hope I can get some face-to-face time."

"Wow, I don't even get to know who the clients are for most of my work. Just keep reviewing documents. We are nearly two years out of law school and I haven't spoken with a client yet. Certainly haven't seen the inside of a courtroom. I don't think any of the partners would trust me with that. Dammit, you and I were two of like twenty-five lawyers who worked on the hedge trimmer case. We drafted the interrogatories and the requests for production of documents. I can't imagine how many thousands of hours have been billed to that case or the millions of dollars we have charged the client in fees. But Wagner has never talked to me and now you are getting to make a presentation to the client. That bastard loves having associates kiss his ass. I went to school in the south, not in the Ivy League like him and I'm not good at playing politics..." Gamble's voice trailed off.

"Do you think I can run through with you what I'm going to say before I get to my meeting with Wagner?"

"Absolutely, I got nothing but time."

Jack stood erect and began: "In the case, the plaintiff, a forty-year-old man living on a small farm in Shady Elm, Indiana, was pruning trees with a hedge trimmer when he lost his grip. The automatic shutoff did not function, so when the trimmer grazed against the man's thigh it sliced a six-inch gash close to his groin and cut open his scrotum, severing one of his testicles. The man nearly bled out from the wound on his leg and his nicked femoral artery. His wife's quick reaction in placing a tourniquet on his leg saved his life. He would, however, be short one testicle for the rest of his life."

"I probably would leave out that last part," Gamble interjected.

"Good point." Jack gently rubbed the inside of his thigh and continued. "The case was filed in state court here in Chicago nearly five years ago. Our firm has worked diligently to investigate the extent of plaintiff's injuries and to evidence our client's efforts to make hedge trimmers as safe as possible. We believe we have viable defenses and can make a good argument that the plaintiff misused the trimmer."

Jack stopped suddenly and looked at his watch. "I need to get to his office. He doesn't like it if I show up late. I'll figure out exactly what he wants me to do and get this presentation together. See ya." Jack waved at Peggy and headed down the hall to Ed Wagner's office.

When Jack arived at Wagner's doorway, he was once again struck by the sheer size and opulence of the office. Wagner's desk and credenza matched and a large picture of a man riding a stallion hung on the wall, framing the desk. Wagner's diplomas, evincing his graduation from multiple Ivy League universities, framed in walnut, were hung with precision over the couch in the office's conference area. A furry, black and white rug lay under the glass table. The sun poured in from the floor to ceiling windows that lined the wall facing the desk.

Wagner was on the phone, leaning back in his leather chair, when he spied Jack poking his head into the office. Jack took a seat in the mauve suede chair immediately in front of the desk, attempting to hide his nervousness. Wagner finished talking on the phone and yelled for his secretary to bring him a letter he had received the day before. He turned his back on Jack and composed an email that to Jack sounded to be to Wagner's wife. After completing this task, Wagner turned to Jack with his best 'I'm your buddy' smile. Jack smiled back. Ed placed his hands on his mahogany desk and said, "How's it going, sport?"

"Fine, I'm working on some fascinating cases, but none quite as interesting as the hedge trimmer case," Jack said, without attempting to hide his zeal.

Wagner accepted the not-so-subtle complement and ran a hand through his short, grey-tinged, black hair. Cufflinks poked through the sleeves of his jacket. He smiled again, revealing perfect teeth. Jack admired the press of his suit and the way his tailored shirt accentuated his physique.

"Tomorrow is the pretrial hearing in the hedge trimmer case," Wagner said.

"Of course, trial is scheduled in three weeks. We put all of the exhibits together so you and Dave can focus on getting ready."

"Jack, you know the company has significant exposure in this case. Including the punitive damage claim, I've told them they could get hit for fifty to seventy-five million."

Jack nodded. Wagner continued, "I'm glad you have been so efficient working up this case. I wanted you to observe how things went during court conferences so you would be prepared when you got a chance to take the lead. Pete Daniels, the president of the company, is coming with us tomorrow. You met him when you helped to defend his deposition. He said complimentary things about you, so I thought as a reward you would come with us."

Jack beamed. Court appearances for anyone less than five years out of law school were unusual at his firm. Cases rarely went to trial because of the high stakes of litigation. He made a mental note to inform Gamble where he would be the next day.

The following day, Jack got into the office early. After reviewing the case notes, he organized the file materials they would be taking to court. Thirty minutes before the pretrial conference, the firm's van dropped the three lawyers and the president of the hedge trimmer company off at the courthouse.

Dressed in suits, the four members of the team sat on the long wooden bench outside of Judge Valley's courtroom. Wagner signaled to Jack to take a walk with him and they casually headed down the hallway. Wagner wanted to make sure they got out of earshot before saying to Jack, "I brought you here today so you can observe how these things are done. When we go into chambers, I will speak with the plaintiff's attorney and we will resolve this case."

"How can you be sure?" Jack replied with a modicum of astonishment.

"Listen Jack, both sides have too much at risk. Our client doesn't want an excessive verdict and Sabato can't spend so much time on this file and not get anything. I've talked to Pete Daniels so many times about settlement value and he believes if we can settle this for under twelve million dollars it would be a coup for his company. Well, counsel and I have discussed this case also. We probably could have settled this two years ago for three million dollars, but we wouldn't have had the chance to work the file up and do proper discovery." Wagner stopped and stared at Jack. Jack stood dumbfounded, realizing this was all prefabricated.

"So, we put in a few more years taking depositions and sending ridiculous interrogatories." Wagner locked eyes with Jack. "Our firm gets to bill some more hours. Counsel and I reached an understanding that he will receive his settlement and because he waited until now it will be a little better than what he would have gotten earlier. We will settle at a figure well below what our client thinks is reasonable, so they will be thrilled. Everyone ends up happy and we don't worry about any messy trials."

"Are you sure it will happen?"

"Absolutely, happens every time. You just have to learn how to dance." Wagner gyrated his hips in a small circle. "Jack, you are a part of this because you're an up and comer. The client likes you and you can become a player at the firm. You understand what I am saying?"

Jack didn't, but nodded his head anyway.

They returned to the bench outside Judge Valley's chambers. Wagner introduced Jack to the plaintiff and his attorney, Tony Sabato, who was short and balding, with a glint of perspiration on his forehead. Sabato appeared nervous and Jack wondered if he was worried the prefabricated settlement might dissolve.

A few minutes later they entered Valley's chambers for the pretrial conference. Elected eight years earlier, the judge sat comfortably behind her outsized desk and motioned for the lawyers to sit. The clients waited outside in the courtroom, unaware of exactly what was transpiring.

Judge Valley spoke about her courtroom procedures as the court reporter took everything down for the official record. She pointed to a stack of pretrial motions on her desk, many of which Jack drafted and asked if now was an appropriate time to wade through the papers to simplify the issues for trial.

Wagner interrupted. "Your Honor, before we argue these motions, I would like to report plaintiff's counsel and I have engaged in some settlement discussions and I was wondering if, with the court's assistance, it might be beneficial to at least explore the possibility of reaching a resolution."

Judge Valley's face radiated approval. "Counsel, the court is always happy when parties are willing to enter settlement negotiations. How can I help the parties?"

Taking his cue from Wagner, Sabato said, "Your Honor, Mr. Wagner and I have made significant progress on certain issues, but we still are somewhat apart. Both of our clients are present in the courtroom, so I think if we speak with them and then with each other, we might find room to bridge the gap."

"Let's take a thirty-minute recess so you can discuss these matters with your clients. Please report back to me if you make any progress. "

The attorneys left the Judge's chambers and Wagner made a beeline to his client, motioning for the other lawyers to give him some space. Sabato also grabbed the plaintiff and led him to the hallway.

For the next ten minutes, Wagner and Sabato went back and forth talking to each other and meeting with their respective clients. After making the rounds four times, Wagner and Sabato shook hands and approached the other lawyers. "We agreed to a deal," Wagner said to Jack and Dave White. "Let's inform the Court."

Wagner walked lightly towards the judge's chambers. He turned his head slightly to get Jack's attention and once again gyrated his hips.

Inside, the two attorneys reported the parties settled the case for 4.2 million dollars. The judge was pleased and praised both sides for their willingness to compromise their claims.

The court reporter transcribed the settlement for the record, while Jack calculated in his head everyone's take from the lawsuit. Plaintiff's counsel would put about 1.7 million dollars in his personal bank account, noting this was probably about 400,000 dollars more than he would've made if they agreed to the original three-million-dollar settlement. Jack added the bills for the injured man's medical treatment with the estimated costs his law firm incurred to prepare the case for trial. Jack figured the plaintiff would receive a check for nearly two million dollars.

Jack sat in silence at the back of the judge's chambers as the primary lawyers listened to the judge's war stories. Their client remained in the courtroom, and Jack presumed he was on the phone telling the home office what an amazing settlement they had negotiated. Even adding in the legal fees the company paid Jack's firm, it would pay out significantly less than it allocated for this case.

Wagner regaled the judge with a story about his last case. Jack sat in awe, knowing he was watching a concert master. Everyone was happy. They either would make more money than they thought, or pay out less than they planned. This was genius Wagner had orchestrated over years with the crescendo happening in the courtroom right before Jack's eyes. No wonder Wagner always was at ease. His clients paid their firm millions of dollars for representation and Wagner never worried about the cases actually going to trial.

Jack stared at Wagner leading the conversation with the judge and realized that was exactly where he wanted to be, and he would do whatever it took to get there.

Chapter 13

December 17, 2010–First Year of Law School

BOYS, IT'S FRIDAY, it's ten o'clock, and we are done studying for the evening," Jeri commanded as Mike banged his head slowly against his Civil Procedure textbook.

"Good, I'm never going to get pendant jurisdiction and right now I don't care," Mike said starting to put his books in his backpack.

"That's right. We are done, so let's go hit Loopers, and let's hit it hard," Jack added, already standing by the exit door.

The three friends left the law school and were hit by frigid gusts of air blowing on the mid-December night. The street lights were illuminated, casting a haunting glow as they walked past the fast food joints and apparel stores that lined the sidewalk.

"Damn, it's cold," Mike said, zipping up his jacket. "I need to get a heavier coat."

"You are such a wimp," Jack said, running past Mike.

Mike took off after Jack but couldn't keep up with his taller friend. He slowed to wait for Jeri, watching Jack's breath rise in billowy puffs as he chugged down the sidewalk.

Jack slowed his gait once he got near to their destination. To his right, a voice came from the shadows of the unlit foyer of a cellphone store. "Hey buddy, can you spare something for a vet?"

The unwashed man, huddled up against the storefront, wearing a tattered flannel shirt and army pants, caught Jack's attention, causing him to stop in his tracks. A soiled woolen hat topped his head but didn't hide the grey growth sporadically covering his face. He looked at Jack and said, "Anything you can give will help."

Jack caught a glimpse of the vet's lifeless eyes and reached into his pocket to grab his wallet. Seizing the only bill bigger than a ten, he reached out and stuffed it into the man's bare hands. "Here you go buddy, hope this helps."

Jack turned and ducked into Loopers and didn't hear the vet mumble, "God bless."

An empty table sat near to the billiards room and Jack grabbed it. Thirty seconds later Jeri and Mike joined him and took off their jackets.

"Dude, you are fast," Mike said. "Couldn't keep up with you."

"It's cold out there. I wanted to get here quick," Jack responded while straightening his hair.

Jeri sat and gawked at Jack, who tried not to notice, but finally said, "What the hell are you staring at?"

Jeri smiled. "I don't know. That was so nice."

"What are you talking about?" Jack said defensively.

Jeri lowered her head and stared up at Jack. "You know, what you did out there."

Jack said nothing.

Jeri continued, "You saw the homeless guy. You stopped and gave him money."

"Shut up Jeri. Let's drink."

"C'mon Jack. You do something selfless, you deserve some credit."

Jack appeared annoyed. "It's just something I do sometimes. That's it."

Mike leaned into the conversation. "Why? None of us have a lot of money."

"Fine. Let's delve into my psyche. You guys are going to have a field day with this."

Jeri pulled her chair closer to Jack. "Go ahead Jack. We're all ears."

Jack paused and then said, "When I was about nine there was a bad fire at our home. It burned down the house. My mom and I were able to get out, but the house was gone. My mom hadn't been working and we didn't have a lot of money and I guess the insurance on the house wasn't enough, but we couldn't get a new house. My parents had already split up and my dad was working in another city at some important job. He said he would send us money, but it took him a while to get it together for some reason. We were shuttled between some friends and some relatives, but they had troubles paying the bills. For a few weeks one winter we didn't have a place to live so a couple of nights we spent sleeping in the park. It was scary, but I knew we would find somewhere to live. My mom ultimately got a decent job and we were able to rent a house."

Jeri stared at Jack in amazement. "Holy shit. I never knew any of this."

"I know. It's just not something I want to talk about, but I see guys living on the street and I think that could be me. It's got to be really tough on those guys."

"Tell us what is was like when you slept in the park," coaxed Jeri.

Jack lowered his head and looked down at the table. When he lifted his gaze, the huge smile was back on his face. "I'm done with the Dr. Phil show. We are here to drink some beer."

Jack turned and flagged down a waitress.

Jeri looked at Mike and whispered, "There are some serious family issues in this group."

Chapter 14

January 14, 2016–Two and a half Years after
Graduation from Law School

AT THE BACK of the courtroom Jeri corralled her witnesses for the three cases she was handling that afternoon. They included two rapes and one aggravated assault, which meant she would be in court for hours. She rubbed her scar as she glanced through the files. She had spent time with the witnesses earlier in the day and had organized the evidence for each case, so she was hopeful she would get convictions on all three.

The courtroom was buzzing as Jeri stood by the door to the bull-pen studying her files. She rehearsed in her mind the framework of her opening statements. She reviewed the list of police officers who would be testifying. Although she hadn't been handling sex crimes for long, she'd already seen enough cops testify that she knew which could handle difficult cross-examination and which presented poorly on the witness stand.

The first file, a rape case, involved allegations the 23-year-old defendant date-raped the accuser. Jeri had already determined that the evidence of a crime was relatively weak, because no witness stepped forward to corroborate the accuser's story and the lab results turned up negative for any of the typical date rape drugs. The investigating officer, a gruff and overbearing cop, came across as lazy and willing to stretch the truth. Jeri focused on how best to present the case to limit the testimony of the cop. Unaware of the activity going on around her, Jeri startled when she felt a tap on her shoulder.

"Hey Jeri, can we talk for a few minutes?" asked Ingrid Blakely, a petite public defender whom Jeri had tried a few cases against and respected for her ability to make the best of the evidence for her clients.

"Sure Ingrid. What can I do for you?"

"You've been working in violent crimes for about more than a year, haven't you?"

Jeri nodded.

"I have a couple of cases against some of your co-workers. I'm not going to name names, but some of them are really cutting some corners."

"Why are you telling me this?"

"I don't know," Ingrid continued. "Most of my clients are guilty and I should be happy if I'm able to get one off, but a couple of times in the past few months I've had cases where the assistant DA has missed some pretty compelling evidence. I'm not telling you guys how to try cases, but I don't think it looks good for your office. You certainly aren't one of the people I'm talking about. You don't miss anything and you keep sending my clients to jail."

"I hear you Ingrid. We got a lot of younger people in the office, but they're getting weeded out. My boss is getting rid of people who don't know how to try a case. It's not like it used to be where you pretty much had a job for life. Now you actually have to know what you are doing. Tell you what, I'll talk to my boss and tell him I got a heads-up. I won't mention your name."

"I think that's a good idea. I'm just trying to make the justice system have a little more justice."

Jeri smiled and asked if they had the next case.

"Yes, I have Wilson Davis, the accused date rapist in the next case. Can we get this resolved?"

"I'm not sure. I saw you have four cases this afternoon. You PD's are always looking to settle. Are you scared to try this one?"

"Jeri, you know I'm not scared to try any of these cases. What's the worst that happens, my client goes to jail? I'm kind of used to that. Let's talk about what we can do on this one."

"Hey, we're about to be called. I'm ready to open, but what do you want?"

"My client says the sex was consensual. In fact, extremely consensual, is what he is going to say."

Jeri looked pulled the photographs from her file. "Did you see those pictures? Victim's bruised on her neck, her back, and let's not talk about what he did between her legs. Strap marks on her arms. Damn he tied her up and raped her. She says she was sleeping and doesn't remember it. Says he put something in her drink and violated her."

"Jeri, you don't have anything. Toxicology came back negative. No witness to anything. My guy said it may have been a little rough, but it was all consensual. Plus, the accuser, she has something of a track record if you know what I mean."

"Come on, you aren't going to try this by bringing up her prior sex history?"

"Of course I am, it's right on page nine of the playbook for this kind of case. She apparently has a bit of a reputation. Quite a little tart."

Jeri considered this, then recognized opposing counsel had made a few strong points. The public defender interrupted her thoughts before Jeri could counter her arguments. "Listen, this kid is twenty-three years old. He comes from a decent family and never caused any trouble. Let's get rid of this one."

Jeri felt a bit defeated, not wanting to lose a conviction, yet recognizing this might not be one of the scum she pledged to keep off the streets. All she had was the mediocre cop who was about to be a mediocre witness and she had nothing to corroborate the victim's story. It was a recipe for failure.

She put on her best weary expression. "What are you thinking?"

"Misdemeanor aggravated assault. Probation for six months."

"Not enough–felony agg assault, one year in a state facility," Jeri countered, understanding the drill. The public defender started too soft, she countered too hard. They knew they would meet in the middle.

"No. No jail time. Oh hell, let's try this," Ingrid said resignedly.

"Enough bullshit. I will let it go at misdemeanor agg assault, but three months of house arrest, followed by one year of probation."

"You drive a hard bargain Jeri, but it's a deal."

The public defender shook Jeri's hand and walked over to tell his client, who smiled broadly. Jeri saw his reaction, and regretted the plea bargain, but immediately let it drop. She had too many cases to worry about them once they were over.

As she watched the defendant, Jeri heard the tipstaff call out the defendant's name. She approached the bench with the public defender and informed the judge they agreed on a plea bargain. In thirty seconds, they put the deal on the record and the court moved onto other matters. Jeri's next file was the third on the list so she wanted to review it to prepare.

She walked deliberately towards where she had left her materials, but felt a hand gently touch her shoulder. She jerked, always concerned about the scum who skulked in the courtroom waiting for their trials. She was surprised to see the white-tooth smile of Alan Corcoran.

"Came to see my star litigator do her thing, but she goes and pleads the case. What's happening here, you losing your nerve?"

Jeri smiled brightly and reminded her boss it was rare she pled cases. "Alan, you understand there are times when you take the best deal possible. I hope you still think I know what I am doing."

"Absolutely, in fact I came down here to tell you something of some significance."

He put his hand on Jeri's shoulder and guided her to the corridor leading to the bullpen, out of sight of the courtroom.

"Go ahead, let me know what kind of trouble I'm in," Jeri said, semi-seriously.

"Not bad news at all. I've been talking to the powers that be in the party…you know, the ones who control everything that goes on in this building. There is an opening because Judge Weksel retired last year. Well, they wanted to know who they should put up to be on the ballot and with a little prodding from me, I suggested you. If you want, they will support your candidacy for judge. They want a woman, they want an anti-crime person and there is nobody better than you."

"This is a little quick. I haven't been with the DA's office for three years."

"I know you are young, but you've done so much in your three years here and people have noticed. Don't question it. Say you will do it."

"Oh my god, yes, of course." Jeri scanned the area to make sure no one could see them, and engulfed Alan in a hug. He let her squeeze his body and lowered his hand to quickly grab a chunk of her butt. Jeri yelped with pleasure.

"This is so exciting. I can't wait to thank you properly," Jeri whispered in his ear. "Tonight, come over and I will show you my appreciation."

"Just like you always do."

Chapter 15

April 19, 2016—Almost Three years after Graduation from Law School

THE WIND WAS blowing hard when they opened the door to exit the courthouse. Dressed in suits and wrapped in overcoats, Mike and Stan covered their faces as another gust blew back their hair. Holding his file folder tightly, Mike jumped back as a car sped by them and sprayed slush onto the sidewalk.

Stan laughed as the spray narrowly missed Mike. "Close call," Stan said to Mike, who smiled at the near disaster. "That would've sucked if he got me."

"This could be our lucky day," Stan said as they continued to walk in the direction of the public garage to retrieve Stan's car. "You deftly handled the tidal wave coming towards you just like you dealt with the summary judgment argument."

Mike beamed at the compliment. "I think it went well enough. I worried they might get our case dismissed, but ultimately the judge saw it our way."

"Mike, you did an excellent job countering their arguments. The Pennsylvania Supreme Court case you found allowing landlords to seek money from tenants if the tenant's guests cause damage to the building essentially gave the judge no choice. He had to let our claims proceed. Now the other side has to deal with the claims we brought against them. They are going to be more willing to settle. Certainly not a case I would want to try if I were them. Let's hope we can get them to offer a fair amount of money,"

They arrived at the car and began the drive to Stan's home and office thirty miles away. "It's too bad you couldn't find your friend Jeri."

"I'm not surprised. Those assistant DAs are always trying a case somewhere. Nobody could tell me where she was, but I left her a note. I think she is doing pretty well there. I hear she keeps getting promoted."

As they exited the parking lot, Stan switched subjects. "Mike, there is a potential new client I want you to interview. Sounds interesting."

"Sure, Uncle Stan, what's it about?"

"I don't know much. Her husband called me last week and said it involved false imprisonment at a department store. He told me his wife is having trouble leaving the house, so she can't come down to the office. Can you go see her?"

"Sure, does tomorrow work for them?"

"I assume. After you talk with them, let me know if you think they have a case."

The next day, Mike drove to Connellsville and found the small, but tasteful house where he was meeting his potential new clients. Mike approached the red wooden front door carrying only a yellow pad and pen.

At the door he was greeted by an unsmiling beefy man in his early forties. Following the man inside, Mike noticed no lights on in the house and all of the shades on the ground floor drawn. The man directed him to the kitchen where Mike sat at one of the wooden chairs encircling a round table.

"I will tell Martha you are here and see if she will come down," the man offered.

Mike nodded and waited. Minutes passed as he gazed out of the window into the backyard. Swings swayed in the wind, a basketball hoop drooped precariously from the blue one-car garage situated at the back of a narrow concrete driveway.

"Excuse me, Mr. Reigert," the man's voice echoed from the entrance to the kitchen. "This is my wife."

Martha Gebbert, dressed in a bathrobe, peeked out from behind her husband.

"Mrs. Gebbert," Mike said trying unsuccessfully to make eye contact. "I am Michael Reigert, but please call me Mike."

"Please call me Martha," said the small woman with short brown hair and dull blue eyes. "Paul, will you get this young man some water?" she instructed her husband.

They took a seat at the table and after some small talk Mike asked Martha to tell him what happened. Paul tried to speak for Martha, but she insisted on telling the story.

"I went to Wendell's department store in Irwin like a thousand times before." Mike knew Wendell's was a typical national chain with at least five locations in the Pittsburgh area. Neither upscale nor completely discount, the chain catered to Middle America with a variety of departments where useful products could be purchased at reasonable prices. The store advertised heavily in local newspapers and offered coupons for additional savings on sales that occurred virtually every week.

Martha Gebbert slumped in her chair, her brow furrowed. Paul sat next to her with a hand on her arm. With a yellow pad in front of him, Mike waited for Martha to tell her story.

"It was a Thursday, about five months ago when I decided to go to Wendell's because I wanted to get some bath towels. They were having a good sale. The kids were at school. I walked into the first floor of the store and started to browse. I picked out a couple of things I wanted to buy. I'm not sure what department I was in, but there was a counter with a box of chocolates on it. I thought they were offering samples, so I took one and ate it."

Mike took notes on his yellow pad and asked her what happened next.

"About thirty seconds later, this guy came up to me and told me to go with him. I had no idea who he was. I actually thought I had won some prize. I asked him why and he said I stole something. I didn't know what he was talking about, but he said it was about the candy."

"You mean the sample you took?"

"Yeah, he laughed when I told him it was a sample. He said it was a returned box of chocolates. I asked him if he was certain and he said, 'like a heart attack.'"

"Wow, so where did you go?"

"He took me in an elevator down to the basement and led me into a room. He told me to sit at the table which I did. He pulled out a pair of handcuffs and locked me to a bar on the table. He put a form on the table and told me I could leave once I signed the paper."

"What paper?"

"Some kind of confession, I guess. It said something like I admit I stole something and I would pay some fine to the company."

As he leaned back in his chair, Mike tried to imagine the setup of the room in which Martha Gebbert was held. He couldn't fathom why Wendell's had such a room in the first place. "What did the security guard do?" he asked.

"The guy told me he would come back in when I signed the paper. I think there was a camera in the room and he was watching me. He came back in the room every thirty minutes and asked if I signed the form. I would tell him no and he would leave. At first, I kind of thought it was funny, but then I got scared, I didn't know how long I might be in there."

"Did anyone else come into the room?"

"No, the security guy was the only person who ever came into the room. I asked him to get me someone to talk to, but he said he was the man in charge."

"How long were you in there?"

"I'm not sure. They didn't put a clock in the room and they took my purse, so I couldn't use my phone. I don't wear a watch. The guard came in at least six times, so I'm guessing around over two hours."

"How did you get out?"

"I told him I didn't do anything wrong and he kept telling me to sign the form to get out of the handcuffs. I started crying, but he didn't care. I think I yelled and screamed, but I'm not sure. Finally, I told him I didn't take anything, but I would sign the form anyway. He let me out of the cuffs. I stood up and tried to grab it back, but he was too fast. He let me go at that point."

Intrigued a company would incarcerate somebody to coerce a confession, Mike pondered the merits of case. He helped his uncle on many different types of matters, but not any false imprisonment or retail theft cases. The image of Mrs. Gebbert locked to the table angered Mike and he wondered what kind of company would implement a policy like that.

Mike felt Mrs. Gebbert had a potential claim against the corporation, but also remembered his uncle taught him to look for three things before accepting a case. First was liability—whether the defendant did something legally wrong. Second were injuries and damages, and third was whether the defendant was able to pay. Mrs. Gebbert provided enough information to indicate there was a decent chance the company had done something improper. He knew Wendell's could satisfy a judgment. The only question left was whether the company's actions injured Mrs. Gebbert.

"What you told me so far is helpful Mrs. Gebbert, but what I would like to understand is how has this affected you?"

At this point Paul jumped in. "My wife is the backbone of the family, but something happened to her. Right after she came home she just went up to her room and cried. She stays in the room most of the time. She's tried to go out with friends, but she wants to stay in the house all of the time. I don't know what's going on with her, but she is scared to leave. She sits around in the dark most of the time."

"Do you have any children?" asked Mike.

"Yes, Stacey is a ninth grader and Tanner's in seventh. Martha hasn't been able to take them anywhere. She isn't there for them and they are used to her helping them."

Martha listened to her husband and stared blankly past Mike. Paul described how she spent most of her time sitting on the couch vacantly watching television.

"Mr. Gebbert," Mike said, trying to show compassion, "has Martha seen anyone about what happened?"

Paul glanced at his wife and then back at Mike. "I'm not a believer in those types of things, and neither is Martha. She's never talked to anybody before and I'm not sure why she would do it now."

"I'm no expert on psychologists and mental health doctors, but I think she may need to talk with someone."

Paul nodded. "We'll consider it."

"Sir, I think you and your wife have a solid case. I want to speak with my uncle, but I am going to recommend we handle this." Mike stood and extended his hand towards Mr. Gebbert who grasped it firmly.

"You seem like a smart, young man. Martha and I would sure be happy if you could help us."

Mike left the Gebbert house wondering who had come up with the idea of locking people in the basement of a department store until they confessed to a crime. He looked forward to figuring out the answer.

Chapter 16

July 13,2016–Three Years after Graduation from Law School

J ACK SAT BACK in his high leather chair admiring his surroundings. His new office three doors down from Jack Wagner wasn't quite as large as Wagner's, but to Jack it felt palatial. The desk, covered with neatly arranged stacks of papers, sat close to the small row of windows so that Jack, when he craned his neck, could get a glimpse of Lake Michigan. A credenza sat against the wall behind Jack; on this he placed his telephone, computer, and a small picture of his father. His diplomas hung over the credenza framed in the same wood Wagner had used for his diplomas. The office was spacious enough so that Jack, on occasion, could stand and practice gyrating his hips.

Jack examined the two unfinished assignments on his desk. Both analyzed an esoteric point of law for one of Wagner's product liability cases. Jack had spent nearly a week on both memos, researching any potential defense the client could conceivably raise if the case went to trial. Trial was unlikely–or at least years away. Jack felt little motivation to put the finishing touches on his work. He was holding a memo in each hand, pondering which to finish first, when Wagner poked his head into the office.

"Got a minute?"

"Sure, what's up?" Jack asked, understanding he was to drop whatever he was doing. Motioning to the leather chairs in front of his desk, Jack offered Ed a seat.

"Your new office looks nice. A lot better than the crap we give new associates on the eighth floor." Jack nodded as Wagner continued. "Some of your buddies are still down there, aren't they? How many are left from your class?"

"We started with nine. There are four of us left."

Wagner smirked. "That sounds about right. You're the only one who's moved out of the starter office, aren't you?"

Jack leaned forward eagerly, "That's true and I hope to keep moving on up."

"I assume you realize that if your friends still have those midget desks, they probably will never get off of that floor."

Jack wasn't sure how to respond, but accepted the implication he was the lead dog among the attorneys who had started with him. "Is there anything I can do to help?"

"Got a new case for you to work on," Wagner said, placing a blue file folder on Jack's desk.

"Thanks, what sort of research are you looking for?"

"No, Jack, you misunderstand. This is yours. You are handling it and in charge. It's a personal injury matter for a potential new client, a national retailer, but it's not much of a case. I perused the file, I doubt there's any liability, and I don't think the plaintiff was injured. I wanted you to get a chance to run with this."

Jack grinned. "I'm flattered. I will handle it."

"By the way, it's filed in your old stomping grounds in Pittsburgh. Since you went to law school there, I assumed this would be fun for you.

I talked to the client last week. Told him I thought it's not too significant of a case. I got them to set the reserves at half a million dollars. You should be able to settle this for perhaps one hundred thousand, so you already have yourself some wiggle room. Work it up, bill some hours and get the other side to dance. It will make everyone happy."

"I hear you," Jack said, thumbing through the papers as Ed spoke. He reviewed the cover sheet to the complaint and let out a laugh. "I think dancing on this case is going to be easier than either of us could imagine."

Chapter 17

September 20, 2016–Three Years after Graduation from Law School

RED WINE SLOSHED around in bulbous glasses as Mike and Jeri relaxed on Jeri's floral printed couch. Mike listened to Jeri talk about her life, but his eyes took in the design of her condominium. The dining room table to their right was set for three. Yellow-striped cloth napkins rested on bone white china with two crystal glasses identically placed in front of each plate. Light blue irises floated in clear vases in the middle of the cherry table.

As Jeri continued her soliloquy, Mike mentally compared Jeri's functional condo with his two-bedroom farmhouse thirty-five miles away, with its hand-me-down furniture, the same off-white colored walls in every room, lacking even one piece of hung art or print.

Mike was proud he was able to find and pay for his own place after having lived with his uncle for over a year after law school. Other than a few garage sale items and the furniture his uncle had given him, Mike had yet to update the interior of the farmhouse.

Mike interrupted Jeri, realizing he had lost track of the conversation. "Wait, we never get to see each other. I want to hear about the election and everything going on in your life." Mike sat back, intent on listening to Jeri, who placed her right hand gently on his knee.

"Everything's going so well. Like I was saying, I tried lots of cases for the DA's office when out of the blue my boss asked me to run for judge. I never thought about being a judge before, but I said I would do it. The process is so time consuming. All sorts of events I have to go to, lots of hand shaking—that sort of thing, but I've met so many people and it turns out its sort of fun. The election is only three weeks away. Everyone at the DA's office is supportive. I hope I don't disappoint them and lose."

"I doubt that could happen," Mike said. "Just like in law school, the people who know you, also respect you. I thought back then you would make an outstanding judge. What else is going on with you?" Mike asked, pointing at the extra setting on the dining room table.

Jeri blushed. "Oh that. You and I are going to be joined by a friend of mine."

"Friend?" Mike did not try to hide his salacious tone.

"Well, my boyfriend, as ridiculous as it sounds, but I guess it's the right word for it. His name is Alan and he was my boss at the DA's office."

"Nice."

"No, it's nothing like that. He was my mentor. He's brilliant and he *gets* me. As you know, I have issues trusting men." Jeri gently touched the scar under her eye.

"I get it. How significant is this relationship?"

"We've been seeing each other for over a year. We kept it private for a long time, but now everyone knows. He still keeps his own place, but we talked about moving in together. I don't know. We are at an interesting place in our relationship and I don't want to screw it up."

"You are not the kind of person who screws things up. I think you will be able to figure this one out." Mike smiled at Jeri.

"I hope so. I bet you'll like him. He should be joining us any time now."

Jeri stood up to check the fish in the oven and returned with some cheese on a platter. They sat reminiscing about law school and how familiar it was sitting on a couch and hanging out.

"Now it's your turn." Jeri touched Mike's elbow as he picked some cracker crumbs off of his green striped sweater. "What's going on in farming country? Tell me something juicy."

Mike groaned inwardly, feeling insecure as to how his life compared to those of some of his classmates, including Jeri. "First of all, it's not farm country. It is a small community of over twenty-five thousand people, only a few who actually own farms."

Jeri laughed, nearly spilling her wine. Mike continued, "It's not what I expected to do when I was in school. I thought I was going overseas, but my uncle needed me. We do a lot of interesting work, a little criminal, a little family law, but mainly people come to see us because they've been hurt and we try to help them. We handle a lot of smaller cases with some larger ones mixed in, but we are in court all the time trying to move our cases."

"How's your uncle?"

"He's doing fine. He's pushing seventy now, but he's in the office every day. He's been my mentor and he's taught me so much. I think I am learning to be a competent lawyer and if I am, it's mainly because of him." Mike stopped for a moment and a sly smile came to his face. "He's been an amazing mentor for me, but we don't sleep together. Do you think I should?"

Jeri shrieked and smacked Mike on his elbow. "You bastard, I think my situation may be a bit different than yours, and no, I think you should leave your relationship with him the way it is."

Jeri quieted down and the silence felt comfortable to Mike. She lowered her head onto his shoulder and Mike touched her hair. "I missed you," Jeri said. "I miss the simplicity and intensity of law school. I like what I have going on now, but I feel like time is moving too quickly and I am missing something. You know what I mean?"

Jeri's question was interrupted by the doorbell. Jeri excused herself and returned seconds later to introduce Alan, who deftly took off his coat and shook Mike's hand. Mike admired the crispness of Alan's clothes: the dark green wool pants that contrasted the fitted light grey sweater. Mike immediately felt comfortable with Alan and happy for Jeri.

Mike and Alan sat on the couch and began lightly bantering about subjects dear to both of them: Pittsburgh sports and politics. Jeri watched as the two men she had been closest with in her adult life bonded.

While enjoying their beer and wine, Jeri beckoned her guests to the dinner table and welcomed them with a toast. After some soup and salad, Jeri inquired about their other law school friend, Jack.

Mike frowned. "We talked about two years ago, but since then, only a couple of texts. Nothing of substance—he was out drinking with some co-workers and he told me I should fly to Chicago and go out with them."

Jeri peered over at the framed pictures arranged neatly on a shelf in the living room. Some of the images captured the three of them on the couch in the boys' apartment during law school. "I know, it's been so long since I've talked to him. Last time he told me he was on the fast track to partnership and he was going to jet us all to some island for a vacation. I never thought it would happen, and it didn't."

Alan grabbed some chicken off of the tray. "It sounds similar to my law school friends. We were close back then. Everything was so important, but people move away or get too busy and then you don't see them anymore. I'm still in touch with some of my buddies, but some I don't know what happened to. Not so long ago they meant more to me than anyone else in my life."

Mike wanted to talk about how things had changed since graduation. "I don't know. The three of us were so tight in school. We spent virtually every day hanging out and then, poof, it's gone. I don't think I will ever find anything comparable to what we had then. My uncle is a stand-up guy, but I don't want to hang out with him all day, every day. We need to find a way to get Jack here so we can spend some time just the three of us. Alan, you can join us and see how cool we were back then."

Alan and Jeri laughed. Mike wondered when the three law school buddies would ever spend time together again.

Chapter 18

September 29, 2016–Three years after Graduation from Law School

JACK RAISED HIS beer and clinked glasses with the mugs of his three co-workers. Foam sloshed onto the metal table, mingling with the pretzels and already spilt beer.

"Thanks Jack for organizing this trip," Bill Pycheck said as he wiped a splotch of beer from his striped button-down.

"Don't worry about that, Bill. We're going to spill lots more before I begin talking with the young ladies in here." Jack swept his arm behind him and his group trained their eyes on the packs of young women engaged in conversation, but who were still aware of the men at other tables. "At least you're not wearing that five hundred dollar suit you had on at work," Jack said loud enough for others in the bar to hear and hoping they were noticing him in his stylish blue jeans and form-fitting long sleeved t-shirt.

Jack turned his attention back to his group. "Gentlemen, and lady," Jack said with feigned seriousness, forcing his face to contort pompously, "we must say goodbye to our dear friend Vy Bock, a man we spent a lot of time with, but one we hardly knew."

The group chuckled and each member simultaneously tossed back a swig of beer. Pycheck threw an arm around his departing friend. "Seriously, you will be missed. I thought out of all of us, you would be the first one to make partner, you are so damned smart."

Bock caught Pycheck's gaze. "Thanks man. It's been more than three years and I need to be doing something else. I'm burned out and too young to be spending sixty hours a week in the office. I never could see the light at the end of the tunnel.

"So, what are you going to do?" Pycheck asked.

"I'm not sure. I realized last week I can't do this anymore. I don't think writing memos for legal issues tangentially touching cases brought by multi-billion-dollar companies is for me. I saved some money, so I'm going to take some time and travel. After that, who knows? I want to put my law degree to some socially meaningful use."

"Oh, I thought *everything* we did had significant social meaning," said Jack, not attempting to hide his sarcasm.

Peggy Gamble was morose. "We began with nine of us and now there is only going to be three. They work us until we drop. Kind of like horses, aren't we?"

"But we are better dressed," retorted Jack to the chuckles of his friends.

"Come on, take this seriously," Gamble said. "Does anyone care that at this rate none of us will be around in a couple of years?"

"Hold on," Jack said, starting to get his ire up. "We are still here and there is a reason. So far, we worked harder and performed better than everyone who started with us. We are all on partnership track if we keep on doing what we're doing."

Gamble's face flashed red. "What makes you think you are so much more talented than the rest of the group? The only reason we are still here is because we are willing to work two thousand five hundred hours every year and not make waves. Dave Remback, remember him? The partners told him to leave after eight months because he dared to ask for two days off when his aunt died. They told him an aunt didn't count as close enough of a relative and if he took time off, not to come back. So, he didn't come back."

Gamble stood and paced around their table before sitting again to continue: "Bev Norvack–she hinted about getting married and possibly having a kid–so at her next performance review the partners suggested her work was substandard and gave her two weeks to find another job. It's bullshit. We are only here because we tow the company line and kiss some ass." She locked eyes with Jack, whose eyes narrowed.

"Hey, all I am doing is trying to get to know everyone at the firm. It's called being friendly. Perhaps you've read a little about it?" Jack lowered his head and gave his best doe-eyed impression. "You know, a few well-placed blowjobs usually do the trick. You should try it sometime."

Gamble faked dumping her beer on Jack and said, "By the way, I don't think any of us are on partnership track. When we are all gone, nobody will remember our names."

"Speak for yourself," Jack said, leaning forward on his stool. "I am planning on making partner in three years. I actually have a couple of cases of my own. A few of the partners assured me if those go well and the clients are happy, I could be looking at a long career here."

Gamble slumped back into her chair. Silence hung for a minute as each stared off in different directions.

"Well, I'm thrilled for Vy," Pycheck said. "I'm sure he's going to be a success at whatever it is he ends up doing." Bock smiled warily. Turning to where Jack had been seated he inquired, "Don't you think so, Jack?" No response greeted his question and the group turned to find his seat unoccupied. Further up the aisle, Jack was resting his arms on a table while talking to a leggy brunette. She threw her head back laughing at Jack's banter, causing her permed hair to bounce.

Vy grunted in astonishment. "At least we know Jack is going to be where he wants to be tonight."

Chapter 19

November 9, 2016–Three Years after Graduation from Law School

JACK TRIED TO sit straight as possible in the leather chair. He forced himself to breathe, but didn't want to make any noticeable movements. Ed Wagner stalked around his office yelling at the bronze statue on the bookshelf and in the direction of the windows, but Jack knew he was the subject of the tirade.

"Two weeks ago, I asked you to cover a deposition in a relatively simple matter because a federal judge summoned me over to court on another case. This was a chance for you to impress–take your first deposition. You seemed so eager to please, but then I read the transcript."

Wagner sat back into his chair and began waving the transcript over his head. "It's not so hard–you ask questions, you get answers, and you show you are in charge."

Not sure if Wagner wanted him to respond, Jack remained silent, wondering why his mentor was so mad.

After Wagner had given him the file, Jack spent the next three days reviewing every pleading and all of the discovery that the parties had taken. Jack learned the plaintiff, an overweight Mexican immigrant, claimed their client, a national supermarket chain, spilled some pickles in an aisle and failed to clean them up. The store employees said they weren't aware of the spill until the plaintiff fell. The spill was significant, so the clerks questioned how the plaintiff did not see it while walking through the aisle.

After questioning the witness, Jack reported back to Wagner that everything had proceeded as planned. He summarized the plaintiff's testimony and was surprised when Wagner did not respond with enthusiasm. "Let's wait until we review it on paper," Wagner had said.

As Wagner waved the transcript over his head, Jack wondered what he had missed and why Wagner's cheeks were so fiery red.

"Do you know what a deposition is for?"

Jack guessed he was supposed to answer this question. "Yes, I was trying to find out what knowledge the plaintiff possessed and what he didn't know."

"Of course, but don't throw back at me what you learned in school. This isn't law school anymore. With a deposition your job is to demonstrate who's in charge. Scare them. Show them you mean business. Then you get the information from them. It's not social hour. You are not there to make friends with the other lawyer or to provide hospitality. You're to put on a display for our client."

Jack was confused. "But you told me we are supposed to teach the other side how to dance so ultimately we can reach a settlement without a lot of risk."

"True, you're correct, but who's your audience for this deposition?"

"Well, the other attorney was there and so was the plaintiff's wife."

"No," Wagner bellowed as he interrupted Jack. "You are doing this for the client. Don't you realize our clients read every transcript—exactly what I want them to do. They review the deposition and they learn how hard we are fighting for them. We are not telling jokes with the other attorney. We are not worrying if everyone is comfortable. We are showing the people who pay our bills we are kicking ass and we are always protecting their interests."

"But what if I am getting all the information I need without kicking butt?"

"Doesn't matter. I spend lots of time with our clients educating them about how lawsuits are won. I build up their expectations so they think every case is World War Three. By being a hard-ass at the depositions I'm only doing what they expect of me. Ultimately, I try to set their expectations at a high level so when we settle for less, they are thrilled."

Wagner rubbed his brow and sighed before continuing. "You didn't do any of that. You sound like a little pansy. Our client is going to be extremely concerned about who we are letting handle their cases. Now I'm compelled to do damage control."

The blood drained from Jack's face. He thought he had handled the deposition perfectly and assumed Wagner would shower him with praise. Instead, Wagner was berating him.

Jack peered at Wagner inquisitively and, trying to save some face, asked what he could have done differently.

The question caused Wagner to interrupt his rant. He slowed and sat back in his chair. He patted the deposition now resting on his desk. "Jack, you have a lot of outstanding qualities and I think you are going to make the kind of lawyer that will do well at this firm and make our clients want you."

Jack relaxed ever so slightly and tried to take in what Wagner was telling him.

"The point is," Wagner began, "you know where the case is going before you walk into the conference room to question their witness. You've talked to the plaintiff's attorney and begun dancing with him. You've managed his views of the value of the case and you've already set the client's expectations for something worse. So when you go into the deposition, you want to demonstrate to the client you're in charge and you control everything.

"For example, make sure once you enter the conference room everything is on the record. Make sure the court reporter is ready to begin transcribing the minute everyone is in the room. Don't ask people where they want to sit, tell them. Don't make pleasantries or ask the plaintiff if he wants something to drink. Just start. Everybody gives instructions to witnesses at the beginning of a deposition, but yours didn't do anything. This is the time to throw out some scary stuff–clients love that."

Jack sat quietly and wrote notes on his yellow pad as Wagner lectured. "Give them the usual instruction about if they don't hear a question they should ask you to repeat it, but also remind them they are under oath and outline the penalties for perjury, including the possibility they can go to jail. This may never happen, but our clients think you are hard hitting when you throw it in.

"When you start the interrogation, don't begin with the personal information, you can ask for their home address and kids' names at the end of the deposition. Start right with the meat. I don't want you to ask open-ended questions. Lead the witness right to the correct answers. When you let them pick their own words they talk forever. When you tell them what the answer should be, the other attorney may object, but it reads better on paper."

Wagner's instructions on how to take a deposition amazed Jack. His advice contradicted everything Jack learned in law school. Although Wagner was more concerned about the client's reaction to what was said than the reality of the case, Wagner explained if Jack made the other attorney dance, the facts didn't matter. What mattered more was the client's belief that it might pay a huge verdict compelling it to allocate more money to a settlement.

Wagner spent the next two hours instructing Jack on how to take a deposition. No textbook Jack studied in law school mentioned any of these concepts. When Wagner finished, Jack had nearly filled his yellow pad with notes. Wagner summarily dismissed Jack who left his office in a daze. Although he had practiced law for over three years, Jack still couldn't grasp the complete puzzle of litigation. His stomach churned with the craving to attain Wagner's status.

Chapter 20

January 12, 2017–Three years after Graduation from Law School

THE STEAM ROSE from the coffee as Mike wrapped his hands around the cup, trying to gather some warmth. He sat in the vinyl booth directly across from his uncle as they did most days before trudging to the office. Patrons filled the booths along both sides of the diner. Waitresses rushed to bring food as quickly as the cooks prepared it. The din enveloping Mike and his uncle did not interfere with their conversation.

"We've dealt with who the Pirates should trade and you've listened to my diatribe on the Steelers' defense, but you haven't told me anything about your visit with Tony Walters," Stan said.

"Not much to say," Mike said, looking down at his coffee. "He's an old high school friend who was visiting some family. We went out last night. Not much to do to impress a friend here in Pottstown. We had a couple of beers and now I'm not feeling so great. Just trying to shake out the cobwebs and keep up with topics you keep throwing at me."

"Now I understand why you are not looking your best. You should probably start eating a little healthier."

"Thanks Uncle Stan, that's a big help." Mike leaned back in the booth and yawned. "Any cases you want to talk about before we head to the office and deal with the phone calls and emails? You know how much I appreciate your questions early in the morning."

Stan smiled as the waitress silently placed their oatmeal and bagels in front of them. They dug into their food in silence. Stan wiped the remnants of oatmeal from his lip. He hesitated before beginning, "I wanted to tell you something, but I am not sure what to say."

"Go ahead Uncle Stan, say what you were going to say," said Mike, almost reflexively.

Stan took a sip of his coffee and cleared his throat. "I went to the doctor's last Friday. He called me yesterday with some test results."

Mike sat up, the press of the vinyl sticking to his shoulders. "What did the doctor say?"

"Unfortunately, he said I had renal cancer. Early stages, decent chance they can take care of it, but...," his voice trailed off.

"Oh Uncle Stan, I am so sorry." Mike's eyes welled up. His heart pounded, creating a swelling pain inside of his body. Mike wanted to say more, but nothing would come out.

He wanted to tell his uncle how much he appreciated him for coming to his assistance after his parents' divorce and for teaching him how to be a lawyer. To tell him everything would be okay and he would do anything to help. He needed to say so much, but his throat tightened and his eyes lowered to focus on the oatmeal. He reached over and touched his uncle's hand. They finished their meal in silence.

Chapter 21

May 15, 2017—Four Years after Graduation from Law School

THE AUDITORIUM IN the courthouse was the jewel of the antiquated building. The gleaming rows of wooden benches and the overhanging balcony lent a unique setting for highly publicized trials or other public events. Alan Corcoran stood proudly at the podium. Jeri sat in a high-backed red velvet chair next to the president judge and the city's mayor. The four hundred people in the audience included many of the finest lawyers in the county, as well as Jeri's family and friends. A sprinkling of dignitaries added luster to the event.

"Jeri Richards was among the best and brightest at her law school and has been the most successful prosecutor ever since she started at the District Attorney's Office three years ago. Like everyone who starts as an assistant DA, Jeri cut her teeth prosecuting small crimes. But that didn't last long–her talents kept propelling her higher.

"After a series of promotions, moving up through the divisions, she began to prosecute sex offenses. I offered Jeri the opportunity to work in any division, but she wanted to deal with society's filth and to handle rape and pornography cases. To say she pursued these criminals with a vengeance would be an understatement. In her two years dealing with rapists and molesters she not only handled more files than any other assistant DA, but nobody else could challenge her results.

"You hear about some prosecutors who settle the hard cases to keep their conviction rate up. Not Jeri, she doesn't think like that. She only settled when circumstances forced her to, and even though she tried more cases than any other lawyer in the DA's office, she maintained the highest conviction rate of any prosecutor."

Corcoran paused as he gazed out at a captivated audience. He had taken a risk by suggesting to the county's democratic leadership that Jeri run for the recently vacated seat held previously by Judge Wecksel, who unceremoniously retired after pictures of him pleasuring his secretary on the desk in his chambers became public. Corcoran was able to promote Jeri's prosecutorial record and avoid any discussion of her relative lack of experience.

"Jeri was a tireless campaigner. She was savvy with the party members and had an unmistakable ability to connect with the voters. She won endorsements from all the major unions and from many of our local officials who have joined us today. Her opponent may have run for judge four times before this, but it was Jeri whom the voters recognized at election time, leading her to win the race by nearly forty percentage points."

When the applause died down, he continued: "As unhappy as I am to be losing a talented assistant district attorney, I am pleased the county bench will be strengthened by the wisdom and determination of Jeri Richards. Congratulations to our newest judge and here's to many more years of public service."

Jeri let the applause roll over her. Standing, she faced her audience and strode to the lectern. "I am so proud to be a judge of the Commonwealth," she said. "As I said so many times during my campaign, we are now in a better position to rid our city of malingerers, evildoers, and anyone else who thinks he can take advantage of the weak. I feel it is my job to protect those who are at risk from the actions of criminals and I will do everything to fulfill that responsibility."

Chapter 22

May 15, 2017—Four Years after Graduation from Law School

JERI WORKED THE room after her swearing-in, making sure she spent some quality facetime with those who helped her get elected. In the span of twenty minutes she shook hands with the mayor, the president judge, the head of her election committee, the party chairwoman, and others who either contributed to her campaign or who had worked to make the day a reality.

As she shook hands with a donor, Jeri noticed Mike and Jack at a small table and her heart leapt. She ended her conversation and nearly skipped over to the boys, who pulled her into a hug. Jeri took a step back and appraised them both out from head to toe. She nodded her approval and said, "Mike, I want to hear what's new in your life, but I get to see you fairly regularly." Poking an index finger into Jack's chest she continued, "You bastard. I text you. I email you, but you never respond. I haven't spoken to you for almost two years. That doesn't matter now. You are here and I am so happy. What is going on?" A smile overtook her face. She bounced on her toes waiting for Jack to speak.

"We would never miss this. You're a judge. So unbelievably cool," Jack said while grinning at Jeri. "Will you take us on a tour of your chambers?"

"Sure, sure, in a few minutes." Jeri grabbed Jack's arm. "So, how is legal life in Chicago? You must be a partner already, come on, give me some dirt."

Jack's face flushed at the attention. He recovered quickly, stood up straight and adjusted his tie. "I've not yet reached that vaunted status, but I am working hard and think I have a chance of making it soon. Sucking in with the right partners is a lot of work, but somehow, I'm getting the hang of it."

Mike and Jeri laughed. "Probably nobody is better than you at your firm," Jeri responded. Mike smacked Jack on the back and the three friends continued to catch up. After a few minutes, Mike suggested Jeri mingle with the other lawyers and dignitaries.

"Guys, we never hang out anymore. Once I walk away, I may not see you again for years," Jeri sighed. The two boys grinned while Jeri gazed at them questioningly.

When they said nothing, Jeri begged, "What are you guys not telling me?"

Mike and Jack exchanged glances before Jack spoke. "You're never going to believe it, but we may be seeing each other more than any of us want."

Mike added, "We appear to have a case together in Pittsburgh."

"Seriously?" Jeri said, her face scrunching up.

Jack put his lanky arm around Mike's shoulder. "My firm represents a national department store chain with a few stores in Pittsburgh. Seems like Mike's client stole some things and the employees detained her. Typical stuff, but she is suing for false arrest."

Mike gently removed Jack's arm and explained, "It's not so simple," he said. "My woman is a sweet lady and the company didn't treat her well. From what her husband tells me, this little incident as Jack refers to it, messed her up. Before the family didn't have many problems. This event caused them a lot of anguish."

"Sounds like an interesting case," Jeri said, almost to herself. "Are you two able to play nice?"

Mike stared right at Jeri. "My uncle taught me lawyers should always act professionally. Whether the other attorney is a saint or the biggest asshole, we should always remember to remain above the fray."

"Beautiful speech Mike. Thanks for the professionalism lesson, pal," Jack said. "My firm taught me it doesn't matter who is on the other side because we always play to win. I hope you remember that when the jury comes back with a defense verdict." Jack stared right at Mike. Neither flinched.

"I guess we'll find out tomorrow," Mike said. "Jack is actually in town to take my clients' depositions. We scheduled them around him coming in for this event. Perhaps he'll play nicer in the morning." Mike focused his attention directly on Jack. "You do know how to question a witness, don't you Jack? How many depositions have you taken so far in your career?"

Jack winced. "Dude, I work on multi-billion-dollar litigation. Your client's little claim isn't going to keep me up at night. I think my firm knows how to handle a case like this." Nonetheless, Jack felt a small drop of sweat run down his back.

Jeri looked at her watch and quietly excused herself from her friends, having caught sight of the mayor.

"She is awesome and has the perfect temperament for a judge," Mike remarked.

"I don't think I would ever want to be in front of her, especially unprepared. She's going to bust some lawyers real good someday," Jack said, causing both of them to laugh.

"I should be getting home to check on my uncle," Mike responded. "I will meet you for breakfast like you wanted. I guess I will see you bright and early in the morning."

"Looking forward to crushing you and your hopes of a large verdict."

Chapter 23

May 15, 2017—Four Years after Graduation from Law School

MIKE LOUNGED ON his couch, the Gebbert file spread out on the coffee table. His client's responses to the department store's interrogatories rested on his lap. He had read them a hundred times and knew what his clients had said by memory. His cellphone buzzed and he saw Jeri's name pop up on the display.

"Your Honor," Mike said, "twice in one day we get to chat."

"Shut up Mike. It's Jeri, not Your Honor."

"Hi Jeri, what's up?"

"I was calling to thank you for coming to my installation today, but also to talk about you and Jack."

"You're welcome. What *about* Jack?"

Jeri hesitated before saying, "I don't know. I'm a little worried about you having a case with him."

"Why? I don't think it's a big deal."

"Maybe not, but his firm has a reputation for being pretty aggressive. They're known for doing scorched earth litigation."

"I know that already and it's probably accurate. Truthfully, when we filed the complaint we were hoping this would be rather simple. I think we have a good liability case, but damages are going to be more difficult to prove. I thought we would get their attention with the complaint, but they seem to want to file motions. So far, we have gotten two motions to dismiss and a set of preliminary objections. I've done a lot of work on this case, but really, we haven't gotten anywhere yet. Plus, my clients are already talking about having their day in court."

"Sounds like Jack's firm is trying to get their billables in early."

"That's what we thought. I was surprised when I saw Jack's name on the Answer. We wondered if Jack was assigned to the case knowing that we were friends trying to get some leverage over me."

"I doubt that would work. Do you think you can handle a case against a big firm?"

"Sure, we do it all of the time. That's the big advantage of working with my uncle. I've taken a ton of depositions and I've even tried five jury trials. I'm sure working at that huge firm Jack hasn't tried any cases."

"Have you had any big cases go to trial?"

"Not yet, but I'm learning something with every trial. Last trial I had my uncle was in the back of the courtroom watching, and I neglected to object when the defense attorney brought up some other accidents when he was questioning my client. Turns out the jury thought this evidence was significant and found against my client when they likely would have given him some money if they hadn't heard the evidence. My uncle took me out to the woodshed for that one. Told me I need to think through every contingency so I am prepared to object and be ready to respond to anything that may come up during trial. It was a good lesson to learn."

"Sounds like a rough lesson. I'm worried that two friends trying a case against each other may test the limits of the friendship."

"I thought of that also. Well, Jack wanted to meet for breakfast tomorrow. Maybe he wants to discuss the rules of us trying a case opposing each other."

"Let's hope so. I wanted to let you know I was worried."

"Thanks, Jeri."

They ended their phone conversation and Mike wondered if his uncle had any sage advice to help him try a case against a friend.

Chapter 24

May 15, 2017—Four Years after Graduation from Law School

STRETCHING OUT ON the hotel bed, Jack listened to the voice on the other end of his cellphone as he pushed his room service meal to the side. The conversation pleased Jack. He had the full attention of Ed Wagner, who was offering him some inside information.

"I met with the president and CFO of Wendell's. We were joined by someone with a lot of authority from their insurance company. Did you meet with your law school buddy?"

"Yes, we met today and we are going to meet before the depositions tomorrow. Anything I need to know?"

"I'm getting to that. The officers from the department store were stuck on the fact that the security guard followed policy when he took Mrs. Gebbert downstairs. They don't think the company's exposure in this case is terribly significant. I had to spend a lot of time explaining that maybe the policy wasn't appropriate. I told them they faced significant potential exposure, especially considering the punitive damage claim in the complaint."

"Sounds like you had them wrapped around your finger."

"Something like that. The bottom line is that they were convinced that a jury could award in excess of a million dollars—not likely, but possible. I knew that just by throwing out that number the insurance company would raise its reserves and throw more money at a settlement. At the end of the meeting the insurance company gave us authority to settle this case for anything under six hundred thousand dollars."

"Holy shit, Ed, that's a lot on a case like this. Were the company execs okay with this?'

"Hell yes. What do they care? It's not their money. Their exposure is on the punitive claim because that claim is not insured. They just want this claim settled. They were very clear about that."

"With that type of money, I would think I can settle this case."

"You better get it done. The company will be quite happy with us if we get rid of this. We will get lots of business from these guys if we keep them satisfied."

"I think there's going to be a lot of dancing tomorrow. You'll buy me a beer when I get this settled."

"Absolutely."

Chapter 25

May 16, 2017—Four Years after Graduation from Law School

THE WIND WHISTLED a high-pitched tune every time the door opened to the diner. Mike and Jack were huddled in a booth in the back near to an outdated radiator, keeping firm grasps on their steaming mugs of coffee and wearing their overcoats in an attempt to keep warm while they attacked their breakfasts.

As they ate, Mike said, "It's weird eating in this diner with you. My uncle and I eat here a lot."

Jack gaped while Mike shoveled the remaining forkfuls of his omelet and hash browns into his mouth. "Wow, you can still eat like a champ. Amazing, you don't weigh three hundred pounds yet," Jack commented as Mike leaned back in the booth.

Mike suppressed a burp, patted his stomach and said, "Unfortunately, I am getting closer to that every day. The practice of law is not the best way to maintain a healthy lifestyle."

Jack nodded. "I wanted to discuss our case. I was hoping we might be able to reach some common ground." Jack pictured his mentor Ed standing in his office, his hips gyrating.

"Sure buddy, what do you want to talk about?"

"Well, I've reviewed the file and talked to our people at the store and they think we have strong defenses." Jack leaned back and waited for Mike to respond, but Mike kept his gaze locked on Jack's face, forcing Jack to continue. "I thought we should decide where the case is going and see if we could get it resolved."

Jack was stammering and did not like how he was starting this conversation.

"We are at the beginning of discovery. We haven't taken any depositions yet. What are you proposing?" Mike asked, somewhat perplexed.

"Well, I don't think your case is very strong, but I thought we could figure out a way to get some money to you and your woman."

Mike's skin flushed as he grabbed the edge of the table with both hands. "Jack, I'm not sure how we can begin this discussion. Nothing's been done yet. I am waiting for you to send me some discovery. You don't know anything about my client. Let me say I disagree with your contention our case is not very strong. Remember what your people did to my client. Mrs. Gebbert is going to scare you. Your department store damaged a really nice woman."

"Hey, slow down buddy," Jack interjected. "I know this is early, but I think we can agree that after some discovery and some motions it would be helpful to put some money in your client's pocket. I don't want to speak out of turn, but if we play nicely here, I'm sure my people will pay something like seventy-five grand to you and your client."

Mike continued to look at Jack, his hands grasping the table ever tighter. "Jack, I don't think you know the case well enough to try and settle it yet. Let me repeat—my client is hurt—and hurt badly by your department store. I'm not sure what this ultimately is worth, but settlement isn't happening now."

Jack's heart sank. He assumed he would have little difficulty making Mike dance.

Anger then quickly took ahold of Jack when he realized settling wouldn't be as simple as he planned. He slammed his hand on the table. "Fine. You don't want to make some easy money. Let's see how you act after I destroy your client at her deposition. Once she starts crying, you'll be begging me to offer her scraps. Mike, my firm is going to bury you in a mountain of discovery."

Jack knew he probably had gone too far. He put his hand on Mike's arm and flashed his smile. Mike yanked his arm away and threw a twenty-dollar bill on the table. "Breakfast is on me. I'll see you in a couple of hours. Jack, you better make sure you don't cross the line."

Mike picked up his papers and walked quickly through the diner's glass door into the cold, brisk air outside.

Chapter 26

May 16, 2017—Four Years after Graduation from Law School

STEPHANIE REGALSKI SAT calmly at her desk that faced the door to the law office, prepared to greet anyone who dragged themselves in from the frigid cold. The trim redhead attempted to appear busy by scribbling on her note pad, but her attention was riveted on the commotion coming from the conference room immediately to her right. Dressed in a red blouse and dark woolen pants with spotless leather boots, she looked more like a lawyer than an assistant or paralegal or receptionist or any of the myriad of other positions she held at the law firm.

Stephanie had worked for Stan for over 20 years, beginning when she was fresh out of college, and believed her employment was a steppingstone to a job in fashion or real estate in New York City. Marriage at age twenty-two and three kids in five years disrupted her long-term plans. She and her husband settled in Pottstown with the thought that it would only be temporary..

After starting with the firm and working six months answering phones and scheduling appointments, Stephanie went to Stan seeking more responsibility. Stan had already recognized Stephanie's innate intelligence and common sense. He gradually assigned Stephanie a greater variety of tasks. Soon she was the firm's expert in probating wills, navigating the bureaucracy of workers' compensation, and conducting legal research.

Stan and his now deceased partner had long considered hiring a younger attorney to help with their workload. But he found in many ways Stephanie was more competent, less expensive and easier to deal with than an opinionated newly-minted lawyer.

Stephanie understood her worth to her firm, but so did Stan. She never needed to ask for a raise and every Christmas she received a generous bonus. In a sense, their lives were symbiotic—Stephanie providing a growing array of legal services as Stan's practice grew and Stan offering support, financial and otherwise, Stephanie could not receive elsewhere.

Perhaps Stephanie's greatest attribute was her ability to relate to Stan's clients. Comprised primarily of individuals who were physically hurt or financially aggrieved, they differed from corporate clients who generally understood how litigation worked and the amount of time and energy necessary to move from the filing of a complaint to a verdict.

Stan's clients, on the other hand, had one lawsuit and to them it was the most important thing in their lives. They didn't understand it was common for months to go by with nothing happening on a case. The majority were looking for constant updates that Stan, like most other busy plaintiff lawyers, couldn't provide.

Many of the calls the firm received came from people wanting reassurance their cases were moving forward and that Stan had a plan specific to their case. This task gradually fell to Stephanie, who with a nearly encyclopedic familiarity of all of the files in the office, was able to tell a client exactly what was happening with their case.

The turmoil in the conference room was interfering with the tranquility of the office, preventing Stephanie from getting any work done. The anguished cries breaching the walls beckoned to Stephanie, who wanted to offer her assistance, and was working on an excuse to enter the room.

As she was about to intervene, the glass door swung open, revealing Mike, weary and disheveled. He approached Stephanie's desk wide-eyed with fear. She kept silent, waiting for Mike to volunteer information.

Mike met her gaze to exclaim, "Oh my god, this is a disaster."

Stephanie maintained her silence, but cocked her head.

"She is a mess and losing it before my eyes. I can't settle her down."

"You've been in there for nearly three hours. What's going on?"

"I'm not sure. I met with them twice at their house already and I didn't sense any major problems. They came here today and it's a complete disaster. For some reason just coming to the office has raised her anxiety off the charts."

"You don't have to tell me. I've been hearing her wails through the walls and they are only getting worse. The depositions are supposed to take place in less than an hour."

Mike peeked at his watch. "I know, it's a serious problem. She doesn't think she can do it. She says she doesn't want to relive what happened. Her husband tried. I tried. Nothing is working. This case is about to go down the toilet."

Stephanie stood and patted Mike on the back. "I've talked to Mrs. Gebbert some on the phone. I've communicated with her spouse a lot. Can I try talking to her?"

Relief passed over Mike's face. "Please, would you? I think it might help," he said. "Whatever you can do would be great. I like these people. Somehow I want to help them deal with this."

Stephanie peered into the conference room. Paul Gebbert was staring out the window overlooking the neighboring industrial park while Martha meekly sipped coffee from the cup she held with both of her hands. Even with only a quick assessment, Stephanie could tell the situation was precarious.

"Hi Martha, how's everything going?" Stephanie asked as she approached the conference room table. Martha did not look up, but replied, "Oh, not so well."

Stephanie smiled directly at Martha as she sat down in the chair next to her and placed a hand gently on her arm. "This isn't easy, is it?" Martha stared out over the table, but at nothing in particular. Her eyes were glassy and the little bit of mascara she was wearing was running. "No," was all she mustered.

Mike stood silently a few feet behind Stephanie and Martha, his brow furrowed. Stephanie, probably better than Stan and Mike, understood the toll lawsuits took on the litigants. Even though someone suing another company might be completely in the right, and entitled to significant compensation, the litigation game posed difficulties for those with little experience. Not just answering discovery requests and getting documents the other side requested, but the constant uneasiness of being in the dark, of not understanding the process, and never knowing when the game was to finish, all sucked the life out of litigants.

Stephanie placed a hand on Martha's elbow. "Hey Martha, why did you decide to sue the department store?"

Martha took a deep breath. "Paul wanted me to do it. He thought they messed up our lives. I'm not worried about making any money from this, but I didn't want anyone else to go through what I did."

"So what's the problem now—why are you so upset?"

"Every time Mike starts to question me about what happened at the store, I picture the security guard and the smile on his face. I think he enjoyed what he did to me. I can't force the image of his face out of my head." Martha started to take in air rapidly. "I see him and I can't get out of the room. I'm stuck there."

"Martha, are you still chained in the room?"

"Yes, every day."

Stephanie let Martha catch her breath and handed her a tissue. "I'm not much of a psychologist, but I think I can help you out of the room." Martha eyes locked with Stephanie. "If you can talk about what happened, if you can stand up to their lawyers and show them they can't get the best of you, I think you could find your way out of the room. If not, you may be stuck for a long time. The other thing, Martha, if you are able to find your way out of that room, I think you might prevent a lot of other people from ever having to go into the room again."

Martha continued to search Stephanie's eyes.

"I don't know. Their attorney is going to ask me a bunch of questions about what happened."

"Do you remember what happened?"

"Absolutely, every detail."

Mike nodded and bent down so he could look Martha in the face. "In every conversation I've had with you, you've told the same story, with the exact same details about your detention at the department store. It's still in your head. You just have to let it out."

Stephanie was now squatting on the other side of Martha. She said, "Do you have any problem telling the truth?"

"No."

"What if the store's attorney challenges you on what occurred?"

"He wasn't there. He doesn't know what happened."

"Martha, what do you think will happen if you can't go through with the deposition?"

"I guess my lawsuit will be over."

"True. Anything else."

"They probably won't change anything they are doing."

"Martha, that's right. Nothing will change and other people might end up in that room."

With her husband now standing behind her rubbing her neck, Martha gathered her thoughts. Everyone else waited for her to make the next move.

After a few minutes of silent deliberation, Martha stood up, faced Mike, and stated emphatically, "I think I'm ready for my deposition."

Mike turned to her husband, seeking confirmation she would be able to get through the questioning. Paul shrugged his shoulders. "If she says she's ready, then she is ready."

Chapter 27

May 16, 2017—Four Years after Graduation from Law School

NOTHING IN THE law office appeared out of the ordinary when Jack Rogers entered pulling his stuffed, wheeled briefcase. No evidence of Martha Gebbert's near meltdown remained and Jack had no idea how close he had been to winning his lawsuit only minutes before. He strutted to Stephanie's desk and announced his presence.

Mike soon emerged from the conference room to shake Jack's hand. Mike's demeanor evinced no residual anger from their earlier encounter at the diner.

Mike guided Jack into the conference room and introduced him to the Gebberts, who timidly stood and offered handshakes. Jack ignored the Gebberts and strode immediately to the head of the table while asking the court reporter if she was ready to begin.

Martha Gebbert sat across from Jack while Mike eased himself into the seat next to her. He placed his hand lightly on her arm and whispered into her ear. Martha indicated she was doing fine, but her gaze did not rise above the table top. Mike placed his yellow pad in front of himself and jotted a few quick notes.

After unpacking binders and papers from his briefcase, Jack avoided making eye contact with Mrs. Gebbert, and asked the court reporter to swear in the witness. Once Martha indicated she would tell the truth, Jack began to give her instructions as to how the deposition would proceed.

He started by informing her that the court stenographer would be taking down all of her testimony so she needed to respond clearly and verbally. Martha indicated she would be able to do that. She also agreed she would wait until Jack completed his question before she would begin to answer and Jack said he would not speak over Mrs. Gebbert while she gave an answer. Mike did not contest these instructions, as they were given in some form at every deposition.

When Jack told Martha she must answer every question he asked her without consulting with her attorney, Mike interrupted and told Martha that if she wanted to ask him anything at any time they would confer. Jack countered that if a question was pending, Martha had to respond before doing anything else, to which Mike told Martha that if she ever wanted to discuss anything with him at any point during the questioning, she should say so and they would find a private place to talk.

Jack shook his head at Mike's interruption and continued his instructions. "Mrs. Gebbert, you are aware you are under oath, aren't you?"

"Yes."

"You understand what being under oath means?"

"Yes. I am supposed to tell the truth."

"Correct, and I am informing you if you aren't completely honest, you can be brought up on charges of perjury and if you are convicted, the court can impose sentences including substantial fines and jail time."

Mike jumped out of his chair, his face turning fiery red. "Hold on right there," he spat out. "What the hell is that, Jack?"

"I am instructing the witness about what will happen if she lies during the deposition."

"No you aren't. You can tell her about the procedures in this room, but don't you tell her anything about what the law is. That is my job. Don't suggest to her there may be any penalty for how she testifies today, because there aren't. Don't you ever try to threaten my client. That is garbage, and if you try anything like that again, we are walking out of this deposition and we will seek sanctions against you for your behavior. How's that for a threat, Jack?"

Mike took a deep breath and sat down. "Jack, we may be friends, but don't think I'm going to let you try anything improper. My first allegiance here is to my client and I will do everything within the bounds of the law to protect her, you understand?"

Jack did not respond, keeping his eyes cast downward, looking at his yellow pad. Mike did not let up. "Well Jack are you going to begin your questioning?" Martha perked up watching her lawyer come to her rescue. A small smile came to her face as she waited for her first question.

Chapter 28

May 17, 2017—Four Years after Graduation from Law School

THE SMELL OF the hospital had been the same every time Mike walked down the hallway over the past few weeks: clean, antiseptic, with a slightly sweet tinge that made him wonder whether the odor was the result of overzealous cleaning in an attempt to fight the viruses that had recently plagued the hospital.

Arriving at the semi-private room his uncle had been in for nearly three weeks, Mike was relieved to see Stan sitting up in bed, perusing a baseball magazine. Knocking softly while peeking into the room, Mike said, "Anybody up for some visitors?"

Seeing his nephew entering the room, Stan tossed the periodical aside. "Please, come in. Talk to me, let me know what is happening in the real world."

Mike pulled a chair to Stan's side and sat looking at his uncle in his pale green hospital gown. "Your attire has not improved much since last time." Stan chuckled and turned off the television.

"How are you feeling, Uncle Stan?"

"Not bad. This new medication is taking a toll, but my doctor says I am doing much better."

"Sounds like you are ready to get out of here. Can't wait to have you back in the office."

"I'm looking forward to it too. I feel like I've been gone forever. Tell me what's going on there, Mike."

"Come on Uncle Stan, you know exactly what is going on. I know you talk to Stephanie for two hours every day. I'm sure you know how many paper clips we bought last week and every motion I filed since you arrived here," Mike said.

"Humor a sick man, won't you Mike? Tell me how things are going at the office."

"Sure, play the sympathy card. I've been here every day for the past three weeks and have told you what is happening. I know you think this will help your recovery, so I will give you a brief update."

Stan adjusted his pillow behind him and sat up straighter.

"Things are going fine so far, but we miss you," Mike began. "As we discussed earlier this week, I settled a few cases so we got enough money in to make payroll."

Stan rolled his eyes. "I'm not too worried about the firm's finances. We can all survive a few more days with me in the hospital. This isn't like it was in the old days when all of us were living paycheck to paycheck. Come on, give me some real information."

"Fine." Mike began to reach for his yellow pad with the notes he took during the Gebberts' depositions, but hesitated. He then leaned in and told Stan about Jack's hard-handed ploy at the diner and how Mrs. Gebbert nearly imploded before the questioning began. When he mentioned that Jack suggested Martha could go to jail if she lied, Stan flushed with anger, but said nothing.

"I was worried about how Mrs. Gebbert would do. We met three times to prepare but as the deposition got closer she got more nervous. I told her she would be okay and after he asked a few easy questions at the beginning of the deposition—like 'What is your name?' and 'Where do you live?'—that she would relax, but Jack's first question was, 'You stole the chocolate didn't you?'"

Stan gripped the rails of his bed, his eyes widening. "That was his first question? Did Mrs. Gebbert collapse?"

"No, the exact opposite. Perhaps it was the audacity of asking it, but she collected herself, locked eyes with Jack, and said, and I quote: 'No, it was sitting right on the counter like samples are laid out in any store and I took one. The chocolate was so tasty I wanted to buy a box, but before I got a chance your security guard grabbed me.'"

Stan laughed. "A perfect answer."

Mike nodded and continued: "I actually think Jack was thrown a bit by how easily Martha handled the questions about the incident. She kept right on answering even when the same question was asked two or three times. She kept giving consistent answers. You know she has always said the same thing about how the incident occurred since I met her."

"How long did her deposition take?"

"It was a little over five hours. He spent about two-and-a-half hours on the incident and almost as much time on her damages and then asked for all of the education and prior hospitalization information at the end. Martha's problem was answering questions about how this incident has hurt her. She didn't say much and wouldn't, or couldn't, open up about how this incident still causes her problems."

"Is that an issue?" Stan grinned like a grandfather watching his grandson score his first soccer goal.

"I hope not. Jack also deposed her husband, Paul. I think he's rock-solid. He painted a grim picture about what their life is like now. I felt Jack was rolling his eyes when Mr. Gebbert talked about his wife's injuries. But that is the nature of these types of injuries—it's not like a broken bone, it doesn't show up on an x-ray. Jack is going to have to come to grips with that. Am I putting the pieces of the discovery puzzle together well enough for you?"

"Absolutely. I just want to think through how you are going to prove your case. It's never too early to start getting ready for trial. How else are you going to be able to demonstrate to them this injury is real?"

"We have the two kids. I met with them once already. Pleasant kids who've learned how to manage their lives independently, without as much help from their mother as they had before. Martha, however, questioned whether the kids should testify at all. She said they suffered enough and didn't want them exposed in court.

"Her doctor will also testify. I haven't met with him yet but she trusts him. I'm not sure what to make of a psychologist and how well he might hold up under cross-examination. They are so touchy-feely and like I said, there is no x-ray which will show a definitive injury. Who knows what a jury is going to think about when we are trying to sell them on a brain injury that happened when she was never hit in the head?"

Stan adjusted his sheets and leaned forward. "You're right. You never know what a jury is going to do. With this type of situation, it's more of a crapshoot—a jury can do almost whatever it wants. It's always safest to settle. A jury may not perceive things the same way you do." They both sat in silence, letting Stan's last comment hang in the air.

"I know, Uncle Stan. You tell your witnesses that if they make a funny face at the wrong time, a jury can turn off leaving them with no chance of winning—and this can happen at any time without anyone in room knowing."

"I know you know this, but juries are fickle. They are given virtually no assistance to guide them in valuing a case. They have no idea if what they award is adequate. Settle your cases, then there are no surprises."

Stan continued to probe. "What type of experts do you think you will need?"

Mike pondered the question. "Like I said, her psychologist will offer testimony about her injuries, but I think he should be the only medical expert we will need. I've been thinking a lot about experts who can testify about what a company should do when it encounters a shoplifter. Ultimately, I must find some sort of security expert with knowledge of the retail industry."

Stan almost jumped out of his bed when he heard Mike's plan. "Wait, ten years ago I tried a case where I used a security expert for a shooting in small store on the south side. He knew his stuff. Worked hard getting himself prepared and could recite the entire file backwards and forwards. He was an attractive man. The women on the jury loved him."

"Did you win the case?"

A sheepish expression overtook Stan's face. "Well, no, we actually lost. But he did an excellent job and I never blamed him for the loss. I can't remember his name, but Stephanie will find it for you. Even if you don't use him, he may give you leads where to find another expert."

"I will get a hold of him as soon as possible. I want to get on top of everything I need to do to get ready for trial."

"How much more discovery do you have and when can you complete it?"

"I'm not so sure Jack will take much more. He subpoenaed all of her medical information. He told me they want whatever doctor they retain as an expert to examine Mrs. Gebbert, but that may be all they have left to do. I still have to take all of their depositions—the security guard, the manager of the store and I told him I want to take depositions of the corporate people who developed the policy and a person who can talk about how the company has implemented its shoplifting policy in the past."

"You still have a lot of work to do, don't you?"

"I do, but we scheduled all of their depositions in a couple of weeks, so I should be okay with the discovery cutoff in a few months."

"Sounds like you have it under control. What are your thoughts about whether the case can be settled?"

Mike shifted in his chair and replied, "It's unclear. Jack offered a chunk of money at the beginning of the lawsuit and suggested there is more available. The offer did not impress Martha and Paul, but it's more than I expected. I'm not sure what our clients would accept, but they aren't going away cheaply. If all goes well when I question the company's witnesses, who knows, but this may not be such a bad case."

"Don't start falling in love with your cases, Mike," Stan advised.

"Oh, I know, but this one is interesting in a weird way. There is a lot of stuff we still don't know and I can't wait to find it out."

"Every case has lots of risk. If they make a decent offer, find a way to get the clients to accept it."

"I hear you, Uncle Stan."

At first Stan didn't respond. He looked out the window and then back at his nephew. "Mike, I wanted to thank you for handling all of our cases. It's hard being alone in a law firm, especially when you get sick. Having a partner is much better. I've rested so much easier knowing that you and Stephanie are on top of the cases."

"You're welcome. By the way, when are you getting out of this place and back to the office? I want to ask you some questions about a bunch of files and this is not the best setting to discuss the intricacies of the law."

"I don't know for sure, but I am hoping in a couple of weeks. The doctors are revising my treatment regimen and seem hopeful they got it right this time. Can't say I enjoy it in here—even with all the attention I get at odd hours of the night. I want to be able to come into the office and yell at people again."

Mike smiled. "I haven't seen you yell at anyone since I started working. We need you there. More accurately, I need you there. The Gebbert's case might go to trial at some point and I'm not sure I know how to get it ready. This is much bigger than anything I've handled before and I could use some help." Mike cocked his head.

"Don't worry, I'm getting out of here soon and I will be back to drive everyone crazy again. You should be careful for what you wish for."

Chapter 29

May 24, 2017—Four Years after Graduation from Law School

JERI SAT AT her desk behind a stack of papers. She alternatively read the briefs and the Westlaw cases she had pulled up on her computer. Kathy Wolfson entered without knocking and dropped a stack of mail in front of her. Jeri startled. "Thanks Kathy, these briefs weren't that important," Jeri said with a hint of a smile.

"Sorry Judge, but I thought you might want to see what's on top."

Jeri picked up the first letter. "You're right. It's my case list. The President Judge has finally given me all of the cases the other judges wanted to dump on me. This is going to increase the amount of work we have."

"I suspect it will. There are about a hundred and fifty new cases we have to deal with in addition to the ones you already have."

Jeri nodded, but her eyes were riveted on the paper. "This is interesting," she said. Kathy did not respond, waiting for Jeri to explain. "I'm not sure what the ethics of this are. I need to do some research before I can accept this case."

"That's fine, Judge. Is there anything I can do to help?"

"No, Kathy. This one is a little tricky, but I think I can work my way through it."

Chapter 29

February 20, 2018—Four Years after Graduation from Law School

SITTING BEHIND HIS office desk, Mike leaned back in his chair, raised his hands over his head and stretched, reaching out as far as he could towards his framed diplomas on the wall behind him. His back hurt and he felt like he had shrunk three inches since hunkering down three hours earlier to work on his still incomplete Superior Court brief. Mike's phone rang with a loud metallic jangle, surprising him and causing him to nearly topple backwards from his chair. Grabbing the phone from the cradle, he answered with perhaps a little too much annoyance.

"Mr. Reigert, will you please hold for one minute while I connect you with Judge Richards," the pleasant, but authoritative voice responded from the other end of the line.

"Sure," mustered Mike, at first confused why he was receiving a call from a judge and then realizing it was Jeri, calling. He chuckled, realizing Jeri was having other people place calls for her so she didn't waste her time dialing. He made a mental note to give her a hard time for pulling rank on him and waited for her to speak.

After a few minutes of mindlessly checking his email and silently cursing Jeri for preventing him from finishing his brief, Mike's attention was drawn back to the phone when he heard Jeri happily talking to a third person, also on their call.

". . . Chicago is awesome. My firm is doing well. I'm trying to get a bigger office. Hopefully soon," said the voice on the other end. Instantly Mike realized Jeri had conferenced Jack Rogers into their conversation.

"Jack, it sounds like everything is going well for you. Say 'hi' to Mike. I figured out how to conference him on the line with us."

"Hey, buddy, long time," Jack said.

"Hey Jack," Mike replied, not necessarily happy he was speaking with Jack as they hadn't spoken since they clashed at Martha Gebbert's deposition, but still curious why they were all on the phone together.

Jeri interrupted. "Guys, I got you on the phone for two reasons. One is personal and one is professional."

Jeri's comment was met with silence. Mike was not sure how to respond.

"We are listening, Your Honor," Jack said with mock seriousness.

"Cut out the crap, Jack. You don't have to say that—unless we are in court. Let's focus. Please."

She began again. "Like I said, I got you on the phone for two very different reasons, but both are important. I thought we could deal with some personal issues and then I have a professional matter to discuss."

Mike immediately relaxed. This was the Jeri he expected, wanting to be in charge, but not overbearing. He wanted some way to demonstrate to her he could still be her friend, yet respect her authority. "Don't leave us hanging Jeri, tell us what you have to say."

Jeri paused. "You remember Alan. Well, we've been seeing each other for a while. I wanted the two of you to be among the first to know Alan and I decided to get married. He's such a wonderful man and it feels so right."

After the briefest moment of silence, Mike said, "Jeri, that is incredible. I only met Alan a few times, but I thought he was awesome. When did this happen?"

"Last week. The news is still fresh for us. We told our families a couple of days ago, but you guys are like family to me, so I wanted to let you know as soon as possible."

Jack reinserted himself into the conversation: "Jeri that is incredible. Personally, I never could consider getting married at twenty-seven, there are too many more women to meet, but if I met the right person, I think I could settle down."

"Thanks Jack, I think. I'm glad my impending marriage won't affect your personal life too much."

"Jeri," Mike asked, "when is the wedding?"

"Here's the thing," Jeri began, "we wanted to let people know as soon as possible to make sure they can make it in for the weekend. We would love it if you guys can make it to Detroit for the ceremony. I'm not giving you a lot of notice—we scheduled it for three months from now. If you can't, we will understand, but I want you to know—you better come to the wedding."

"Jeri," Mike asked with empathy in his voice, "is there something you're not telling us?"

Jeri hesitated. "Yes, there is. It appears Alan, in quite the considerate and sensitive manner, may have knocked me up."

"Damn Jeri, things sure are happening fast for you," said Mike.

"First, judge by the time she was twenty-six and now you may be a grandmother by the time you are fifty. You don't waste any time," Jack added. They all laughed at the thought of Jeri as a young grandparent.

"Don't you worry, Jeri, we will be there," Mike said. "Nothing is going to stop us from coming. By the way, do we bring a wedding gift or a baby gift?" This again caused everyone on the call to break out in laughter.

"Please come. That will be enough of a present. It's really so wonderful letting you guys know my good news. It's been so much fun telling everyone close to me what's happening."

"What do you mean?" asked Mike.

"Here's the story. When I told Alan I was pregnant, he came back the next day and proposed to me. He told me he had planned to do it anyway, he just moved it up a few weeks. He already had this beautiful diamond ring and at dinner, he gave me this speech that included all of the reasons he loves me and the ways I make his life better. He never mentioned the baby during the proposal, so I am certain that he wanted to get married, whether or not I was pregnant."

"Aw, that's so sweet," Jack swooned.

"Shut up, Jack Ass. Let me finish. It wasn't quite so easy telling my mom. I was worried how she would react to me being pregnant, but not married. The next day I called her. I was crying before I could say anything. Then my mom started crying because she thought something horrible had happened. It took fifteen minutes before I could convince her that nobody was dying. We both started crying again at the thought of my dad."

Hearing her news, Jack and Mike promised that no matter when the wedding took place, they would be there. "Just tell us is what we need to wear," Jack quipped.

"Okay boys, the personal part of the conversation is over and thanks for letting me share it. Now to the professional portion of the call and I will put back on my judge's hat."

Mike swallowed hard as he sensed the tenor of their discussion about to change.

"I became judge seven months ago and there have been a lot of other changes since that time. The President Judge mandated that everyone clean up their dockets. The court administrator assigned me a number of newly filed cases, but the other judges also transferred files to me. The process is almost complete.

"It turns out one of the cases I recently received is the one the two of you have against each other, *Gebbert v. Wendell's department store*. This is now mine. Because I know both of you and are friends with you, I did some research and I don't think there is any conflict with me handling the matter. If either of you think for any reason I shouldn't oversee the case, speak up now and I will recuse myself."

Jeri let her buddies momentarily consider but heard only silence. "Outstanding, neither of you indicated a desire for me to recuse. This is now my file and our prior dealings will not factor into any decision I make or how I will preside. I will not allow you to attempt to use our relationship in any way during the pendency of this matter. Agreed?"

Neither lawyer offered an objection.

Jeri stayed in charge. "I don't know much about the specifics. The administrator hasn't sent me the hard file yet, but I reviewed the docket and some of the court filings. This matter is already scheduled for trial in September. Is there any reasons to change the date?"

Mike decided weeks ago he wanted to do his best to make sure the trial date did not move. He had scheduled the depositions of the store's local witnesses and the corporate employees who knew something about the incident. He retained the security expert his uncle used years before and received an expert's report from him, which he sent to Jack as required by the court rules. Jack's security expert also prepared a report detailing his opinions why the department store was free from blame. Having also received a report from Mrs. Gebbert's psychologist, Mike believed he would be ready to go to trial as scheduled.

"Judge," Mike began, not sure at this point how he was to address Jeri, "the plaintiffs are prepared to go to trial and hope the date in September is firm."

Jack groaned. "Jeri, I mean, Your Honor," Jack began, "the defendant in this case hoped to try the case next year. I have a motion sitting on my desk requesting a continuance. I know these types of motions are usually granted."

Jeri interrupted to ask, "Next year? The court already scheduled a date for this year. What's the problem?"

"My calendar is fairly full for September and the client informed us September is a busy month in the retail business due to the back to school season. Making so many witnesses available would be detrimental to its bottom line."

Mike wanted to jump up and scream "Bullshit," but before he could, Jeri said, "Jack, you should have blocked this off months ago. Your client is a national retailer. It employs thousands of workers. I'm sure it can spare a few for this trial. How long is it going to take anyway?"

Mike jumped in, saying "I don't think it will take long. We have a few witnesses and a couple of experts, but I think we are looking at about three days, don't you agree Jack?"

"I think it will take much more time," Jack said. My cross-examination of the plaintiff could take one day alone. We have medical experts and security experts. It's looking like this could be a major trial."

"Well I'm not going to tell you how to try your case," Jeri stated, "but I suspect a whole day grilling a witness may be a bit of overkill. Here's what I am going to do. We are getting lots of pressure from the Superior Court to move our cases along and reduce our dockets. With that mandate, I believe keeping the date firm will best serve the interests of both parties and the Court. I am going to block off the entire week for the trial and Jack, if you need more time, we will go into the following week. Is this workable?"

"Yes, your honor," Jack mumbled.

"Final matter. Does either side believe it will file a motion for summary judgment?"

Mike did not expect to file a motion and hoped Jack would indicate he wouldn't file one either. To Mike's disappointment, Jack informed Jeri the defendant intended to move for summary judgment and argue the court should dismiss the case because, he claimed, Mike would not be able to prove the department store did anything wrong legally.

When he heard Jack's intention, Mike inwardly groaned, not because he was especially worried the court would dismiss the case, but rather because of all of the work Mike would have to do to prepare a brief opposing the motion.

After hearing Jack's intention to file a motion, Jeri ruled all briefs would be due six weeks before trial so she could hold argument two weeks later.

"Hey guys," Jeri said in a light-hearted tone, "I'm glad we are going to be spending so much time together. I think we will handle this without much trouble, don't you?"

Sounding more hopeful than he was, Mike offered his agreement.

Jeri tried to end the phone call on a positive note. "I guess I will see you guys again for argument on the motion. Looking forward to it." Jeri clicked the 'Goodbye' button on her phone, ending the conversation. Mike swiveled his chair and inspected his law diploma. He thought about how law school now seemed so distant.

Chapter 30

March 5, 2018–Four Years after Graduation from Law School

"ARE YOU A fucking idiot?" Ed Wagner roared in the direction of the floor to ceiling window overlooking the Chicago skyline, yet clearly directing his venom towards Jack.

Jack believed the pending question was rhetorical, so chose not to respond, allowing Wagner to continue his tirade. "I am trying to teach you how to play the game–how to be a player, but you are fucking it up. Wendell's could be an amazing client. They have four hundred and fifty locations nationwide with annual revenue of thirteen and a half billion dollars. They get sued in commercial claims, labor disputes, workers' compensation—so many ways. They want us to advise them on how to manage their property portfolio, tax issues, benefit analysis. We could receive fifteen million in fees every year from this client. All they want us to do is handle one little PI case properly and you are trying to piss it all away."

Wagner turned toward Jack, who saw his mentor's face was now a bright shade of red with the sweat stains under his armpits creeping down to his waist. Running his hands through his thick, closely cropped hair, Wagner took a deep breath and walked towards the couch where Jack was seated. Wagner's face briefly contorted in a smile before the scowl returned.

"How are we going to solve this problem?" Wagner demanded.

Jack wanted to appear confident and in control. "I think I can still settle this."

A nasty smirk stretched across Wagner's face. "You are not in a position to settle at this point. You are facing a trial in a few months. Maybe opposing counsel is a friend of yours, but you didn't teach him how to dance. From what it sounds like to me, he is in control and not you."

Jack wanted to disagree, but decided not to interrupt. "Let's see," Wagner continued, "the client again raised the reserves on this case to the ridiculous figure of six hundred and fifty thousand, which in my estimation would be a huge windfall for the plaintiff. Unfortunately, you don't know if there is any chance they will take your offer. If you can't convince them to take the money, you will have to take your chances in front of a jury. Are you prepared for that?"

"Absolutely," Jack said, his voice sounding more exuberant than he hoped.

Wagner turned his back to Jack again and walked back to the window. He began to speak again in a more measured voice. "Let's go through this from the beginning. Our client likes you and wants to let you run with the case. However, I am concerned you are blowing this, but they, for whatever reason, still think you are in control. It's good, but if we can't settle this for less than the shitload of money they allocated to settlement or at least bring a verdict in under that figure, we are screwed. I know these guys and if you don't satisfy them, they will pack up shop and take their business to another firm and we will lose the chance to bill them for millions of dollars every year. You understand what's happening here?"

"Yeah, I better settle this."

"Let me paint a clearer picture for you." Wagner turned to stare directly at Jack. "If you get this case resolved and the client remains happy, you will likely be a partner within a couple of years." An enormous smile appeared on Jack's face as he pictured himself in a corner office receiving all of the perks of a shareholder of the firm.

"Before you stain your pants fantasizing about your huge paycheck," Wagner stated, "let me finish what I was saying. If you are not able to keep our client happy, you are done here. It will be 'pack your bags and be on your way'. You will be walked out the door with no recommendation and you will be forgotten by the time you board the bus to travel home to mommy."

The images in Jack's head of luxury goods and other trappings of wealth immediately morphed into images of walking into small law offices and begging for a job. This was the first time since he began school that his view of his legal career did not involve an upward trajectory with accompanying financial rewards.

Jack stood and took a step forward. "I know what to do and please don't worry, I will handle it—no matter what."

Wagner nodded paternally. "I think this talk has been a benefit for both of us. I'm glad we are on the same page."

Recognizing his cue to leave the office, Jack turned and left. As he was walking down the hallway, he felt bile burn in the back of his throat.

Chapter 31

April 24, 2018—Five Years after Graduation from Law School

STEPPING FROM THE elevator, Mike tried to appear inconspicuous, carrying the oversized green dinosaur, stuffed and dressed in a suit and tie he had purchased the day before. Mike walked down the brightly lit corridor, his stride impeded by the five-foot animal he attempted to grasp in his left hand while carrying his briefcase in his other.

"Do you need any help?" a kind voice asked from behind the nurse's station. Conscious of his awkward situation, Mike indicated he could manage his load. This did not dissuade the young LPN, who came out from behind her post and grabbed the dinosaur before Mike could offer further protest. The nurse placed both of her arms around its neck, and gave it a quick kiss on the cheek.

"This is clearly a full-service hospital. Thanks for the help. I probably would have dropped the poor dinosaur five times before I got to the room," Mike said.

"Which room are we headed to?"

"My Uncle Stan's room."

"Stan Rotmen? He's my favorite. I'm so happy he's ready to leave the hospital, but we're going to miss him. He's such a sweetie."

"Everyone says the same thing, but he's actually quite the bastard," Mike said.

"I doubt it. You can't fake being so nice with IVs sticking out of you."

Holding the stuffed dinosaur in front of her, the nurse asked why he was in a suit.

"I would think that should be obvious, but perhaps you've only seen my uncle in his hospital-wear–not flattering. He's kind of like you," Mike said, "he also wants to help people. You wear a nurse's uniform when you treat your patients, but my uncle wears a suit when he helps people solve their problems. So, I wanted to tell him I'm tired of seeing him in those ugly hospital outfits and everyone is looking forward to him getting back to the office."

"What a kind thing to say. But why a dinosaur?"

Mike blushed a little. "I tease him–that he's a dinosaur. I consider it a compliment. He does things the old-fashioned way, like treating people with respect, listening to people, and being honest–stuff a lot of younger people have difficulty with these days."

The nurse held the stuffed animal in front of her face as they walked, speaking directly to it. "You are going to a wonderful home. Stan is certainly a sweetie and his nephew appears to have many of the same traits." Initially taken aback by the compliment, Mike was at a loss for words as they turned into the hospital room.

"There's my favorite nurse," Stan said while sitting up in his bed. "Finally, the two of you have met."

"Sort of, Uncle Stan. She agreed to help lug your present into the room, but we actually never introduced ourselves." Mike turned to the nurse, extending his hand. "Hi, I'm Mike, Mike Reigert."

"And I'm Megan O'Malley. It's a pleasure to meet you Mike Reigert." She shook his hand and approached her patient, who rested the dinosaur on his lap with its short arms around his neck. "Mr. Reigert, now is not the time to be playing with dinosaurs. We must take you downstairs for your final tests so we can release you this afternoon."

"You're making me so happy. Seeing my favorite nurse and my nephew with this amazing dinosaur just makes me smile. I ache and I'm exhausted, but get me out of this place and into my own bed and I will be even happier. I can't wait to get back to work in a couple of weeks."

Megan swiftly transferred Stan to a waiting wheelchair. As she wheeled Stan out of the room, she casually said to Mike, "I need to drop him downstairs and then come back up here to change some sheets. I hope you will still be waiting for your uncle."

Mike was not sure exactly what she meant, but nodded to indicate he would remain in the room. He noticed Megan's small frame and the bob of her red curls as she wheeled Stan out of the room. He made a mental checklist of things he could do to make sure that he was still there when Megan returned, no matter how long it took.

After twenty minutes of sitting in an uncomfortable chair, trying to review a deposition, Mike startled when Megan returned to the room. With high-speed efficiency, Megan began to break down Stan's IV tower and remake the bed. Mike admired not only the precision with which Megan made her hospital corners, but also the manner in which she filled out her green nurse's uniform, and the spirit which she brought to mundane tasks.

"Do you do this to everyone's room when they leave? I'm not much at changing linens," said Mike, cringing when he realized how trite his questions sounded.

"Oh good, you do actually speak. I thought you were going to let me finish everything I had to do without saying a word."

"I was trying to think of a witty opening line."

"Perhaps you should take a little more time to come up with one." Megan's comeback would have stung except for the way her eyes sparkled at him when she said it. He fumbled for some other area to discuss, but was momentarily flummoxed.

Megan continued with her tasks, and as she finished turning off the monitors behind the bed she said, "Mike, I have lots of other patients to deal with. I would love to chat, but I must attend to another in about two minutes. I think I should be direct. Your uncle's raved about you since he got here. I've wanted to meet you in person, but I usually pull the early shift and you come to visit your uncle after work. Today when you came with the stuffed dinosaur, I thought it was so damn cute. So, Mike, would you like to go to lunch sometime?"

Megan's directness nearly floored Mike. Once again, he had trouble formulating a response. He nodded and as he did Megan handed him a piece of paper saying, "My cell number is on here. Call or text me and we can meet. I think it would be fun."

Before Mike could respond, Megan threw the old sheets in the used linen hamper and walked out of the room. Taking a deep breath to modulate his heart rate, Mike immediately entered Megan's number in his cellphone.

Chapter 32

May 5, 2018—Five Years after Graduation from Law School

THE SUN SHONE onto the hillside, warming the grass and creating a glow around the neighboring trees. A bevy of children played on the jungle gym rising from the foam padding, their screams and laughter converging, background noise for the entire park.

A football field's length away from the playground was a secluded location shaded by three sprawling oak trees. A gentle breeze caressed the two lone figures sitting casually on a tartan blanket. Scattered containers of food and a near empty bottle of wine littered the blanket. Mike tilted his head backward to allow the wind to rush over his face. Megan rested on her side, her hand supporting her head, as she and Mike took a brief respite from their conversation.

Mike pointed out two birds making large, swooping circles in the sky. "Look they are coming right for us," Mike yelped.

"Stop it. They are just having fun. So, tell me what do you like to do for fun on dates?"

"That's a loaded question," Mike responded. "I haven't had a lot of fun dating recently."

"I can't believe that. I've found you rather easy to talk to. Even when you called me that first time when I was just getting off my shift at the hospital you were easy to talk to. What problems have you had dating?"

"Since I've moved to Pottstown it's been a series of interesting experiences to say the least. The first time I went to dinner with a woman here within ten minutes she told me we couldn't go out because I didn't fit her picture of long-term dating material. Another time, a client of mine tried to fix me up with his neighbor. I met her at a bar and she was really nice. Only problem was she was twenty years older than me. She played billiards like a pro, but we didn't have much in common."

Megan laughed. "I think I can match what you have to offer. I met this guy at a friend's house. Funnier than anybody I had met before. When he picked me up at my apartment, he saw a picture of me with another woman. He told me how hot the other woman was. I told him it was my mom. I kicked him out when he asked me for her number. Seriously."

"Maybe it hasn't worked out well for me so far, but I like meeting people and I keep trying. Gives me some good stories."

"Hopefully you won't get too many of those stories from today."

"I doubt it."

Megan looked at the spread of empty containers covering the blanket. "You must have spent all day putting this together. It's impressive."

Mike looked down and then glanced into Megan's green eyes. "I wanted to make it different, but we had never talked about what you liked to eat, so I just got a variety of spreads, salads, and fruits. I figured you would like something. Speaking of recent dates, last week I had dinner with a woman. I ordered a hamburger and listened to her chastise me the whole meal about my food choices and the benefits of a vegan lifestyle."

"You won't get that from me. You pretty much could have brought anything and I would have eaten it. There aren't many things I won't eat.

I'm no vegetarian. In fact, my dad has always called me a 'foodasaurus'. He thinks it's funny."

"It is," Mike said while surreptitiously looking Megan over in her casual shorts, denim top, and sandals. "Plus, nobody would ever guess how much you like to eat."

"Thanks. You know we are way past that hour time limit we put on this picnic."

Mike looked at his watch. "Wow, we blew way past it."

The sun was beginning to fall behind them and the children abandoned the jungle gym as evening approached. "I'm going to take a risk and declare this picnic a success," Mike said.

Megan took a sip of the wine they'd been drinking stealthily out of blue Solo cups. "We may not agree on the definition of success, but throwing together some food you bought at the supermarket hardly counts as successful," she teased. "Until you spend some serious money on me, don't think about success."

Mike guessed she was joking, although given his recent track record with women, he was not totally sure. "I want at least one more chance to impress you."

"Fine." Megan stifled a fake yawn. "I will allow you one more opportunity."

Mike clutched her arm and said, "I'm not kidding. I want to take you out again."

Smiling, she answered, "I'm not kidding either. I would love to go out with you again."

Chapter 33

May 11, 2018—Five Years after Graduation from Law School

THE BEDROOM, NEAT and tidy, held a hodgepodge of collections. On the shelf over the bed, staring open-eyed towards the ceiling was an assortment of dolls, looking worn, but obviously loved through overuse. Tacked to the closet door were three band posters evidencing a hard rock phase that coincided with high school and the corresponding pot experimentation period. Barely visible in the closet were a series of t-shirts emblazoned with slogans that seemed so important in college. Shirts she had received as a member of the Young Republicans Club and the Sierra Club. Next to the bed was a bookshelf containing law books arranged by year including Prosser on Torts, Kamisar's Constitutional Law casebook, and the other books necessary to gain an education and ultimately a degree in law.

Stacked neatly next to the legal casebooks were a series of binders holding notes, course outlines, and other school materials. She had not touched any of these resources since graduation, and likely she would never utilize them again. But she wouldn't sell the books back to the bookstore or destroy the binders and class scribbles because doing so would implicitly suggest the years in law school never happened or at least weren't so significant.

Not much had changed in Jeri's bedroom since she left for school. Sandy Richards didn't need the extra room, and hadn't changed it. Every now and then Jeri's mom would wander into Jeri's room, sit quietly on the bed and marvel at how quickly time passed. She would rub her hand on the quilt Jeri used starting in fifth grade and remember how Jeri would clutch it trying to force herself to go to sleep when the issues of the day like why Martha Kellerman dumped her as a friend or why Mrs. McClelland refused to raise her score on the science fair project raced through her head.

Sandy Richards, though in her mid-fifties, still looked thirty-something. Outwardly, she maintained the positive outlook that allowed her to overcome a childhood being shuttled from foster home to foster home, to becoming the proprietor of Detroit's second largest flower boutique, Flowers in Bloom. Living alone, even with an active group of friends and social life, Sandy was still not ready to consider opening up her life to anyone new.

Sandy sat on Jeri's bed and beckoned her over so they could speak. "Sweetie, I have enjoyed these last two days so much. Now that you are a judge, we just don't get to talk or see each other enough. Soon you are going to be married, and then have a kid. It's just happening so fast to my baby."

Jeri rolled her eyes. "Mom, we talk all of the time. Maybe not quite as much as usual, but I let you know what's happening with me. Thanks for helping me get through my checklist for the wedding. It's coming up faster than I thought it would."

"You must be worn out. Planning a wedding is not easy, but I loved having you all to myself this weekend."

"So did I Mom, but there's a lot I need to do in Pittsburgh. I know you want me to stay longer, but I need to get out of here."

"I know you want to go home." Sandy stuck out her lower lip and pouted. "I know we've covered this territory all weekend, but let's make sure you have everything ready for the wedding."

"Awesome idea Mom, because something probably changed in the last hour since we went over this," Jeri said, realizing that most of her attention to detail had been inherited from her mom.

Wanting to placate her mother, Jeri good naturedly went through the checklist again. "Dress—I will have the final measurements on Tuesday to allow for any last-minute bodily changes." Jeri patted her belly which had gotten marginally bigger in the past few weeks. "The hotel's confirmed. Caterer has the menu finalized. We will go over the guest list next week. You are to call Aunt Betty to make sure she brings enough of her medication and takes it before she arrives. I spoke with the band and will give them your playlist when I meet with them. Is that everything?" Jeri smiled at her mom, knowing she only wanted the perfect wedding for her.

"One more thing I wanted to talk about," Sandy said, again caressing the quilt on the bed. "I thought of this and couldn't imagine what you were doing about it, but who is going to walk you down the aisle?"

Of all the details which Jeri, with the help of her mom, planned with bureaucratic zeal, this was the one she did not want to think about. When her mother posed the question, Jeri realized she had been unconsciously ignoring this issue. With her father having been killed when she was in high school, and no close relative available to step into that role, Jeri was at a loss.

"Why can't you, Mom?"

"I don't think I should give my daughter away. Your dad would've been so proud to walk with you down the aisle. I'm worried I would want to keep you rather than give you away and that just wouldn't make for a happy wedding, would it?" Jeri pictured her mom desperately holding onto her arm as Jeri tried to finish her walk to Alan.

"You are probably right. I don't need that video on YouTube the next day." Jeri stopped, turned her head to the side as an idea emerged. "I have a thought. I don't want to tell you now, but I have a possible solution. I will tell you when I finalize it. Is that okay?"

"Sure, honey, whatever you want."

Jeri stood to signal she was ready to leave. She walked to her mother and embraced her. Sandy still appeared sturdy to her, but for the first time Jeri noticed a subtle frailty in her shoulders and her back.

"I love you, Mom," Jeri said as she left the room to head downstairs to leave for home.

Chapter 34

May 15, 2018—Five Years after Graduation from Law School

THE DIN IN the restaurant drifted over the patrons spinning their pasta and sipping their drinks, but didn't seem to reach the back table where Mike and Megan had been quietly conversing for ninety minutes. Mike was still picking at the remnants of his eggplant linguini while Megan tossed back the last sip of wine, effectively killing the bottle. Mike eyed Megan pushing away her dish.

"Damn, you are a good eater," Mike remarked. "We've been to Thai, Vietnamese, barbecue, and now Italian restaurants. I don't believe I've seen you leave a speck of food on your plate anywhere. It's good to see someone enjoy eating so much."

Megan patted her stomach and smiled at Mike. "You do just fine yourself. I think it's good we share this love of food. It gives us more time to talk."

"True. Tonight we've discussed your family. I told you about my disappearing dad. We came to an understanding on action flicks. I guess that only leaves a little time for you to tell me what happened at the hospital."

Megan shifted uncomfortably. "I had an interesting day, but I'm not sure I'm ready to share."

"Come on. I promise I won't tell anyone."

"Fine, but this is a little embarrassing."

Mike nodded, but said nothing.

"Okay, I am juggling three extra patients because we were a little short in the morning. Mr. Davis—I will call him that to protect his HIPPAA rights—is in one of the rooms. He's been in bed for a couple of days for pneumonia. Nothing life threatening, but he's demanding star treatment. Ordinarily, I would be happy to give him a little extra kindness, but I am running from room to room checking IVs and dispensing medicine. You know real patient care stuff."

Megan stabbed a piece of eggplant off Mike's plate and continued. "Every time I go by his room, he's trying to get my attention. I told him I would help him as soon as possible, but that didn't slow him down. He pressed his call button like three times in fifteen minutes, but it was clear he had no medical issues, he only wanted someone in his room with him. I couldn't get to him for a little while, so I hear him singing, really loud. 'oh, nurse, oh nurse, would you please come and help me.'"

Mike started laughing as Megan became animated, telling her story. "This goes on for five minutes. He comes up with three verses about how beautiful I am and how he needs me to come see him. Everyone on the floor hears him: patients, nurses, doctors, families, but nobody is doing anything. It's starting to get embarrassing because everyone knows he is singing to me.

"After about twenty-five minutes, I go to Mr. Davis's room. He's a sweet man, but I think extremely lonely. He smiles at me. Mr. Davis is pushing eighty and his wife died a few years back. He finally stops singing and I stand next to his bed thinking I was going to have to be stern with him. There is a tear rolling down his cheek and he says to me, 'You remind me of my wife. I used to sing to her. I'm sorry I caused so much trouble.'

"I see his small frame lying in his bed and I tell him I loved his singing, but I thought we should keep it between the two of us and he should only sing to me when I am in his room, but not when I am walking down the hall. He agrees it would be our little secret. I go into his room two more times before my shift ended and he sang two beautiful songs. He has a lovely voice when he's not singing at the top of his lungs."

Megan glanced at Mike and caught him admiring her. "You better start singing to me," she said, "or I may be eating my dinners with Mr. Davis."

Mike took a sip of water. "Thanks for sharing your story—not where I thought you were going when you started. By the way, don't count on me singing to you anytime soon. I don't have much of a voice. Sounds like Mr. Davis was looking for some company, and I think he was looking in the right place."

Megan blushed allowing Mike to continue. "I was thinking. We've been spending a lot of time together and I have a proposal."

"Go ahead," Megan said, her voice wavering.

"I told you a law school friend of mine was getting married in a couple of weeks. The wedding is in Detroit and I would love it if you would come with me for the weekend."

Megan took a moment before replying. "I don't know Mike. First of all, you must have RSVP'ed months ago when you didn't know me, so there is no place for me there."

"I told you Jeri is a close friend of mine. If I called her, she would be so excited I was bringing someone. She thinks I don't have much success in the dating department. It wouldn't be a problem."

"Well it sounds like fun, but I don't know if I have anything to wear."

"I will take you shopping."

"I don't know if I am scheduled that weekend." Megan pulled her phone out of her purse and opened it to her scheduler. She blushed. "It looks like I'm off then. But, my dad would be unhappy if I went to another city and shacked up with some guy in his hotel room."

"Hopefully, I am not just some guy and we can reserve two rooms if necessary. I want you to come for two reasons. First, I would have much more fun with you along, and second, I want to show you off to my law school friends. Make them realize I'm doing okay here in the boonies. Please come with me. You will like most of the people I know, I promise."

Megan fidgeted in her seat. Finally, she locked eyes with Mike and said, "Fine, I would love to go with you, but you better be ready to dance all night."

Chapter 35

May 18, 2018—Five Years after Graduation from Law School

THE COURTROOM WAS abuzz with activity. Lawyers huddled together trying to agree on stipulations before they argued their motions. It was forty-five minutes before the scheduled time for all of the arguments, but so far no court personnel had arrived to sign in the attorneys and tell them what number they were on the argument list.

Mike arrived an hour before the scheduled time for the argument, hoping for an opportunity to say hi to Jeri. After being denied entry by her staff into her chambers, he sat alone in the courtroom looking over emails on his phone. A young attorney, wearing a charcoal grey pinstripe suit and sporting the beginnings of a goatee placed himself next to Mike and said, "Mr. Reigert, good to see you again."

Mike recognized the man as an attorney he opposed on a case which had settled a few weeks earlier. "Hey, Charlie, how's it going?"

"Just great. I filed summary judgment in a commercial claim. Got here early trying to get the lay of the land. I'm hoping to get to watch a few arguments before my case is called. Have you had anything before Richards before?"

Mike shook his head. "No, this is my first time in front of her. Although we were law school classmates."

"Really, how do you think she's going to handle the motions? Think she'll be like Weksel and just sit there like a potted plant and not ask any questions?"

"I doubt it. I think you're going to get plenty of questions."

"Good. That makes it easier. It's hard when you have no idea what the judge is thinking."

"Don't you worry. She'll know your brief better than you do."

Charlie chuckled. "Then I better go study my brief a little more. See you, Mike."

A few minutes later Jack rolled a huge document bag into the courtroom. He looked around undecided where to sit or place his bag until he spied Mike sitting on the last wooden bench gathering his materials. He walked over to him and plopped down. "How are things Mike?" Jack asked, smiling.

"Pretty good, Jack. Good to see you again."

"We're making a habit of it, aren't we? I'm glad we got all of corporate depositions out of the way last week."

"Three days in Atlanta and I never left the hotel. We got to spend a lot of time in the same room, but we didn't speak much, did we?"

Jack laughed. "At least you didn't yell at me this time."

"Nope, you were a perfect gentleman and professional during those depositions. Thanks for letting ask my questions without getting in the way too much. Your witnesses were pretty good at spewing the company line, weren't they?"

"Absolutely. That's why they are corporate executives. They know our policies backwards and forwards."

Mike and Jack quickly gave each other personal updates. Noticing the court personnel had entered the courtroom, Jack switched gears. "Mike, I want us to take one more stab at settling this case. We upped our offer to your clients to a hundred and twenty-five thousand. So far you have indicated they would be interested only in a 'substantial payday.' I'm not sure exactly what that means, but I talked to my client who is prepared to offer two hundred thousand. Now Mikey, I will let you know I might have a little more money to close a deal, but you got to let me know where your clients are. If not, we will try this case and you may be looking at a big fat zero."

Mike waited for his annoyance at Jack's comment to pass. "Here's the thing Jack," he began, "we are not worried about getting nothing. We are confident in our position. As I told you repeatedly, your people substantially impaired the lives of my clients by what they did to her. You know I'm not blowing smoke here, Jack. You met the Gebberts. Try and tell me they are full of shit–I know you can't. I've told you they have not given me authority to settle the case. They appear like they want their day in court and whether or not I think you are making a fair offer, if they don't want it, I can't do anything."

Jack gritted his teeth and ran his hand tersely through his hair. His face turned crimson, his eyes narrowed. He tossed the file folder he held onto the seat next him. "Mike, you've made this difficult from the beginning. We are offering real money and you do nothing. We are about to argue summary judgment and your clients may be thrown out of court in the next hour."

"I doubt that and you do too. Jack, your offer doesn't interest my client. In a lot of ways, you're making it easy for them," Mike stated calmly.

Jack bent to pick up some of the papers which had fallen on the floor. When he lifted his head up to face Mike, not a trace of his smile remained. "Okay Mike, we'll play it your way. I'm trying to teach you how to dance, but you keep standing off on the sidelines like you're the prettiest girl at the party. But sometimes the best-looking girl never gets asked to dance."

Dumbfounded, Mike kept quiet, allowing Jack to continue. "I know I am not supposed to do this, but I'm going to make you an offer that will make your mouth water. I've got quarter million dollars for your clients. Tell me they accept and we can walk out of this courtroom still friends."

Jack's offer nearly knocked Mike off of his chair. His first reaction was to leap in the air, throw his arms around Jack and tell him they were going out for a beer. His clients, however, had not authorized him to accept anything close to that and his marching orders were to keep plugging away and prepare for the trial scheduled in less than a month.

Mike shook his head. "Jack, it sounds like a reasonable offer, but like I told you, my clients want their day in court. All I can do is take the offer back to them and once I talk to them, I'll call you. Right now, I think we have to argue your summary judgment motion."

"God dammit Mike," Jack said with undeniable exasperation, "you are crazy. No sane jury would ever give you anything in that ballpark." As his voice rose, their conversation was interrupted by the banging of a fist on the clerk's table. "Please, quiet in the courtroom," the clerk instructed Jack and Mike. "Have all lawyers with arguments today checked in with the court?"

Mike and Jack stood and walked to the front of the courtroom to check in and find out when how long they had to wait for the court to hear Jack's summary judgment motion. Both were a bit disconcerted when they found out they would be the last to argue. They returned to their seats and sat together in stony silence.

Chapter 36

May 18, 2018—Five Years after Graduation from Law School

"ALL RISE, THIS Honorable Court is now in session, the Honorable Jeri R. Richards presiding," the tipstaff announced as Jeri strode out of her chambers and up the three steps to her seat behind the bench. She carried a stack of files and placed them next to the larger pile which was already on her stand. Pushing her black robe down as she sat in her leather chair framed by the flags of the United States and the Commonwealth of Pennsylvania, Jeri gazed out over the packed courtroom.

Before announcing the first case for argument, Jeri motioned for her tipstaff to come up to the bench. Kathy stood on her tippy toes as Jeri leaned forward.

"Hi Kathy. Are you sure we have all of the files up here?" Jeri asked in a whisper, motioning to the papers next to her.

"Absolutely Judge. I think you are ready to go."

"I don't know why I am so nervous. Probably because I haven't handled oral argument yet."

"You've spent the last three days reviewing the briefs for every argument. I think you've read all of the cases in the *Pennsylvania Reporters.* You're ready."

"Do you think all of the lawyers know how much time I spent getting ready for these arguments?"

"I doubt they care."

"Kathy, I'm not sure I told you before but when I used to argue motions, we would stand in the back of the courtroom and make nasty comments about the judge. Things like, 'What a moron, he doesn't know the law?' Or, 'Don't be such an ass, Judge, we're all doing our best here.' Look at all of the attorneys here. You think they are talking about me?"

"Probably, Judge," Kathy said with a smile. "But they are only saying good things."

"Make sure you walk around the courtroom and if you hear anyone saying anything bad about me let me know."

Kathy shook her head. "Sorry Judge. I have to stay up here near you to make sure you are calling the right case. It's going to be up to you to make sure you keep control."

"Fine. Then we should get started. What do we have, twelve motions for summary judgment?"

"Right on, Judge."

"Want to bet how many cases I dismiss?"

"Not really, but if you're anything like my last judge, it won't be too many. He didn't like to write opinions."

"Well, if I grant the motion, I won't have to worry about a trial. Kind of balances out. Let's just see how this goes. I haven't made my mind up on most of them. Hopefully, we'll get some good argument."

"I certainly hope so."

Kathy stepped back and sat in her place in front of the judge's bench. Jeri picked up the first file and called out the case name. She placed her yellow pad with her notes about the case in front of her.

The arguments proceeded quickly and uneventfully. Jeri allocated fifteen minutes per side for argument, but most lawyers completed what they had to say with time to spare. After the lawyers had their say, Jeri decided to make her rulings without taking additional time to make her decision. For the first seven cases, she immediately denied the motions, ruining the moods of the defense lawyers who hoped the cases would disappear without the worry of trial or settlement.

For the eighth motion, Jeri probed the plaintiff's attorney in a car crash case, alleging the car company manufactured the brakes of the plaintiff's car improperly, with questions about why the plaintiff didn't retain the vehicle. When the victim's attorney did not offer any explanation as to why his client allowed the car to be destroyed before the car company was aware of the accident, she granted the company's motion and dismissed the case.

Jack and Mike sat in the back of the courtroom watching their former classmate adjudicate the onslaught of arguments. Mike whispered to Jack, "This used to be Judge Weksel's courtroom. He took forever to deal with motions and we never had any idea why he ruled the way he did. Jeri is getting through all of these motions with efficiency and there even appears to be logic and consistency to her rulings."

"Like we would expect anything else from her," Jack quipped.

"Good point. Looks like she's running a tight ship. I'd make sure you answer her questions directly."

"Absolutely."

"I think we're next. Good luck."

"Thanks. You too."

Two lawyers walked away from the bench after Jeri denied the defendant's motion to dismiss. She tossed the file from the argument onto the pile of the previous motions. She picked up the last file of the day and announced with a slight smirk, "Gebbert versus Wendell's department store."

Mike and Jack rose from their seats and walked together towards the bench. As Jack spread his papers across the lectern facing Jeri, she asked, "Can counsel please approach." Mike and Jack paced around the wooden railing separating the lawyers from the judge to take their place in front of Jeri. They craned their necks slightly as she leaned forward to speak. The court reporter nudged in between Jack and Mike carrying her stenography machine ready to take down what Jeri would say.

Jeri's face lit up. "Oh no, Marianne, this is off the record. Please give us a minute," she said. The reporter dutifully took her equipment and returned to the small desk in front of the witness stand.

"Hi guys, how's it going?" she asked, in spite of the setting.

"Fine, Judge. How have you been?" Mike asked haltingly.

"Mike," Jeri began in a mocking voice, "you don't have to call me judge when we are off the record."

"This is getting quite confusing," Mike mumbled under his breath.

Nodding, Jeri continued. "I brought you up here, not to discuss anything about your case—we'll deal with that in a minute, but to ask you a personal favor."

"Go ahead," Mike said.

She started to talk, and then stopped. Jeri looked down at her friends, her eyes slightly moist. "You know my wedding is in two weeks—and I am thrilled you both are coming. You guys know my dad died a while ago and I was thinking...." Jeri was having difficulty forming her sentences and attempted a smile. "You two are my best friends, and I was hoping you would help me out and walk down the aisle with me at my wedding."

Mike and Jack looked at each other in astonishment. After only a slight hesitation, Mike blurted out, "Of course, we, I mean I, would love to."

"Absolutely," they said in unison.

She reached out to touch her friends' arms resting on her desk. "Thank you, guys that is awesome. I will let you know the details as soon as I can." She paused to gather herself. "Now that's settled we can return to the Court's business. Let's hear some focused arguments."

Stepping back to their respective positions facing Jeri, Jack and Mike resumed their roles as advocates. Standing behind the lectern with his hands gripping its edges, Jack waited for a signal to proceed. Jeri located their legal briefs, noticed the court reporter was ready, and nodded for Jack to begin his argument.

"Your Honor, Jack Rogers for the defendant, Wendell's department store. This is defendant's motion for summary judgment."

"You may proceed Mr. Rogers," she said, inwardly chuckling at the formality which had quickly re-entered their discourse.

"In this matter, the plaintiff came into our store and stole candy from one of our displays."

"Hold on counselor," Jeri said interrupting. "Plaintiff claims she didn't steal anything, so isn't that issue in dispute? You're not claiming it is an undisputed fact, are you?"

Jack shuffled his feet and conceded, "No, you are correct. I am trying to give some background."

"Understood, Counselor, but when you are asking for summary judgment, all the facts you rely upon must not be in dispute. Let's not argue to me like I am the jury in your case."

"I know, Your Honor. As I was getting to, our guard had a reasonable belief Mrs. Gebbert was shoplifting when he detained her and under Pennsylvania law our stores maintain the right to detain people for stealing as long as they have a reasonable basis for believing a crime occurred."

"Mr. Rogers, are you saying I must decide now that your security guard had a reasonable basis—how am I to know that?"

"What I am saying, Your Honor," Jack said with annoyance, while looking down at his prepared outline, "is under the circumstances it was reasonable for the security guard to detain her, which is exactly what he did."

Jeri couldn't help herself but counter, "But he handcuffed her to a table, didn't he?"

"Yes, which is the point, I am trying to make. Under Pennsylvania law, a store owner has the right to detain a suspected shoplifter. The detective reasonably suspected the plaintiff of stealing. Accordingly, the employee did nothing wrong when he detained her. We ask the court to grant our motion and dismiss the plaintiffs' case."

Jack picked up his papers before he finished his statement and once his final words were out of mouth turned to head back to the counsel table.

Mike stared astonished as Jack shuffled away from the lectern. He watched Jack retake his seat and then approached the judge. Placing his papers in the same spot where Jack had argued, Mike looked up at Jeri, who offered a smile.

"May it please the Court," he began, "it appears that the defendant wishes Pennsylvania law allowed for outlaw justice and for untrained store security personnel to act like the police, or worse, attempt to coerce confessions out of unsuspecting shoppers.

"I am going to keep this short because the actions of the company, and not just the security guards–but also the corporate officers who developed the policies this company implemented, are so far beyond what is allowable under the law that granting summary judgment would be an affront to anyone ever falsely accused of a crime.

"First, we will never concede Mrs. Gebbert stole anything. But even if she did, what the store did was so beyond reason that no court should validate their policies by dismissing this case. Second, what they did to Mrs. Gebbert specifically defies explanation and is contrary to the law I provided the court in our brief."

Mike had no opportunity to raise additional arguments as Jeri announced, "Counselor, you can stop where you are. I reviewed the briefs and read the law. Although a store has the right to detain suspected shoplifters, questions of fact remain for a jury to decide. Accordingly,

I am denying defendant's motion and ordering this case to proceed to trial as scheduled."

Jeri banged her gavel and Mike let out a huge breath. Trying to keep a smile off of his face, he turned and observed Jack's back as he headed for the door.

Jeri said from the bench, "Gentlemen, I will see you in a couple of weeks." Mike waved at Jeri as she picked up her folders off her desk and returned through the door leading to her chambers.

After gathering his papers and stuffing them in his bag, Mike left the courtroom and walked towards Jack, who was waiting against the wall underneath the portrait of a bearded nineteenth century judge. Mike warily approached and was greeted by Jack's golden smile.

"I thought we had a shot at summary judgment, but I guess I was wrong," Jack stated. "Not a huge deal, the company is ready to fight this one. I'd ask if you wanted to go to lunch, but I have to catch my plane, so I wanted to say goodbye. Let's spend some time together when we get to Michigan, but do me a favor. Talk to your clients again about settlement. I think we have a fair package for them and with a little prodding from you, they should take the money. Perhaps we can wrap this up at Jeri's wedding to save us the time and effort of preparing for trial."

Jack slapped Mike on his back. Mike began to respond, "I'll try to...," but Jack had already turned and started down the hallway before Mike finished his sentence. Mike shook his head and headed for the elevator.

Chapter 37

June 8, 2018—Five Years after Graduation from Law School

GUESTS SWARMED THE lobby of the hotel, making a beeline for the restaurant situated by the check-in desk. Groups of people at the bar area sat at tables nursing their drinks. A line stretched back from the two bartenders who were trying to handle the influx of people.

Weaving their way through the throng of people, Mike and Megan held hands, each pulling a small suitcase behind them. As they were waiting to check in, Mike was grabbed from behind by somebody jumping on his back and yelling, "I am so thrilled you made it."

Mike broke the embrace and turned to face a grinning Jeri who was bouncing up and down on her toes. Without pausing to take a breath, Jeri kept talking, "I am so glad, so glad and happy too."

Mike gave Jeri a hug and put a finger to her lips to quiet her. "Jeri, you know we would never miss this." Noticing the new pink and blue sleeveless dress Jeri was wearing, Mike exclaimed, "By the way, you look awesome."

Jeri twirled to show off the cut of her new outfit. Spotting Megan standing next to Mike, Jeri extended her hand and said, "You must be Megan. Mike has excellent taste. Thank you so much for coming."

Megan blushed. "Thanks for having me on such short notice. I can't wait for the wedding."

Jeri motioned to the group of people standing around the lobby and said, "We just finished the rehearsal dinner. It was so much fun and mostly about me, which usually I don't like, but for this weekend I'm going to enjoy the attention. Too bad you couldn't make it. The food was awesome. I think everyone is sticking around for a little celebrating. Please let me buy you a drink and you can meet my family."

"We will. Let us put our stuff in our room first." Megan gave Mike a slight elbow in his side. Mike cleared his throat and added, "I mean, after we get situated in our rooms." Jeri laughed, easing Megan's embarrassment, and excused herself to talk to a husky man eager to give her a hug.

Mike and Megan returned to the lobby after dropping off their bags. The bar was crowded with people who had attended the rehearsal dinner, but they were able to snag a table at the rear of the restaurant.

"This should be quite a weekend," Megan said as Mike signaled a server. "Thanks for that quick make-out session in the room. I'm sorry I had to work today, but I'm ready to unwind after that drive."

Their drinks arrived and Mike raised his glass. Megan clinked her glass against his. "So far not seeing anyone I know," Mike offered. "There will be a bunch of people from law school here."

"I can't wait to meet them, but I will enjoy our time alone and watching your friend Jeri soak up the weekend."

A few minutes later, a well-dressed man sporting a stylish haircut pulled out a chair and sat down without invitation. He placed himself in front of Mike, silently challenging his identification skills. Mike stared blankly at the familiar looking man, but could not place his fashionable clothes or confident manner.

"The last time we spoke, you wanted to kick my ass," the man said, smiling broadly at Mike and enjoying Mike's discomfort. Recognition flashed after hearing his voice.

"Holy shit," Mike said, recalling the man from the recesses of his memories. "I know you. John—John Catulla."

"Yes, but you never were going to recognize me, were you?"

"I don't think so, at least not immediately. I'm supposed to say nothing has changed since graduation, but you have—it's amazing. Mike turned to Megan to introduce her. "Megan, this is a law school classmate of ours, John Catulla. I think the last time we saw each other Jack and I were threatening him with bodily harm."

"That's not quite right. You and Jack tortured me our first year in law school. You eased up by third year, but Jack, well, he never stopped."

"I never thought you and Jeri were close in law school. Were you?"

"Not really, but Jeri didn't like the way you guys treated me. She would talk to me when you weren't around and make sure I was okay."

"Did you and Jeri hang out after graduation?" Megan asked.

"Good question. The reality is Jeri and I weren't terribly close in school. She would talk with me, but she mainly hung with this guy," he said, pointing at Mike, "and their friend Jack. A few days after graduation I ran into her and we started talking. I had a job in Pittsburgh so we went to lunch a few times. I got to know her better and came to realize how awesome she was. When I lost my job, she had me talk to Alan—they had recently started to date. He got me an interview with a firm in Atlanta and they offered me a position. I've been plugging away since, handling mergers and acquisitions, and I owe everything to Jeri and Alan."

Catulla's story impressed Mike. "This is all new to me. Sounds like you are doing great John. Congrats."

John smiled confidently. "Awesome to catch up with you Mike and meeting you Megan," he said. "I hope we can spend some time together at the wedding tomorrow. Right now I am exhausted. I'm going to sleep."

They all exchanged goodbyes and after watching him walk towards the elevator, Megan stated, "He seems like a nice guy."

"You're right," Mike responded, "he does, but he was not like that in law school. He was rather insecure. I guess people change with time."

After spending a few minutes conversing alone, Megan and Mike were joined by Jeri's effervescent Aunt Betty, who sat at their table and gave them a brief history of the Richards' family tree, including stories about three different philanderers, two great uncles with undiagnosed mental disorders, and one cousin who had an assortment of animals living with her because she couldn't find the right man.

Mike and Megan sat amused, offering the occasional "uh uh," or "no way," but not contributing substantively to the conversation. After six minutes of unyielding recitation, Mike was struck firmly on the arm. Mike turned to witness Jack Rogers flashing his million-dollar smile.

"What's up Jack?" Mike asked, more wanting to interrupt Aunt Betty's groove than feeling enthusiastic about the arrival of his old friend.

"I'm superb. Just got in from Chicago. Wish I would have gotten here earlier, but we had a classic firm meeting this afternoon and I didn't want to miss it. Hoping to receive some news about partnership, but nothing new on that front."

"Too bad, why don't you pull up a seat?" Gesturing to Megan on his right, Mike introduced everybody. Betty nodded at Jack while talking directly at Megan who was now the only one listening to her.

Jack took the seat next to Mike and asked discreetly, nodding in Megan's direction, "Is she with you?"

"Yes, we've been going out for a little while."

"Congratulations, she appears to be an excellent listener," Jack joked.

"One of her many fine traits."

Jack got the attention of a server and placed an order for a vodka. After the waitress left, Jack changed the subject. "I wanted to talk business with you for a moment. I hoped to deal with our case, put it to bed, and enjoy the rest of the wedding festivities."

Inwardly Mike groaned, not wanting work to interfere with his enjoyment of the weekend, but giving into the inevitability of the conversation, he acquiesced, "Sure Jack, what do you want to talk about?"

"The last time we got together, you agreed to speak with your clients, because we both thought we might settle this case." Mike nodded, indicating he had spoken with the Gebberts. "I think we can resolve this." Jack paused waiting for some reaction from Mike, but none was forthcoming. "I received additional authority from the department store and if you tell me your clients will be reasonable. . ."

"Jack, I told you I would speak with them, and I did. Like I told you, they think the department store treated Mrs. Gebbert improperly and believe they suffered significantly because of it. They are not looking to settle, but they told me to tell you they would take three million dollars for their troubles."

Jack nearly spit out his drink. "Stop being so ridiculous Mike. My client will never pay that."

"I didn't think they would. I'm only relaying their demand."

"I can't believe this. I have a ridiculous amount of money to offer them on a case no one would pay six figures on and they are turning up their noses."

"I suppose you are right. They tell me the three-million-dollar figure is firm," Mike said.

"They are crazy and now they are messing with me," Jack wailed. "Goddamn it Mike, can't you control your clients?"

"It is what it is Jack. This case isn't going to settle." Jack's face turned red as he clenched his vodka. For a moment, Mike thought Jack would throw his drink at him, but Jack angrily rose from his chair and stood over Mike. Pointing a finger, Jack growled, "I can't believe you can't make those old twits take our money. You are weak Mike, and your weakness is going to make life difficult for both of us. You and your clients better watch out for what is going to happen."

Jack slammed his glass on the table, causing ice and alcohol to splash out. He turned on his heels and stormed off without another word. Megan, hearing the exchange between Jack and Mike getting louder, had turned to Mike and was splashed on her arm by Jack's drink.

"What just happened?" Megan asked as Mike tried to collect himself. Aunt Betty, seeing the commotion, excused herself.

"I have no idea, but he is not happy with me."

"Why did he get so nasty? Did you say something to make him angry?"

"I don't think so. This was business, nothing personal. He wants to settle our case. His client is offering a lot of money. I spent hours with my clients last week, but they don't want to settle. Mrs. Gebbert told me she wants to look the company executives in the eye and tell them what they did to her. She says it's not about the money. I don't think she realizes what she is getting herself into. My uncle thinks it's crazy that they won't accept the money, but I can only do what they authorize me to do. I guess I'm going to have to earn my fee in this case. Seems like Jack also thinks it's crazy."

Megan looked shaken. "I don't get you lawyers. I know that litigation is contentious, but bringing all that here to Jeri's wedding? It doesn't seem terribly professional."

"You're right. This shouldn't happen, but it does sometimes. My uncle told me this story about a case he handled which was going on for three years with the clients displaying a growing abhorrence for each other. A perceived slight at a deposition led to a fist fight and broken furniture. Although Stan and the other lawyer each wanted to win badly, the rancor between the litigants never spread to them. They stayed above it all, which allowed them to facilitate a settlement that would have been unreachable if they had been drawn into the dispute. I'm trying to do that here, but I don't know what's going on in Jack's head."

"Keep trying. I don't want to see you act like that. I'm getting tired. I'm going to the restroom and then maybe we should say our good-byes and head upstairs." Megan slipped out of her chair and excused herself.

Mike fidgeted with the ice cubes remaining in his drink while having two brief conversations with other relatives in Jeri's family. Once they left his company he felt a bit awkward sitting alone among the celebrants.

Attempting to distract himself, Mike looked over the floral arrangement on the decorative bookcase in the lobby. Mike then noticed Megan quietly sit back in her chair and bury her head in her hands. He perceived a slight sobbing coming from her side of the table.

Mike immediately put his hand on Megan's arm. "What is going on? Are you okay?"

At first Megan was unable to respond, but gathered herself. "He waited for me. I didn't understand what he wanted."

Mike stared at Megan, not speaking, recognizing Megan needed more time to regain her composure before she could explain.

"I walked down the hall to the restroom," Megan said, while attempting to regulate her breathing. "When I got out, he was waiting."

"Who was?" Mike asked with an air of desperation.

"Your friend, Jack." Mike slumped back in his chair, horrified to hear what Megan would say next.

"He was just there, one foot up against the wall like a model. He had this huge smile on his face.

"I didn't realize he was waiting, but he said he wanted to talk to me about something–something about the wedding, I think he said. He motioned for me to follow him. I wasn't thinking, I just followed him out the door. We went to some trail at the edge of the parking lot.

"Once we were out of sight, I realized I might have made a mistake and turned to leave. He stopped me and said he wanted to talk. When I said we could go inside, he insisted I hear him out. I said fine, but only because I didn't think I had a choice. He started talking about how ridiculous you were because you couldn't convince your clients to accept this huge payday and how weak you must be. He said how this was interfering with him getting his partnership and how he needed to teach you how to dance."

Mike didn't understand what Jack had been trying to say to her.

"He told me if you were going to screw with him, he was going to screw with you."

"Oh shit, Megan, what did he do to you?"

"Nothing really. He tried to be threatening. He touched my hair and suggested he was better than you. He started to push me up against a tree. I don't think he was going to do anything, but I wasn't about to find out. I smacked him and ran away.

"The funny thing is he stood against the tree with a huge shit-eating grin. He yelled at me that I should teach you how to dance or he is going to do something worse."

Megan wiped her nose with a napkin, her eyes pale and bloodshot. Mike squeezed her arm offering some support. Looking up at Mike with a forced smile, Megan said, "I don't know if he wanted to hurt me, but he was so menacing. I think all he was trying to do is threaten you through me. Why?"

"I don't care. What the hell is he doing threatening you? This so far beyond anything I would have ever expected. This is nuts. I thought we were friends, but this proves otherwise. Clearly, to him a lot of things are more important than our friendship." Mike sensed how upset Megan was and asked if they should call the police.

Megan considered. "No, he didn't actually do anything. Nothing would happen to him. I'll be fine."

"Well I am not good with this, nowhere close to it. I'm not sure what I am going to do, but I will do everything to ensure he doesn't get anything he wants. Are you sure you are okay?"

"No, but we need to leave."

Mike helped Megan out her chair, put his arm around her, and walked her towards the elevator. As they waited, she rested her head on his shoulder, shuddering.

Chapter 38

June 11, 2018—Five Years after Graduation from Law School

STAN TWIRLED IN his desk chair enjoying the breeze his movement created. He laughed when the spinning made him a little dizzy and had to remind himself he wasn't quite sure how his body would react with all the medicine he was taking.

"Uncle Stan, stop. What are you doing?" said Mike, having walked into Stan's office.

"Hi Mike. I'm feeling pretty good today. Just going for a spin."

"Funny. You should be careful. I don't want you spewing all over the office."

"I've been back for a week now and I'm ready to work even more."

"Your doctor said no more than three hours a day and you are over that for today."

"I'm glad you're looking out for me, but I'm pretty much back to normal. The doctor said they have the cancer under control and I'm going to try not to worry about it. Coming back to work is the best medicine. I felt better from the minute I came back and saw the ribbons and posters that Stephanie arranged. Now I'm back to dictating letters and reviewing medical records. It's starting to feel normal again."

Mike sat in the chair in front of Stan's desk. "You sent for me. I came running. I'm sure you want to talk about my cases. I shouldn't let you because you are over your time limit, but go ahead and start asking your questions. Don't worry about all the work I have piled up on my desk."

Stan smiled at his nephew, stretched out his arms and said, "We'll only talk for a few minutes." Mike rolled his eyes, knowing their conversation would last longer, but also happy to placate his recovering uncle.

"What's going on with the Briskin matter?" Stan asked, inquiring about the case of a pawn shop selling a client's stolen property.

"Come on, Uncle Stan, you don't want to go over all of my cases, do you?"

"Don't worry, Mike. This isn't stressful for me. You're doing everything on the file. Tell me what's happening."

"Fine. We sent out discovery, they responded. I took the deposition of the pawn shop owner. Not surprisingly, he was a scumbag. He admitted to buying our client's coins. He said when the thief came into the store, he had no idea he was pawning stolen items, so he bought them from him. He never got anything from the guy proving ownership of the coins. Of course, he said he rarely demands proof from anyone. He was not a salt-of-the-earth kind of guy."

"Do you have an expert?" Stan enquired.

"Why do I need an expert?"

"I would think you need someone to tell the court what the coins were worth."

"I will look into getting someone tomorrow. I hadn't thought of that. That's a pretty good idea." Mike flushed, realizing he had neglected to cover an important element of the case. Every time Mike thought he was starting to understand the complete picture of litigation and believed he could handle cases by himself, his uncle pointed out some minor deficiency in his analysis or suggested an alternative method for finding information. Now that his uncle had returned to the office, Mike had a greater appreciation for his insight.

Stan noticed Mike's reaction to his suggestion and changed subjects. "So, how was the wedding you went to in Detroit? Did you tell Jeri congratulations for me?"

Mike leaned forward in his chair to tell Stan about the events of the weekend. "I told her you wanted to wish them all of the best. The ceremony was beautiful. Jeri looked awesome. I think she and her husband are going to be happy."

"Sounds like you had a good time. Did you spend time with your law school friends?"

"Yes, and I'm glad I got to connect with them, but things didn't go so well with Jack." Mike recounted his conversation with Jack and the large settlement offer. Stan expressed his disappointment that Mike couldn't accept it. Stan pressed Mike to talk to the Gebberts about accepting the money and to emphasize the possibility they could receive nothing at trial.

Mike told Stan how upset Jack was and what Jack did to Megan. After listening to Mike recount Megan's reaction, Stan stood from his chair, shook a finger in Mike's direction and yelled at Mike that he had to do something about Jack immediately. Stan suggested filing disciplinary charges against Jack or reporting him to the police, but Mike declined, noting that Megan was questioning her recollection of the events and didn't want to make a bigger deal out of the situation.

Stan retook his chair shaking his head. "I don't get it. Why can't some attorneys handle themselves? Nothing good will come out of attorneys threatening each other." Stan threw his hands up in the air. "I'm going to not think about this for now. Tell me what happened with you and Jack during the wedding?"

The question made Mike grin ever so slightly. "Jack and I walked Jeri down the aisle. She was glowing, but I would not look in Jack's direction. I was smiling, but inside I wanted to throw Jeri to the side and punch out Jack. But the wedding was Jeri's day and I think the pictures will verify I covered up my anger. Jeri had no idea what had happened."

"Are you going to say anything to her at the trial? She *is* the judge."

"I don't think I will, but I am still mulling my options."

This did nothing to alleviate Stan's concerns. "What is your plan, Mike—how are you going to deal with this?"

Mike pondered, before saying, "I don't think this changes anything. You always tell witnesses their answers don't change if the lawyer asking the questions is the nicest guy in the world or a complete ass. Don't ever argue with the other attorney. I think the same advice applies here. As far as we are concerned, I try the case the same way we planned all along. The only thing different is my relationship with Jack. I will deal with him professionally during the trial, but our friendship is over."

"I don't know Mike. I'm not sure I would remain so calm and collected under similar circumstances."

"I'm not sure I can either, but we will find out." Mike let out a sigh. He wondered if he would be able to mask the considerable anger he still harbored while together in court with Jack for a week. He knew it wouldn't be easy. "You're still planning on coming to trial and helping me out, aren't you?"

"Of course. I'm doing much better and looking forward to you trying your first big case. Aren't you glad you tried some others before this?"

"Absolutely, questioning witnesses in court for the first time with this much on the line would suck."

Chapter 39

June 11, 2018—Five Years after Graduation from Law School

JACK ONCE AGAIN took a seat in the suede chair in front of Ed Wagner's desk. This time the seat didn't feel so comfortable. Instead of relaxing as Jack had done many times before, he felt an odd stiffness and a sense of dread. Jack did not examine any of Wagner's art collection or the photos Wagner displayed on his walls of the trips he had taken throughout the world; instead Jack struggled not to blink as Wagner returned his gaze without uttering a syllable.

Wagner let the stare-off linger. Jack knew that Wagner was enjoying his discomfort and thought about how much Wagner liked to lord his authority over him. Jack respected Wagner's position of power over most of the lawyers in the firm, and how Wagner designed virtually every move he made to maintain his status. Jack wanted to be like Wagner and bring in the desired clients with their massive legal fees. Jack knew it didn't matter if others were better lawyers or cannier cross-examiners. The superior lawyers received their rewards, but it was the lawyers who brought in the clients who got the biggest paychecks and enjoyed the most influence at the firm.

Wagner broke eye contact and turned to a stack of letters on his desk. He began to peruse the correspondence. His eyes narrowing with anger as he read one letter, Wagner threw it aside, rested his arms on the desk, and grasped his hands in front of himself as he sighed deeply. Jack recognized this as the signal the meeting was about to begin.

"You had one easy assignment. Meet with your friend and get the case settled. Apparently, that was too much for you. When things didn't go as planned, you had to let me know, but all you did was write me an email," Wagner said while holding up a piece of a paper. "Let me read it to you and then you can tell me if there might have been a better way for you to handle this."

Jack nodded.

"You wrote: 'Just talked to opposing counsel. Doesn't seem like we are going to be able to settle. The wedding looks like it's going to be lots of fun, '" Wagner sneered at Jack, who slunk a little lower in his chair. "Do you think I give a shit about the wedding? No. I care only about getting this case settled. Don't send me an email because you are too big of a pussy to hear my reaction. If you had called we might have come up with a different plan and you could have avoided my brilliant response, 'nice job, stupid fuck. You are one step closer to being booted out the door.' That was a pretty good response, wasn't it?"

Jack didn't answer.

"Okay Sherlock, you have this simple case. Your friend is the attorney on the other side. Two old farts are the plaintiffs, yet you can't convince anyone to accept the huge amount of settlement money I arranged with our client. What the hell am I going to do here?"

Jack pondered this question, hoping it was rhetorical, but when Wagner's silence persisted, he uttered, "I will try the case and kick their ass."

This provoked only a grimace from Wagner. "I don't know, Skippy. This is getting real dicey. Our client is now extremely worried, which makes me more nervous. I spoke with them last evening for an hour.

They still trust you, but not as much as they did before. They insist I go with you to Pittsburgh to help you try the case. I'm not sure you understand the significance of this. The last trial I had was in nineteen ninety-nine, but they want me there to make sure nothing goes wrong. This is exactly what I don't want to do. Now I'm coming to this trial, holding your hand and every evening reporting back to the CEO. This does not make me happy."

"Yes, sir," was all Jack could muster through his dry lips.

"Here's the deal. You are still preparing all of the witnesses. You are still doing all of the legal research and brief writing. You are still questioning all of the witnesses at trial. I am going with you and I will watch you. But you better hope I report nothing bad to the client. Understand?"

"Absolutely, sir."

"Exactly what I wanted to hear. Go back to your office and prepare to win this case."

Jack stood up and left Wagner, who had returned to the papers on his desk. As he approached his office with the six boxes containing the pleadings, medical records, and reams of correspondence, dread spread through his body at the realization that even though Wagner was now coming to trial, he was still on his own.

Chapter 40

September 4, 2018—Five Years after Graduation from Law School

MARTHA'S GEBBERT'S FACE contorted, the lines around her eyes deepening. She twisted a paper napkin in her hand until it wrapped around her whitening index finger. Her eyes darted from side to side, while tears dripped onto her wooden kitchen table.

"For the past two years I have been trapped here. I think I am going out of my mind. The thought of doing what you are telling me makes me want to retch," she screamed, pointing directly at Mike.

Once again, Mike Reigert was staring at his star witness and picturing his case imploding. Mike had been meeting with Martha and her husband for over two hours to prepare the Gebberts for their time in court.

"Martha," Mike said pleadingly, "I'm doing everything I can to try to make you comfortable with what will happen once we walk into the courtroom."

Martha stared blankly at Mike and then looked up at her husband.

"I've brought everything I have in the file with me," Mike continued. "I'm showing you every possible exhibit that will a part of the trial. What is the problem?"

Mike dropped the papers he was holding onto the table and turned his back on his clients. Paul Gebbert grabbed Mike's arm and guided him out of the kitchen and into the living room.

"I don't know Mike," Paul began, "when we were meeting last week she seemed fine. I guess trial is pretty close and she's realizing that."

"I understand the pressure trial puts on people. I get it, but I can't spend all day here going over the same thing. Do you know how much I have to do to get ready for the trial? I'm still summarizing depositions and making witness outlines. Stephanie is back at the office getting all of the exhibits organized and I have to know them all backwards and forwards. I have to finish the jury instructions and do pretrial motions and briefs. I thought preparing the two of you would be the simplest task I had." Mike shook his head in frustration.

"I get it. I'm trying to get her on board, but she just isn't responding."

Mike and Paul returned to the kitchen where Martha was staring out the window. "I can't sit in that courtroom and have them pick me apart," Martha sobbed. "I can't watch the videotape. I can't listen to the security guard say that I'm a thief. I can't–I won't make it through the trial."

The scene in his office months before when Martha melted down prior to her deposition flashed in Mike's head. Mike considered how her deposition was only five hours and these proceedings would be significantly longer and infinitely more intense. Mike wished Stephanie was at the Gebbert home offering Martha some well-chosen words to help Martha overcome her fears. Even channeling Stephanie at this point would do little good–Martha couldn't handle the stress of the trial.

"Paul," Mike directed at Martha's husband, "I don't think she will make it through this trial if she has to watch the whole thing and I don't want this to cause her any more emotional stress and make anything worse for her."

Paul nodded in agreement. "What should we do?"

Mike put his hand to his chin and thought. After a minute of reflection, he smiled. "I think we minimize the potential harm to Martha," he said, "while reaping some benefit for us." He stood from his seat at the kitchen table. "Sometimes, in cases where a person suffered a devastating injury, like ending up in a wheelchair and ventilator dependent, they don't attend most of the trial, but are wheeled in at the end to offer testimony. This builds suspense and supports the impression of significant harm."

"Like in this case," Paul interrupted.

"Absolutely. This might be a way to convey that perception to the jury. I think the less they see of Martha, the better for us. Paul you will be the face of the family. What do you think?"

"Sounds acceptable to me."

"I still want Stacey and Tanner to tell the jurors how Martha's injuries have affected their life," Mike said, returning his attention to both his clients.

"Absolutely not," Martha responded. "I don't want my kids questioned by that attorney. I won't be there to protect them."

Mike wanted Paul Gebbert's support, but Paul said, "She says they shouldn't testify. I think she knows best."

Mike hoped one of them would change their minds. When they didn't, he said, "Fine. Paul you are going to be the only Gebbert at trial until Martha testifies. I hope you can tell the jury what's happened to your family. The plan is risky—it might turn off the jurors who may want more of Martha. But given none of us think she should attend the whole trial, I believe we have to implement this strategy and keep our fingers crossed. Are you two on board?"

Martha appeared relieved to pass the burden of being present to someone else. Paul turned to Mike and said, "I think that is the best we can do under the circumstances."

Chapter 41

September 5, 2018—Five Years after Graduation from Law School

J ACK STARED AT the expansive plate glass windows in the conference room and wondered how much force it would take to shatter them and what it would feel like to fall 57 floors to the concrete below. He felt ragged and distraught, unable to sort through his thoughts, like a person feels right after a family member dies without warning.

"Hey snap out of it," Peggy Gamble said from the doorway to the conference room. "I've been watching you for the last two minutes and you had no idea I was standing here."

"That's true," Jack replied, rubbing his eyes. "I'm having troubles focusing on what I need to do." He pointed to the myriad of documents strewn about the conference room. "I've been in here for the past two weeks. Wagner took away all of my other assignments. It's Wendell's department store one hundred percent of the time."

"Are you ready for trial?"

"How the hell should I know? I've never tried a case before. I know every deposition backwards and forwards. I've memorized every word of the company's policies. I've got witness outlines and jury instructions.

I know her medical records better than her doctor, but I'm not sure if that is enough."

"How are your witnesses?"

"The corporate reps came into town last week so we can prepare them. Ed spent some facetime with them and then left me to do all the work. I yelled at them because they were a little too at ease. They are confident the company didn't do anything wrong. I tried to get them to see it from the other side's perspective. I don't think I succeeded."

Jack walked over to the windows and stared out at the lake. "I think I'm doing a good job getting this case ready for trial, but I don't know. I've read their expert reports, but I'm still not really sure what they are going to say. Wagner's not helping much and nobody here can tell me if I'm on the right track. You want to know the worst thing? It's trying to sleep at night. I don't get much sleep. I just lie there and the case runs through my head and I can't stop it. I think it's normal, but this constant sense of dread is killing me. I guess the only good thing is that I'm billing the shit out of this file."

"Wow, sounds rough. I would love to offer you some sage advice, but I've pretty much only reviewed documents since I've been here, so I don't have much insight to give to you about how to try a case."

"I appreciate you stopping by to check on me. When this is over, let's get some lunch."

Mike watched Gamble walk out of the conference room, jealous that she was going to sit in her office and review a box of documents without worry. He looked at the stack of boxes piled against the wall. He thought with only two more days to prepare before flying to Pittsburgh he had to buckle down for his final push. He wanted to find someone to give him a last-minute tutorial on how to try this case. A melancholy gloom hovered over him. He could think of no one to ask for guidance.

Chapter 42

September 6, 2018—Five Years after Graduation from Law School

THE DINER WAS not as crowded as usual. It was late afternoon and only a few people occupied the counter seats. Mike stood at the door, unsure of what to do, then spied him when he waved at Mike to come over to his booth. Mike dithered, taking off his coat and hanging it on the hooks. He couldn't avoid the conversation now despite his growing apprehension.

The man in the booth stood and attempted to smile. The effort fell flat. Mike walked towards the far side of the booth and when the man reached to hug him, Mike stepped aside and tumbled into the seat.

"Mikey, it's good to see you. How have you been?" the man began after they both were seated.

"I've been fine. Fine for the last six years since I've seen you."

The man looked down and took a sip of water. "I deserved that. I know it."

Mike nodded and looked at the menu. They sat in silence.

"Your mom told me you were working with her brother," the man started again. "Stan's always been a good guy."

"He is. He's always there when I need someone to talk to."

The man winced. "This isn't going to be easy, is it? I know I haven't been around. I just wanted a chance to catch up."

Mike leaned back against the vinyl. "I gave you chances for years. You never seemed to want them then. Why are you trying to be my dad now?"

Mike's father looked up at the ceiling. Mike observed that he had aged so much since the last time he'd seen him. His hair was now grey and wrinkles had formed around his eyes and jetted across his forehead. "I know I haven't been good to you," Mike's dad said. "I know."

Mike thought about being six and finding out that his dad had left. He pondered the times he had tried to connect with him, but only felt rejected. He knew he couldn't let himself feel like that again.

"Great, Dad. You're forgiven. Is that good enough?"

"No, that's not what I'm here for. I just want to apologize."

"I'm not sure we have enough time for that."

"Mike, I know, but let me try." Mike's dad took a deep breath. "I'm not sure where to start, but here goes. I'm an alcoholic. Your mom kicked me out before I did real damage to you and your brother. She told me she never told you anything about me and let you draw your own conclusions, but for nearly twenty years I drank every day. I got some help recently and I haven't been drinking, but part of my treatment is that I have to apologize to the people I've hurt. You are probably the one I hurt most, so this is the hardest one I've done."

Mike stared at his father. "I never knew," he said.

"I'm sorry Mike. I'm sorry I was never there for you and sorry that I don't know how to make things easier for you."

"Dammit, Dad. I would have really wanted to hear this—fifteen years ago, but right now I'm not in a position to deal with it. I have this big case going to trial next week and that's all I can think about. I want to invest in what you are saying, but it's too much for me right now."

Mike's dad smiled. "I get it, Mike. Trust me, I get it. Just give me a chance once your trial is over so I can explain."

Mike nodded.

"You know what?" Mike's dad continued. "I'm going to be in town for a little. Can I stop by and see some of the trial?"

"Oh god, Dad. I don't know."

"Please. I want to see how a trial works. I've never been to one. I promise I won't say a word. You don't even have to talk to me."

Mike felt the energy drain from his body. "I can't stop you, Dad. Trials are open to anyone. Please remember, this is really important to me. I need to focus on what I'm doing there."

"You got it."

Chapter 43

September 7, 2018—Five Years after Graduation from Law School

THE TELEVISION WAS broadcasting a college football game. The score was tied. There were less than two minutes remaining and the crowd was going crazy. Mike and Megan sat on the couch, uninterested. Their attention was focused on the stacks of medical records strewn across the sofa, coffee table, and floor.

"Come on, you are Dr. Lawson, don't throw Megan O'Malley into the answer," Mike chastised Megan.

"Oh my god, we've been doing this for two hours and this is the first time I went out of character. Give me a break, you are killing me," Megan responded with exasperation while gently caressing Mike's check.

"Stop," Mike commanded. "Dr. Lawson would never do such a thing. He is a board-certified neuro-psychiatrist hired by Wendell's to examine Martha Gebbert and offer the opinion in his court filed expert report that she suffered no injury from the store detective locking her to a table–essentially calling my client a liar and a faker. I don't think Dr. Lawson is going to be caressing my face. Let's go over this questioning one more time."

Megan sighed and rolled her eyes, hoping they could take a break from Mike's practice cross-examination of the company's hired gun. For the past week Mike had been coming over Megan's tidy apartment and running through the questions they expected the store lawyer to ask, then practicing the questions he expected to ask of every witness.

Now they were moving onto the expert witnesses. Megan had already heard Mike's opening statement three times sitting patiently as Mike attempted to hone in on the company's weaknesses without overselling his case.

Megan knew more about the case than anyone except for Mike. Megan easily comprehended the legal issues in the case and could digest volumes of testimony helping Mike fine-tune his case for the jury.

Mike gave Megan a stern look and said, "It was your idea that we start with the Gebbert's damages even before we present any evidence that the company did anything wrong. You know that's backward and we are taking a risk. If I'm going to stick my neck out like that, then I would think you would want to make sure we prepare properly."

Megan looked wounded. "Can't we take a little break? I want to make out some. Since you started preparing for this trial we never do any of that stuff." Megan immediately felt guilty for asking, knowing this case consumed Mike and it would be all he thought about until the jury announced its verdict.

Mike reached over, grabbed Megan behind the neck, and pulled her close. They kissed deeply and Megan started to melt into his arms. Just as quickly as it began, Mike backed away to ask, "Dr. Lawson, your examination of Mrs. Gebbert lasted a total of forty minutes, didn't it?"

Megan rolled her eyes and said in monotone, "Yes, counselor, you are correct." She turned her back to Mike. "I guess Dr. Lawson isn't going to get any loving right now."

"Not tonight, but after this trial is over, I'm going to take this Dr. Lawson away to some remote island for some thorough attention."

Chapter 44

September 10, 2018, 6:00 a.m.
Trial Day 1

JERI WOKE REFRESHED. She quietly got out of bed hoping not to disturb Alan, who was sleeping soundly after meeting late into the night with the mayor's sub-committee on reducing crime in the city. She patted her belly, marveling at how much the baby was starting to show in the weeks since her wedding. The downtown condominium they lived in still smelled new. Jeri put on a new pale green suit and applied a hint of makeup.

The sun was just beginning to illuminate downtown, backlighting the tall buildings waiting for the workers to come back into the city. Slightly nervous to preside over her first trial, Jeri closed the door behind her to begin the half-mile walk to the courthouse.

Four blocks away, Jack Rogers tipped the bellman who had spent the last two hours transporting Jack's boxes containing the binders holding the pleadings, depositions, and outlines over to the courthouse. Jack stood at the entrance to the downtown hotel ready to head to court.

Ed Wagner approached Jack from behind and slapped him on the back. Jack nearly jumped out of his skin and yelped in surprise. Wagner, smartly attired in his navy pinstriped suit with cufflinks poking out of the sleeves, carried a swanky leather hard-shell briefcase with gold-plated clasps. "Okay Skippy," Wagner said, "let's go watch you try your first case. I got my yellow pad here and I'm ready to help."

Thirty miles to the east, Mike Reigert gently pressed on his horn when he pulled alongside the curb in front of his uncle's house. Almost immediately Stan opened the door and began walking towards the car. He nodded at Mike when he got in, but neither said a word. Mike stared straight ahead, contemplating his plans for the first day of trial.

"I know you're nervous," Stan said. "If you want to practice your opening statement one more time, I'm happy to hear it. I know how nervous you probably are and I want to help."

Mike reached over and touched his uncle's arm. They drove the rest of the way in silence.

Waking up across the county, forty different individuals' routines had been knocked out of whack. These people were forced to call off from work, get babysitters, and make sure they accounted for everything in their lives until they got home later that afternoon. Most rarely made it downtown and didn't know what bus to take or where to park. Many had little idea what to expect and couldn't decide if they were excited to experience something different or annoyed they were being forced to come into town just because they received a piece of paper in the mail. They had their own reasons for wanting to be on a jury or for doing their best to avoid being picked. Today, each would spend eight hours in court and receive twelve dollars for their service.

Chapter 45

THE COURTROOM SHINED with the counsel tables cleared from the day before. The seats in the jury box had been freshly dusted and wiped down. The fluorescent lights, hung from the high ceiling, cast a blanket of light, illuminating the two immense portraits on the wall and made the judge's bench appear to float above the witness stand next to it.

Kathy Wolfson had arrived two hours earlier to make sure Jeri's courtroom was ready for the trial, with no stray piece of paper or chair left askew. The court binder, holding every document filed in the case, sat waiting for the judge's arrival.

A short, stocky woman in her forties, Kathy enjoyed her job as the court's tipstaff, doing whatever was necessary to assist Jeri, from getting her coffee to running through the courthouse to track down wayward court filings. Jeri retained Kathy who had worked for Judge Weksel in the same position. With two kids almost ready for high school, whose deadbeat father had disappeared three years earlier, Kathy was grateful for Jeri's kindness in keeping her in her job when most new judges would have employed one of their friends or family.

Kathy always enjoyed the first day with all of the new jurors confused about the process and looking to her for guidance. As the only buffer between the court and the jurors, Kathy often developed a strong bond with them as a trial wore on. In one previous murder case, Kathy watched the jury members deteriorate upon listening to gruesome witness accounts about how the accused had dismembered his victims and fed the remains to his dog. As the testimony was coming to a close after fifteen horrific days, Kathy presumed the jury was going to convict and ultimately impose the death penalty. But even with the unredeemable defendant, Kathy watched the jurors start to fall apart realizing they were going to sentence a man to die. Not being allowed to talk about the specifics of the case, Kathy took it upon herself to make the jurors' lives as pleasant as possible and tried to say a few kind words to them each day. The jurors recognized she was trying to help them deal with the horrible task assigned to them and after their service ended, got together and bought her dinner at a local restaurant.

At 8:30, Jeri arrived at her chambers and thanked Kathy for organizing the courtroom and getting everything ready for jury selection. With a stack of unsigned motions on her desk, Jeri hunkered down to execute the orders while waiting for the trial participants to arrive.

"Hey Kathy, can you come here, please," Jeri hollered through the open door. Seconds later Kathy appeared.

"What time did we tell our litigants to show up this morning?" Jeri asked without looking up from the stack of papers. Before Kathy could answer, they heard the door open to the anteroom to the chambers, followed by the grinding sound of a heavy cart being rolled across the tile floor.

"Right about now. I will get everyone situated in the courtroom and whenever you want I can call for the jury panel to be sent up."

"Before you do, I want to talk with counsel. So when they are set up, let me know and we can meet in here. Thanks."

Ten minutes later, Kathy notified Jeri the lawyers were waiting to confer with her and they followed closely behind into Jeri's chambers. Jeri motioned for Mike and Stan to sit in the chairs to her left, and Jack and Ed took the seats to the right side of her desk.

"Is everyone ready to pick a jury?" she asked after greeting them. The lawyers nodded and Jeri told them it would be a few minutes before the jurors were brought up from the holding room.

"Are there any preliminary matters we should handle at this time?" Jeri asked. She sensed tension in the room, which was not unusual at the beginning of a trial, and hearing nothing from the parties, she tried to lighten the tone. "Mr. Rotmen," she addressed Stan, "I have not seen you for a long time. How are you?"

"Well, Your Honor," Stan replied, utilizing the formalities of court, despite being forty years Jeri's senior, "I have not had the opportunity to appear before you yet, so let me congratulate you on your election."

"Thanks so much. By the way, I heard you were in the hospital recently. I hope you are doing better."

"Absolutely, I am feeling much stronger." Stan said as he sat up as straight as possible.

Turning her attention to Jack's side of the room, she glanced at Ed Wagner. "I don't believe we've met. I am Judge Richards." Jeri rose and reached over her desk. Wagner grabbed her hand and introduced himself. Gesturing to Jack he said, "This is Mr. Rogers' case, I'm only here for the ride. Jack tells me you and he were classmates in law school—small world. He only has great things to say about you."

Jeri smiled and said, "Let's see what he has to say after the trial is over. I apologize for the mess in my office." The lawyers examined Jeri's chambers, but didn't see anything out of order. "I never realized the time demands there are on judges. I'm never able to straighten anything up here. I was going to do it last night, but I went to a dinner at the County Bar Association. They were honoring all of the young judges–pretty long evening with mediocre food. But I took this home." Everyone laughed when Jeri held up a small statue of a rhinoceros. "I'm not sure exactly what this symbolizes, but it weights a ton." She raised the statue up to her face. "I'd say at least ten pounds."

She passed the trophy around and the lawyers got a chuckle from the heft of the rhino, and after it went full circle Jeri placed it back on the bookcase above Mike's head.

"Jury's ready to go," Kathy informed them, sticking her head in the office.

"Excellent, let's go pick a jury."

Chapter 46

September 10, 2018, 9:30 a.m.
Trial Day 1

ORTY PROSPECTIVE JURORS filed into the courtroom and as instructed took seats in the back of the room by their assigned number. The lawyers seated at their respective counsel tables turned discretely, trying to size up the panel without appearing as though they were over–scrutinizing any individual.

Each prospective juror had filled out a questionnaire earlier in the morning during their introductory session. The court's staff provided the lawyers with copies and told them they had thirty minutes to review the questionnaires before jury selection would begin.

Mike and Stan sat at the plaintiff's counsel table and quickly reviewed their notes for the type of juror they were looking for and to make a preliminary determination as to whether any of the prospective jurors fit their criteria. Stan reminded Mike they were looking for outliers—any individual who they thought would be tremendous on their jury and, equally important, any who they would likely strike because they fit the profile of a juror who would sympathize with the department store's case.

At the table next to Mike and Stan, Jack Rogers and Ed Wagner were performing different functions. Jack reviewed the questionnaires and furiously took notes. Ed gazed around the courtroom, looking at the jurors, attempting to make fleeting eye contact. On his sheet of paper, he made notes about two of the jurors whom he would strike given they did not return his gaze.

Mike and Jack were sitting less than seven feet apart, yet they still refused to acknowledge each other. Jack leaned over his yellow pad, his back turned slightly towards Mike, so he didn't have to make eye contact.

At precisely ten, Kathy instructed everyone to rise and Jeri marched to her bench. She welcomed the jurors, thanked them for their service and moved immediately into the jury selection phase. She gave a brief explanation of the case, read them a list of prospective witnesses and experts each side provided to the court and asked if anyone could not serve for any reason. An unkempt, balding middle-aged man dressed in a torn grey t-shirt and jeans stood and raised his hand. Jeri commanded the man to approach the bench and was joined there by the attorneys and the court reporter.

Jeri asked the man to identify himself and the reason why he believed he could not serve. After fidgeting with his jeans, the man stated, "My name is Michael Young. I own my own business and I can't afford to take off time from work, and if I miss work my family will suffer."

Jeri examined Mr. Young quizzically. "Sir, do you have other employees who can cover for you?"

"Sure, but they don't know the business like I do."

"Will your company still be able to serve its customers?"

"I guess, but I think I should be watching them. Plus, I don't think I like people suing each other."

Exasperation flashed across Jeri's face. "Sir, are you a fair person?"

"Sure."

"Can you listen to the evidence and decide the case fairly and impartially?"

"I suppose."

"Mr. Young, I believe if you are selected, you would make a fine juror. Please make sure your business has the proper coverage. This trial should take less than a week."

Mr. Young timidly walked back to his seat and as he did, Jeri commented, "Being asked to serve on a jury is the second highest form of service one can give to their country. I would think long and hard about making up excuses why you don't want to be on this jury and rather think of reasons why you want to serve. All of you will be missing time from work and the court understands the inconvenience this can cause you and your family. Please understand it is appreciated and respected. Also, remember the thousands of people before you who served as jurors without complaint or excuse." Hearing Jeri's speech as a rebuke, Mr. Young slunk down in his seat.

One by one, Jeri called each jury to the bench to respond to her basic questions and to specific inquiries of the attorneys, exploring whether any of the jurors held potential biases they could not put aside, and to discover information the lawyers might use to strike them from the panel.

One juror, whose family had immigrated to the United States ten years previously from Haiti, answered Jeri's initial questions, demonstrating a possible dislike for corporations. When allowed to question the young woman, Jack probed further, attempting to establish that she was biased. "Are you saying you will hear the evidence more favorably to the woman bringing the lawsuit than you would for my client, the department store?" The wide-eyed woman snapped, "Yes, you are right. I don't like companies like the one you are working for."

Jack instantly turned to Jeri and moved to dismiss the juror for cause. Unable to come up with a valid reason to oppose the motion, Mike shrugged his shoulders. Jeri turned back to the woman and said to her, "Thank you for your service, you are dismissed from this case." Ed Wagner inconspicuously patted Jack on the back, recognizing Jack had saved one of the defendant's four peremptory challenges by forcing the court to dismiss the woman.

The remaining potential jurors were questioned individually. After three hours, the exercise was complete, and Jeri informed the lawyers they could begin striking witnesses. She excused the jurors for a fifteen-minute recess, but told them to return to the courtroom on time so the lawyers could complete their strikes and the trial could proceed on schedule.

The attorneys for each side began to compare notes. Mike and Stan were in agreement about their first three peremptory strikes: the first, the president of his own startup company; the second, a woman who had worked for a major corporation her entire adult life; and the third, a youthful security guard with a remarkable resemblance to the Wendell's store detective who detained Mrs. Gebbert. For their fourth strike, Mike and Stan were going to see who the defendant struck and reevaluate before making their decision.

When Jack turned to Ed to compare thoughts, he recognized Ed had taken no notes beyond indicating Jack should strike based upon the initial eye contact game he played before jury voir dire began. Jack's face reddened, but he said nothing. Hearing from two unemployed steelworkers and a woman who clearly identified with Mrs. Gebbert, Jack mentally allocated three of his strikes.

"I think you need to strike jurors eight and twelve," Wagner said with certainty.

"But both are executives with corporations. They are just what we are looking for."

"I didn't like the way they acted when you questioned them. I can sense these things."

"I don't know, Ed. I didn't get that sense. I think we should keep them."

"Hey, you're in charge, but it's your ass on the line."

After exactly fifteen minutes, Jeri returned to the bench and ordered the parties to begin striking the jurors. Mike took the official court document drew a line through the name of the president of the startup company and handed the form across the table to Jack without acknowledging him. Jack took the paper and immediately scratched a mark through the first steelworker's name, and returned the form to Mike.

Mike inspected the paper, noticing the name struck by the defense counsel. He turned to his uncle and whispered, "He got rid of one of the two African Americans on the panel. I think we should challenge his strike as race based."

Stan shook his head, saying "No, don't. He's clearly a juror they don't want and they will easily come up with a non-discriminatory reason for their decision. Let it be."

Mike deferred to his uncle's experience. He made his second strike and returned the form to the other side.

Mike watched the jurors absorbed in the ping pong of passing the sheet back and forth. He knew the jurors were all guessing what each side was looking for and which of the panel the lawyers were considering striking. Mike wanted to explain to them that each side was getting rid of outliers, leaving generally the least unacceptable people to serve on the jury.

Jack held the paper to exercise his last strike. Jack had ignored Wagner's first three suggested strikes. Wagner glared at Jack, who quickly struck a teacher who acted a little too empathetic. Wagner smacked his hand on the wooden counsel table, the thud echoing off the high ceilings of the courtroom.

Jack passed the sheet with the juror strikes to the tipstaff, who relayed it to Jeri. Jeri reviewed the sheet and dismissed the eight individuals scratched out on the form, thanking them for their service. Kathy directed the remaining twelve to the jury box. The people sitting in the box shifted in their seats, acclimating to their new environment.

They eased when Jeri called for a recess and informed them the parties would give their opening statements once everyone returned from grabbing a quick bite.

Chapter 47

September 10, 2018, 11:00 a.m.
Trial Day 1

MIKE HUNG HIS head over the cracked porcelain toilet waiting for his stomach to empty. Once his insides settled, he returned to the courtroom, arriving right before the jurors filed into the jury box. Stan understood the churning inside of Mike, having done the pre-opening bathroom upchuck routine many times himself. He handed Mike a mint to suck on.

Jeri took her seat on the bench and called the court to order. She gave the jurors preliminary instructions on how the trial would proceed. She explained that the plaintiff presented evidence first and each of their witnesses could be cross-examined by the defendant. The plaintiff had the burden of proof, she informed them, on the matters she needed to prove. The judge would instruct them what the law was that governed the case, but they decided factual disputes and would ultimately render a verdict based on the facts as they determined them. Jeri finally introduced her court reporter and tipstaff and explained if there was any trouble she could summon the sheriff who would be in the courtroom within minutes.

Upon completion of her preliminary instructions, Jeri asked Mike if he was ready to give his opening statement, which Jeri informed those in the courtroom was simply the lawyer telling the jury the evidence he expected to present. Mike stood and walked toward the jurors leaving all of his notes and papers at counsel table

Taking a moment to collect himself and to make eye contact with the jurors, Mike began authoritatively. "Ladies and gentlemen of the jury, on a beautiful April day two years ago, Martha Gebbert went into a Wendell's department store a happy, contented woman and left broken, battered, and shamed.

"This all happened not because of anything improper Mrs. Gebbert did. What was wrong were the policies of Wendell's that empowered untrained, unsupervised, and incompetent security guards to harass and mentally destroy innocent victims like Mrs. Gebbert. And they do this by handcuffing people like Mrs. Gebbert to a table so they can't to escape.

"Why do they do this? For one reason: plain and simple, to make money. Let me state that again—Wendell's department store developed a policy where it takes innocent people to the basement of its stores, handcuffs them to a table, and won't release them until they sign a form stating they committed some theoretical crime. Once they admit to a crime, Wendell's uses the admission to force these people to pay a civil penalty of hundreds and sometimes thousands of dollars.

"Martha Gebbert was one victim of Wendell's' policy, but she suffered from more than just a fine. After being locked to a table for over two hours, Martha relented and said she had stolen a piece of candy, which was when the security guard finally let her leave.

"Except when Martha left the store, she wasn't the same person she was when she came to shop. Because of Wendell's' policy, Martha ended up with post-traumatic stress disorder and what is known as agoraphobia. After this event Martha tried to continue her life, but she couldn't. Soon, she was unable to leave her house. Instead it got worse, until her husband Paul convinced her she needed help.

"She went to a psychologist, a doctor named Byron Rathman. Dr. Rathman, who has been licensed to treat patients with mental conditions for twenty-five years is going to tell you he has treated Mrs. Gebbert for well over one year and she now suffers from agoraphobia–fear of being outside, and has developed other mental issues which prevent her from engaging with her family or friends the way she used to.

"You may be thinking is this a significant injury? You can't see it on an x-ray. Physically she appears fine. This might be true, but as Dr. Rathman will tell you, this incident with Wendell's has caused injuries as devastating as if she were hit in the head with a baseball bat. Her husband will come in here and tell you how their family's lives all changed because Martha sits in her room all day–too scared to go outside.

"At the end of the trial, we are going to ask you in your verdict to find Wendell's department store was negligent–careless in how they dealt with Mrs. Gebbert and careless in how they developed this shoplifting policy of theirs.

"We will ask you to find Wendell's' carelessness caused Mrs. Gebbert substantial injuries and we will ask you to reimburse Mrs. Gebbert for all of her medical expenses, and more importantly to compensate her for the pain she and her family have endured, and for all of their suffering.

"Finally, we are going to ask you to find that Wendell's department store owes punitive damages for their reckless shoplifting policy, because it violates Pennsylvania law, and punish them by awarding the Gebberts money that sends the message to Wendell's that this is not how we do things in a civilized society."

Mike paused, holding the jurors' gaze, and then turned to head back to his chair at the table next to the jury box. The courtroom was silent as Stan reached over and patted Mike on the back.

Jeri looked up from her note-taking. She asked if the defendant was prepared to open.

Jack stood and nodded. He drew back his shoulders and raised his chin as he walked to the front of the jury box. He placed a yellow pad on the jury rail shelf, but walked away from it so nothing was between him and the jurors.

"Good morning everyone," he began. "There are always two sides to every story and I would like to take a few minutes to tell you what happened that day, backing it up with the evidence we will introduce during this trial.

"When Mrs. Gebbert came into the store, she was acting somewhat suspiciously. As you will see on the videotape, she kept picking up items from various displays and she may not have put all of them back. Our security guard, Robert Lombard, followed Mrs. Gebbert on the video as she went through the aisles, never appearing to want to buy anything. He will tell you the suspect was acting suspiciously, which is why he maintained visual contact with her until she actually stole something.

"As Mr. Lombard was watching Mrs. Gebbert, she was looking around side to side, but not appearing to be shopping. Lombard witnessed her open a box of chocolates by ripping off the cellophane and eating the chocolate. He immediately approached Mrs. Gebbert, identified himself as an employee, and asked Mrs. Gebbert to accompany him, which she did voluntarily.

"He took her to a room off the sales floor and asked her what she had taken. Mrs. Gebbert became irate and would not cooperate, forcing Mr. Lombard to put Mrs. Gebbert in handcuffs. Ultimately, Mrs. Gebbert acknowledged she stole the candy, so Mr. Lombard let her leave the store.

"Theft is an ongoing problem for all retail establishments. Everyday people come into stores looking to steal. Most of the time, these criminals look like ordinary people, just like you and me. Laws are designed to help stores prevent shoplifting. Wendell's developed a shoplifting policy and trained its guards to protect the assets of the stores from theft. The policy is tough, but effective. The retail industry recognizes the company as having the best record for protecting its stores against thieves.

"The evidence here will be clear. Security guard Lombard had a reasonable suspicion Mrs. Gebbert was committing a crime. He followed the company's policy in detaining Mrs. Gebbert. She admitted she stole the candy. In short, nothing the defendant did was improper.

"Finally, a world-renowned neuro-psychiatrist named Doctor Bernard Lawson will inform you Mrs. Gebbert suffered no injury as a result of anything Wendell's did—rather, if she has any problems, they stem from her own family situation." Mike shifted uneasily in his chair at Jack's mention of Mrs. Gebbert's "family situation," as he had no context for Jack's reference. Moreover, Jack had turned and glared at Mike when he made this statement. Mike, feeling challenged and trapped, did not respond. Turning back to the jury, Jack concluded his remarks. "Ultimately, the defendant didn't do anything wrong and we will ask you at the end of the trial to return a verdict in favor of Wendell's."

"Let's take a lunch break and then we can begin testimony," Jeri instructed from the bench.

Chapter 48

September 10, 2018, 1:30 p.m.
Trial Day 1

"MR. REIGERT, HOW** many witnesses do you think we can get through today?" Jeri asked while looking down from her seat high at the front of the courtroom.

"I think there should be enough time for two, Your Honor," Mike responded, standing. "For our first witness, we will call Dr. Byron Rathman." Mike felt apprehensive, knowing he was committing to trying his case backwards. Most times, lawyers have the plaintiff testify first to paint the picture of what happened and to create rapport with the jury. Martha was a wildcard and Mike wanted to gain traction before he put her on the stand. His conversations with Megan convinced him his biggest hurdle was convincing the jurors Mrs. Gebbert was injured and establishing this before weariness set in with the jurors as the trial proceeded. Stan signed off on the plan.

Byron Rathman, wearing a freshly pressed olive sports coat and dark grey trousers, took the stand and adjusted his microphone with an unsteady hand. The chair squeaked as Dr. Rathman squeezed his six-foot three-inch frame into the small seat. Rathman had treated hundreds of mentally impaired patients over the past 25 years, but this was the first time one of the people he treated was involved in a lawsuit and the first time he testified.

Speaking in a halting manner and in too low of a tone for Mike's taste, Dr. Rathman introduced himself to the jury and provided his educational background, which was unremarkable compared to the defense expert who would testify later. After the psychologist explained he treated a variety of patients in a solo practice for the past 25 years, Mike offered Dr. Rathman for questioning about the witness's qualifications to testify as an expert.

Jack stood and moved in front of Mike's table so Mike did not have a clear view of the witness.

"You are not a medical doctor, are you?" Jack said, zeroing in.

"No, I am not."

"You are not permitted by law to prescribe medication?"

"No, I am not."

"Therefor, if a patient of yours needs additional treatment that may include prescribing medication, you would refer them to a medical doctor, like the defendant's expert witness, Dr. Lawson, who is a neuro-psychiatrist?"

"I guess you are correct, but I can usually treat my patients without resorting to pills."

"You've never published any scholarly articles, have you?"

"No."

"Sir, you don't maintain admitting privileges at any hospital, do you?"

"No, I don't."

"Finally, doctor, before today, you've never testified in court before, have you?"

"No, I see and treat my patients."

"I suspect no judge has recognized you as an expert in your field before?"

"I guess not, but I know how to treat my patients."

"Perhaps. Sir, thank you. I will question you further when Mr. Reigert is through his questioning."

Mike stood again, this time with less confidence, wondering how much damage Jack had done to his first witness in the one minute he questioned him. Trying to regain his momentum, Mike took the psychologist through his treatment of Mrs. Gebbert. Dr. Rathman indicated he first saw Mrs. Gebbert eight months after the incident. She explained to him that Wendell's security guard falsely arrested her, took her to the basement of the store, handcuffed her to a table, and after being in the room alone, finally released her when she signed a confession.

According to Dr. Rathman's testimony, Mrs. Gebbert suffered post-traumatic injury as a result of the incident. She became wary of strangers and after a few weeks she began to have increasing difficulties leaving the house, often sitting in her bedroom in the dark, despondent and virtually a recluse. She grew increasingly unable to assist her family in functions occurring outside the home. Her children, now both high school students, relied on her to help them with homework and to organize their busy schedules, but as time went on, Mrs. Gebbert couldn't perform those tasks.

Mike wanted Dr. Rathman to explain Mrs. Gebbert's problems in greater detail, so he asked, "Doctor, what is your diagnoses for Mrs. Gebbert?"

"Based on my continued treatment of Mrs. Gebbert, she suffered post-traumatic stress syndrome after being handcuffed at the department store. This led her to suffer panic attacks which became fairly frequent. She began to believe her only safe zone was her home and ultimately her bedroom. The further she gets away from her safe zone, the more fearful she becomes and the more likely she will have another attack. This is known as agoraphobia."

"Doctor, what exactly is agoraphobia?"

"Like I was saying, agoraphobia is an anxiety disorder that causes a person to fear new situations because they think they are going to panic, or will feel trapped, helpless, or embarrassed. So they avoid public places and stay where they are comfortable, usually at home."

"What is the treatment for this?"

"It involves what is known as cognitive psychotherapy. We talk about her fears and develop a plan to overcome them. It is a difficult process because the fear is so real and in this case highly debilitating."

"How long will Mrs. Gebbert need cognitive psychotherapy?"

"We have done it for over a year now with some progress. She and her husband can travel further from her home—for example to a restaurant. But at this point, if she is going to leave the home, she has to do it with a trusted companion, and she is unable to go to places she used to go regularly that might be crowded. She still can't go to the supermarket or to a baseball game. Too many people are around in those types of situations. Mrs. Gebbert is improving, but recently her improvement has slowed. She is going to need a lot work to get anywhere close to where she was before all this occurred."

"How debilitating is her condition?"

"Depends. For Mrs. Gebbert, it is significantly problematic. She has to stay at home or she will likely suffer a panic attack. It's like a car hit her and broke both of her legs, physically confining her to bed."

Mike paused to allow the jury to digest the ramifications of the doctor's testimony before continuing. "Doctor, in your opinion, what caused these problems for Mrs. Gebbert?"

The psychologist looked at the jurors as he leaned forward. "Before she was trapped in that room in the basement of the department store, she didn't have any mental issues. According to what I learned from her husband and children, she was the rock of the family and never had any sort of problem or any type of treatment before. Since this situation, she has fallen apart. There is only one cause for her problems and that is what they did to her at the department store."

"Let me ask it another way, Doctor. If the incident at Wendell's never happened, what would her mental condition be like today?"

"If the store employee had not handcuffed her to a table and kept her in the room against her will, she would be the same person she was before—a well-adjusted, caring woman who is able to take care of her family. Unfortunately, this is not what happened."

Having completed his direct-examination, Mike was satisfied Dr. Rathman had conveyed the seriousness of Martha's condition. As he returned to counsel table, his uncle gave him a wink. Both turned to clean pages on their yellow pads and steeled themselves for the doctor's cross-examination.

"Doctor," Jack said, already questioning the witness before Mike could organize his papers, "can you point me to the x-ray showing the problem you claim Mrs. Gebbert is having?"

"No, her type of issue wouldn't appear on an x-ray."

"How about on something more sophisticated, like an MRI?"

"Of course not, those imaging tests aren't going to show her problem."

"Well if I broke a bone, I would show the jury my x-ray to prove my injury. Some objective test would prove if I sprained my ankle, correct?"

"Yes," the doctor answered, beginning to sound a little defensive.

"How about bloodwork—that often proves when a condition exists within the body—can any blood test conclusively prove Mrs. Gebbert has this problem you say she has?"

"No, bloodwork doesn't detect mental illness."

"Doctor, some test that objectively establishes this problem you say Mrs. Gebbert has exists, doesn't it?"

"No there aren't any. Mental illnesses like these are diagnosed by speaking with the patient, understanding their complaints, and working through how they deal with these problems."

"Has any other doctor reviewed your findings to determine if your diagnoses are valid?"

"No. I am the only doctor who has treated her."

"I guess this jury has to accept your word, because nothing is available other than what you are saying to support your conclusion, is there Doctor?"

"What you are suggesting is completely unfair," Dr. Rathman responded through gritted teeth. "I have twenty-five years of experience diagnosing and treating patients like this, so I am confident in my conclusions."

Jack turned his back on Rathman and walked to his counsel table. Wagner held up a manila folder which Jack snatched out of his hands. He faced Rathman and held the folder up in the air.

"Doctor, you just said you are the only doctor who had treated Mrs. Gebbert for psychological problems."

"Yes, that is what I said."

"That's not true, is it?"

Rathman shifted uncomfortably in his chair. "I am not aware of any other treatment."

Jack pulled documents out of the folder. He handed Mike a copy and placed another copy in front of Rathman. "Looking at these documents, Doctor, it's true that Mrs. Gebbert treated with another psychologist, isn't it?"

Mike stood. "Objection, Your Honor!"

Jeri thought for a moment. "Overruled. The witness will answer."

Rathman glanced through the documents. "Yes, it's true, but give me a minute to look through them." Rathman took five minutes to read through the records he had been provided. He continued, "Looking through these, it appears that Mrs. Gebbert five years ago treated on six occasions by a psychologist after her mother died."

"She withheld that information from you, didn't she?"

"She never told me about it, true."

"Doctor, look at page three of those records. Isn't it true that Mrs. Gebbert complained that her husband didn't pay enough attention to her?"

"Yes, it does say that."

Jack looked at his yellow pad. "You said earlier that you had treated other patients like this, referring to Mrs. Gebbert, but you never had any patient before who was in the middle of suing someone?"

"Yes, but so what?"

Jack smirked. "Because aren't patients in litigation different than your other patients?"

"No, I don't think so."

"Come on doctor, patients in litigation have a reason to stretch the truth, don't they?"

"Perhaps," Rathman conceded.

"Patients who have a lawsuit may not tell the truth to their doctors because it can benefit them financially."

"Yes."

"Thank you, Doctor. I have one last question: Given you are unaware of any objective test supporting your conclusion Mrs. Gebbert suffers from a mental illness, and because she has a reason to lie to you and stands to make money if you believe her lies, isn't it possible Mrs. Gebbert duped you?"

"Oh my god, no. She is a wonderful woman and I have no basis to think she isn't being anything but one hundred percent honest with me."

"No further questions." The smirk returned to Jack's face.

As Dr. Rathman shuffled off the witness stand and walked out of the courtroom, Mike pondered whether Jack's attack on the doctor's conclusions resonated with the jury. Mike put those concerns out his head as he called Paul Gebbert to testify. Looking meek and out of his element, Gebbert ambled to the front of the courtroom to take his oath. Mike hoped Paul would be able to paint a picture of how their family's life had changed since Martha's incident.

Chapter 49

September 10, 2018, 3:15 p..m.
Trial Day 1

PAUL GEBBERT TRIED to ease into the witness stand, but instead sat with a thump, causing his striped blue tie, which hung a tad too low, to bounce against his grey pants. Mike took a position at the far edge of the juror box. He began with simple questions. Paul sat straight when he told the jury that his job as a welder for a local union allowed him to take whatever jobs he wanted and spend the rest of his time with his wife and children. Despite never graduating from college, he had worked consistently since he was eighteen. He directed his gaze towards the jurors as he explained that he was able to provide for his family so Martha didn't have to work and could be home for her kids.

Now 42 years old, Paul said he split his time between working, spending time with his family, and having an occasional beer with his pals. Mike guided him through the preliminaries and turned everyone's attention to the incident.

Paul spoke slowly. "I wasn't there and I had no idea what was happening because she couldn't call anyone. Martha has a cell phone but they took it away from her. I got home early, around three in the afternoon and I was surprised she wasn't there. The kids got home from school and a few minutes later Martha returned.

"I could tell something was wrong right away. I didn't know what, but I asked her if she was okay. She sat down at the kitchen table, and stared out the window. So, I again asked her if everything was alright. She started to cry. The kids got scared so I told them to go do their homework and I would talk to them later. I pulled up a chair next to Martha and she just cried. Finally, I asked her what happened. It took a while, but she told me she'd been arrested and locked in a basement."

"How did you react?"

"First, I had no idea what she was talking about. I didn't know anything about where this took place; I assumed she had been at the police station. A little later she told me it was at Wendell's, but she couldn't tell me why. I called the store and they told me they caught her stealing and she signed a form admitting she stole something. They said they wouldn't talk to me anymore, but their lawyer would be calling to collect the penalty. I had no idea what they were talking about."

"What did your wife do?"

"She went upstairs and went to bed. She told me she never took anything and I believe her because she has never taken anything that's not hers, ever." Paul crossed his arms tightly across his chest and stared at Jack, defiantly challenging him.

Mike relaxed somewhat, because Paul was able to convey to the jury how this incident affected his wife. Paul explained that for the first few days Martha was distant, but nothing to cause alarm. As the weeks went by she became more and more withdrawn, spending more time in the bedroom and less time outside of the house. Her friends tried to coax her to do things, but Martha kept coming up with excuses until they stopped calling.

He took Martha to Dr. Rathman because she hadn't left the house for ten days at the time he'd made the appointment. He drove Martha to virtually all of her appointments and believed the doctor was making progress, but it was extremely slow.

Paul raised his hands and testified that his children probably suffered more than his wife. Before she went to the department store, Martha was actively involved in her kids' lives, taking them to activities, helping them schedule time with friends, and keeping track of homework assignments and school functions. Now, the kids primarily did this themselves. Paul chuckled when he admitted in some ways this gave them greater independence, but emphatically stated they were missing out on so much because their mother couldn't do what she did before. "It's almost like they don't have a mother anymore."

"Let's turn to how this has affected you," Mike said, moving into his last area of questioning with Paul. "Do you think you've been injured by what happened to your wife?"

"*Absolutely*," Paul said. "Everything has been taken from us. Our marriage was strong before this. We spent a lot of time together. We talked and we had fun. Now, she just sits in her room. We barely speak and when we do, I get upset. It's probably not fair, but I'm so mad because she isn't herself anymore. We don't have much left in our marriage."

Paul's testimony pleased Mike. Paul efficiently laid out his family's injuries caused by the changes to Martha since this incident. He didn't oversell what happened and didn't become too emotional. He simply explained what their lives were like now. Mike turned the witness over for cross-examination, hopeful Paul could handle the questioning.

Jack stood and walked over to a video player. He turned on the projector, which was pointed at a screen in front of the jurors. Jack placed his materials on the lectern and carefully set the remote control nearby.

"Mr. Gebbert, you testified you've been hurt because of your wife's injuries," Jack began.

"Absolutely."

"You spend time at home helping your wife."

"Sure."

"And this has caused you to miss out on lots of things outside of the house."

"Yes, it has."

Jack shifted positions, stepping out in front of the lectern and moving closer to Paul. "But you have been able to do certain activities while your spouse remained at home alone, true?"

"Sure, I go to work."

"And you do a lot of other things, don't you?"

"I don't know what you mean."

"You say you lost companionship with your wife, but you found comfort with someone else, didn't you?"

Paul stammered, unable to formulate a response. Jack took another step forward. "Let me play you some video and perhaps you will be able to answer the question."

Sensing impending danger, Mike stood and shouted, "Objection!" Jack turned to Mike almost snickering, his hands on his hips.

"What is your objection, Counselor?" Jeri asked from the bench.

"Mr. Rogers is about to play a video. They did not identify any videos on their exhibit list. They can't offer any evidence if they didn't previously identify it—unfair surprise."

Glancing at Jack, Jeri allowed him to state his position. "Mr. Gebbert testified he has lost the companionship of his wife because of what happened at the store. The videos we compiled show him in the company of another woman and disprove his claim. Rebuttal evidence does not need to be identified on our exhibit list and we should be allowed to impeach the witness's testimony with it."

Jeri pondered the issue and then ruled, "I accept Mr. Rogers' offer the video will be used to rebut Mr. Gebbert's prior testimony and to impeach him. Accordingly, this is not unfair surprise and did not need to be identified in defendant's Pretrial Statement. The defense may show the witness the video."

Mike slumped into his chair, sensing his case was about to be hit with a body blow. Jack nearly skipped back to his lectern to begin the video.

The jurors sat forward in anticipation. When a grainy image of a man and a woman holding hands, ambling through a parking lot, appeared, Jack asked, "Isn't the person walking with the woman, you, Mr. Gebbert?"

The jurors stared at Paul who responded, "I can't tell, the picture quality isn't good."

The shot on the screen pulled back to show a longer view and the couple entering the lobby of the Hidden Pines motel. "You recognize the motel don't you Mr. Gebbert?"

"I think I do. It's by the highway close to our house."

"Have you ever been a guest?"

"I can't remember?" Gebbert offered weakly.

"Perhaps this will help—here's a picture of the same couple coming out of one of the rooms holding hands. Isn't that you, Mr. Gebbert?" This time, Gebbert couldn't deny the implications of the images on the screen—his face easily identifiable.

"Yes, it's me," he submitted.

"Mr. Gebbert, I have lots of pictures here of you with this woman. Going to the movies, out to dinner and spending three hours at the zoo. You will admit these are you, and the woman depicted is not your wife, won't you?"

"Yes," he said even more meekly.

"And perhaps my favorite, you and your little lady friend having a picnic and then sneaking into the woods." The video showed Paul and the woman running off, hand and hand, disappearing among the trees. "You remember going on this romp, don't you?"

"Yes."

"Last question—you spent day after day and evening after evening with this woman all during the time you say you lost the companionship of your wife, correct?"

"Yes."

"I'm done with you, Mr. Gebbert," Jack practically sang as he picked up his materials and returned to his seat. Ed Wagner conspicuously patted him on the back.

The room had closed in on Mike. Jack had inflicted major damage and Mike cursed himself for not knowing Paul Gebbert cheated on his wife. He had to do something to help his case, but was beginning to panic and couldn't think straight.

"Mr. Reigert, any more questions?" Jeri asked from the bench as the jury looked on. Stan, seeing Mike squirm in his chair, leaned over and whispered in his ear. Nodding his head, Mike said, "I have a couple of more for Mr. Gebbert."

Mike took a position in front of his counsel table—the location he ordinarily utilized when he cross-examined hostile witnesses. Paul Gebbert was now an enemy and Mike prayed he could establish one fact to save his case. "Mr. Gebbert, all of these videos were taken after your wife's imprisonment at the department store, weren't they?"

"Yes, they were."

Mike, now taking a stab in the dark, asked, "Did you ever have an affair with another woman before the incident at Wendell's?"

"Never."

Mike turned, heaving a sigh of relief and returned to counsel table. Paul Gebbert slinked off of the witness stand collapsing into a seat in the back of the courtroom. He looked directly at the floor, avoiding the venomous eyes of the jurors.

Chapter 50

September 17, 2018, 4:45 p.m..
Trial Day 1

MIKE LEANED UP against the wall in the hallway outside of Jeri's courtroom and softly banged his head against the plaster. Stan waited
for a few moments, allowing Mike to process what Paul Gebbert
had done to their case. They needed to come up with a plan for how to
deal with this unfortunate development. It was the end of the day which,
at least, provided them with a little time to regroup. Mike's worried words
came out in rapid succession. "How do we overcome this? We might as
well pack our bags. The jury thinks we are a bunch of slime."

Stan put a hand on Mike's shoulder and said, "Slow down.
Unexpected things happen at trial all of the time. We can deal with it."

"Uncle Stan, this is bad."

"Agreed, but think for a minute. Martha is hurt by the department
store. She can't be a real wife for Paul, so he seeks comfort elsewhere.
Paul may appear to be a pig, but Martha is the one who is aggrieved."

"True, but to the jury, Paul is the face of the family."

"That needs to change. You need to get the husband as far away
from this courtroom as possible. You saw the way the jury looked at
him when he got off the stand. He's damaged goods."

Before Stan could continue, Mike was smacked on his back as Jack and his mentor came strolling down the hallway. "Hey buddy, we had some fun in there didn't we? You didn't see that one coming, did you?" Jack said, stopping to wait for a reaction.

"You're an asshole Jack. You take a lot of pleasure in breaking up somebody's family, don't you?"

"Don't blame me. It was your client's own doing. Nice pictures of him going into the woods," Jack sneered. "You screwed with me Mike and now we are going to win this case. You should've accepted our offer." Jack turned and smiled at Wagner.

"You're a poser Jack. You always were. You can't do things on merit, so you'll take any shortcut." Mike's retort hit the mark. Jack took a step towards Mike, raising his hands in threat.

"This is how you like to respond, right Jack?" Mike moved toward Jack. "You want to threaten me like you did to Megan. You're a coward Jack." The former classmates edged closer until Jack shoved Mike with a strong two-handed push.

The commotion was attracting attention. Recognizing the impropriety of two attorneys coming to blows in the courthouse, Stan stepped in between them and barked, "Back off, both of you. Jack, walk away. You two can settle this tomorrow."

Jack glared at Mike as he straightened his tie and backed away. "You should have taken the money. I'm not going to let this cost me my partnership." Wagner slapped Jack on the back as the two sidled down the hallway.

Mike leaned against the wall to gather his nerves, before saying to Stan, "Perhaps Martha can't sit in court for very long, but I think I have an idea. I need to go talk to Martha. I have to tell her what happened today. This will be ugly. I'll let you know if it works." Mike ran down the hallway, leaving Stan alone.

Chapter 51

September 11, 2018, 8:45 a.m.
Trial Day 2

MIKE SLOUCHED AGAINST the wall of the courtroom resting, his eyes heavy and his back in knots. He had spent most of the previous evening at the Gebbert home, formulating a plan to deal with Paul Gebbert while also assisting the family in coping with the revelation of his unfaithfulness.

When Mike arrived at the Gebbert house the drama was already unfolding. Paul had returned home and confessed his transgressions to Martha and their kids. The betrayal devastated Martha, who told Paul to leave the house. Martha was nearly non-communicative while Mike tried to develop a revised trial strategy. It took hours of pleading until Martha finally consented to a change in their plans.

On his way home from the Gebbert house the evening before, Mike briefly explained to his uncle that he had convinced Martha to allow the kids to take Paul's place as the family's representatives in court. Mike understood the risk of having the children in the courtroom and the jury assuming they were trying to engender sympathy, but Mike believed they had no choice. Given what she had learned about her husband, Martha indicated she just wanted the trial to go away. Ultimately, the kids convinced their mother to allow them to testify.

The next day, Stacey and Tanner Gebbert, dressed in their church clothes, followed Mike into the courthouse. Neither had been to a legal proceeding before and both gaped as they walked into the courtroom.

Mike took a seat at counsel table, unable to predict what would happen during the second day of testimony. "Call your next witness, Mr. Reigert," Jeri announced to start the day.

Stacey Gebbert shuffled to the stand, unable to make eye contact with the jurors, the judge, or anyone else in the courtroom. She stepped into the witness box and was consumed by the large wooden chair. When Mike asked her to state what her name was, tears began to stream down her checks. The jurors looked sympathetically at Stacey while Jeri handed her a tissue and offered some reassuring words. Watching the mini-drama unfolding, Mike felt a tinge of guilt, recognizing the family's disintegration might pay dividends with the jury.

Mike introduced her to the jury and Stacey tried to collect herself, but acted confused. Mike decided to start with the hard part. "Stacey, tell the jury what happened at your house last night."

Stacey faced the jurors, but still was unable to make eye contact. "My dad came home last night and there was a lot of crying."

"Stacey, let's take this a little slower. When your father came home did he say something to your mother?"

"Yes, he was upset and he told all of us he did something very bad. He told my mom he was seeing someone else."

"What did your mom do?"

"She cried. She yelled at him and she told him she wanted him to leave the house and not come back. That's why Tanner and I are here today and not our dad." Stacey looked at jury members bewildered. The jurors returned her gaze.

Mike shifted gears. "Stacey, were you aware of any problems between your parents before your mother was chained to a table at the department store."

"No, I didn't think there were any. Everything was fine. After she came home that day, things for my mom got worse. I thought my dad was working real hard to help my mom, but I never knew...." Stacey's voice trailed off and more tears formed at the corners of her eyes.

Watching from the edge of the jury box, Mike thought Stacey was accomplishing exactly what he and his uncle had hoped. Relying on kids' testimony is fraught with danger—they are unpredictable, but if they come across as credible, the emotions they convey can linger for an entire trial. Mike thought that within minutes of Stacey taking the stand the jury began to bond with her, which was inevitable once they saw the pain her parents' breakup was causing her.

"Tell us how your mom has changed since she was handcuffed by the department store."

Stacey considered. "She was always there for us. She helped us in school and got us to our activities. I play soccer a lot. She went to every game and was the head parent for the team. Whenever I had a problem, I would go to her. Now everything is different."

"How?" Mike prodded.

The question appeared to confuse Stacey, but she persisted. "Last week, I needed to finish an assignment for science class and had two soccer games. I was having trouble getting started with the project and I went up to see my mom in her bedroom. It used to be she would come up with a great idea to help me start my homework. So, I asked her and she told me to talk to my father.

"My dad's not good at that kind of thing so I went and got everything I needed for the project. I did it all myself, but it took a lot of time. I missed my games." Stacey paused. "Before this, my mom would have made sure I got this done on time and drove me to soccer. Is that what you wanted?"

Mike smiled at Stacey. "Yes, thanks Stacey. I don't have any more questions for you." Stacey started to stand. Jeri grinned and said, "One second, young lady. The attorney for the department store gets to ask you some questions if he wants to."

Mike sat at his counsel table. As Jack stood and walked to the lectern, Mike recalled Stan telling him that at trial jurors usually root for the witnesses over the attorneys because all of the rules favor the attorneys—more so when the witness is elderly or a child. Every attorney knew to tread lightly when questioning these types of witnesses and to make perhaps a single point and immediately sit down. If the jurors thought the lawyer was beating up on the young or the infirmed, the jury might penalize that side when handing down its verdict.

Jack placed his hands on the lectern, glanced at Stacey, and then at the jurors. "We have no questions of this witness," he announced.

Wanting to maintain his momentum, Mike immediately called Tanner Gebbert to the stand. Now a seventh grader, but yet to have a growth spurt, Tanner looked younger than his actual age. Tanner took his seat with a bit more confidence than his sister. After being sworn to tell the truth, Tanner waved at the jurors. Two of the women jurors waved back.

Tanner sat with an impish smile and had no difficulty speaking directly to the jurors. Mike's questions were simple, and Tanner's answers were even simpler as he offered little in substance, unable to articulate how his life was different since his mom had returned from her detention at the department store. Mike presumed that the jury sympathized with Tanner, no matter how unaffected he acted.

Mike did not ask a lot of questions of Tanner, again wanting the jurors to see that he and his sister were good kids caught up in a bad situation. Tanner was another face of the travails the family had endured.

Jack didn't rise when he said, "No questions for this witness."

Stan nodded to indicate Mike had covered Martha's damages appropriately. Mike worried that the jurors were focused on her lack of physical injuries. If the jurors didn't buy that Martha was hurt, they had lost the case. Calling more witnesses to testify about her problems wouldn't serve any purpose. Mike was ready to shift to putting on the people who would establish the company's liability for handcuffing Martha Gebbert to a table.

Mike glanced at the jury, wanting some sign they supported him. All he saw were blank faces impassively staring towards the window, waiting for the trial to continue.

Chapter 52

September 11, 2018, 9:30 a.m.
Trial Day 2

"**THE PLAINTIFF WILL** call Steven Lombard for cross-examination." Jeri turned to the jurors. "Parties are able to call witnesses associated with the other side as witnesses in their own case. Because Mr. Lombard is employed by the defendant, plaintiff may call him as a witness in her case and cross-examine him."

The jurors nodded and turned their attention to the witness stand, seeing a young, well-dressed man, take his place in the box. Mike stood at the edge of the jury box, ready to put on testimony to prove the company's liability.

Within two minutes of putting Lombard on the stand, Mike established that the witness was 26 years old, already divorced, and had held three jobs for less than six months before the department store hired him. He was a high school graduate, but received no further education and had no background in security or law enforcement before he became a detective for the company.

Mike moved to question Lombard about the training the company provided. "Before you began as a security guard, you went through a training course."

"Yes," Lombard said.

"The course lasted three days."

"Yes."

"A man named George Magnuson ran your training."

"Yes, Mr. Magnuson taught us a lot."

"Mr. Magnuson was a store detective for the company who was fired by the company three months later."

"I believe that is true."

"For, and I read from his personnel file, 'gross incompetence.'"

"News to me."

"Other than what Mr. Magnuson taught you, you received no training from anybody else."

"Also true."

"Mr. Lombard, did you receive any written guidelines from the company on how to handle shoplifters?"

"Yes, in our training materials."

Mike held up the binder of materials. He began reading, "When you locate a shoplifter, you are to take him or her off the sales floor to the designated shoplifter detention area."

"Yes, you are reading correctly."

"The rules of Wendell's encourage you to handcuff a suspect to assist in your investigation.'"

"Yes, they taught us to place shoplifters in cuffs."

"I'll read further: 'A suspect who is handcuffed will remain in handcuffs until they sign the theft admission form.'"

"Exactly."

"They taught you to handcuff suspects to a bar on the table in the designated shoplifter detention area."

"Yes, so they couldn't do any harm to us."

"So let me get this straight. Whenever you handcuffed someone, you chain them to a table until you decide to release them and you only release them if they sign the theft admission form admitting they stole something."

"Correct."

"Sir, what if your suspect didn't' steal anything?"

"I'm sorry, I don't understand."

"What if they didn't steal something?"

"Oh they stole something. If we detain them, we're positive they've taken something and they taught us not to listen to their excuses and trust what we see."

"So, once you decide to stop someone, you take them downstairs and handcuff them to the bar on the table, and they will stay there until they sign the form admitting they've committed theft."

"You got that right."

Mike informed the witness he wanted to discuss the day he handcuffed Mrs. Gebbert.

"Mr. Lombard," Mike began, "you were stationed in a small office off of the sale's floor."

"Yes, I was monitoring the surveillance system."

"More to the point, you sat in a room spying on the people who come to buy things at your store."

"I wouldn't call it spying."

"You watched people when they didn't know you were watching them."

"Everyone is aware there are cameras in retail stores," Lombard returned.

"You were spying." Mike wanted Lombard to concede this point.

"Objection," Jack said, trying to protect his witness. "Plaintiff's counsel is arguing with the witness."

Jeri held her hand up to prevent further discussion. "The objection is sustained. Mr. Reigert, move on."

Mike changed tack. "Your job is to watch your customers and decide from the small room where you are watching if they are stealing."

"My job is to protect the assets of the company and make sure any item that leaves the property has been paid for."

"You watched Mrs. Gebbert select three different products."

"True."

"She was carrying them to a register."

"I couldn't tell where she was going. She was wandering through the store. She appeared to be walking aimlessly. "

"You would agree she didn't try to steal those items."

"Well, she never paid for them. I didn't know if she was going to pay for them. It looked like she might have tried to conceal them, but I stopped her before she got to the register."

"Meaning you arrested her before you gave her a chance to buy those items."

"I detained her after she took the chocolates without paying for them."

"Let's watch the surveillance footage so we can discuss why you arrested her."

Mike turned his back on the witness and signaled Stan to play the tape. Black and white video images formatted in a 3x4 grid appeared on the screen.

"These are the twelve monitors the company placed in the ceilings throughout the store."

"Yes."

Movement was evident on all twelve camera displays simultaneously.

"You are responsible for watching all of the monitors at once and you may be viewing the screens for your entire eight-hour shift."

"I guess you are right, but usually I will go out on the floor and patrol after watching the cameras for a while."

Mike directed Stan to pull up camera six alone on the full screen.

Mike turned toward the witness. "Camera six is the only camera you used to determine Mrs. Gebbert did something wrong?"

"That is correct."

An image of Mrs. Gebbert was displayed on the screen. The grainy and imprecise picture suggested the system utilized by the department store was not of a recent vintage.

"You watched Mrs. Gebbert while she selected three items to purchase."

"Yes, I was watching her."

"She didn't do anything unusual to get your attention, did she?"

"I think she was acting a little bit suspicious, but I have learned sometimes the ones who appear to be the most trustworthy do the worst things. I guess that proved true here," Lombard said.

"Really, let's watch what happened that day."

On the video, Mrs. Gebbert casually walked through the aisles until she arrived at a counter in the candy section.

"By the way," Mike interjected, "you actively followed Mrs. Gebbert with the camera system, didn't you?"

"Yes, I was using a toggle switch to move the camera so I could watch what she did."

Utilizing a red LED pointer light to direct Lombard's attention to a particular portion of the image on the screen, Mike continued, "Mr. Lombard, Mrs. Gebbert approached the display and saw an open box of candy."

"I wouldn't agree. The box was not opened."

"The lid on the box was off."

"That is true."

"Which allowed her to easily take a piece of the chocolate to sample."

"Didn't look so easy to me. She had to break the cellophane covering the candy."

"Mr. Lombard, the image you watched on your eight-by-twelve-inch screen provided you all of the information you utilized to decide to detain Mrs. Gebbert, correct?

"What do you mean?"

"She didn't do anything suspicious before that. She ate the candy conspicuously like a person would eat a sample. So the only reason you detained her was because you thought she opened the box of candy with her finger?"

"Yes, that is true."

"Did you retain the box of candy so this jury could examine it?" Mike asked, sweeping his hand towards the jurors to suggest he was including them in the process.

"No, I left the box at the candy department. They probably threw it away."

"Mrs. Gebbert was completely surprised when you stopped her," Mike continued, boring in. "She acted as though she didn't steal anything, correct?" Mike pointed to the video which showed Martha covering her mouth with her hand when Lombard first approached her.

"Most people who commit theft act like they didn't do anything. The stuff some people do amazes me when they are caught red-handed."

"She told you she didn't take anything."

"And I told her the video caught her opening up the chocolates," Lombard said, sitting erect and not twitching.

"Exactly what I wanted to talk about," Mike said, excited that Lombard had helped him jump to his next area of questioning. "Let's watch the video." Stan anticipated Mike's plan and jumped the tape to the section where Martha selected the chocolate. "I can see the box of chocolates sitting on the counter, and my client reaches in to grab one. Nothing is on the video to suggest she opened the cellophane, is there?"

The video displayed an image of Mrs. Gebbert reaching into the box of candy and picking a piece and eating it. Mike had watched this portion at least one hundred times, yet couldn't see any reflection to suggest the covering was intact and certainly couldn't determine if she broke the wrapping. The camera image lacked sufficient detail for him to make that determination. The jurors intently watched the screen.

Lombard studied the images, which in the courtroom were much bigger than when he watched them on his workplace monitor. On the video, Martha grabbed the chocolate. "There, you can see a glimmer of the cellophane as she breaks it."

Stan and Mike had discussed how to deal with this issue many times before and decided to replay the video multiple times because they did not believe anyone could definitively see anything on the videotape. As the video depicted Martha approaching the candy display, the jurors leaned forward to examine the images. Once they sat back to indicate they had completed their inspection, Mike moved on to another area of questioning.

"Let's talk about what you did once you took Mrs. Gebbert downstairs," Mike said, inching closer to Lombard. "When you took her to the basement, you didn't allow Mrs. Gebbert to leave."

"I guess you are right. I took her off the sales floor so I could complete the appropriate forms and to give us privacy so she wouldn't be unnecessarily embarrassed."

"You had no concern about her privacy. You wanted to maintain control."

"Objection, he is arguing with the witness again," Jack said, jumping to his feet.

"The objection is sustained. Ask a question Mr. Reigert."

"Isn't the reason you take a person who you stop for shoplifting into the basement is because the person becomes disoriented and has no chance of walking away."

"I took Mrs. Gebbert to a room to process her. She didn't ask to leave."

"You took her to that room. You took all of her possessions and handcuffed her."

"Our procedures are clear. To protect the people in the room we handcuff all suspects. There were some situations where people became violent and tried to hurt our security guards, so for our protection, we cuff everyone. Here, the suspect got agitated, so I put her in handcuffs to make sure."

"I can only wonder why people become upset when you falsely accuse them of shoplifting."

"Objection, that is outrageous!" Jack again jumped to his feet. "I move to strike counsel's statement."

"The objection is sustained and the jury is to disregard Mr. Reigert's statement. Mr. Reigert, be careful. You are getting close to the line with those remarks." Mike turned with his back to the jurors and smirked at Jack, knowing that despite the objection being sustained, they heard what he said.

"Mr. Lombard, Mrs. Gebbert told you she didn't steal anything and she refused to sign your admission form, didn't she?"

"True."

"So she is locked to the table and you tell her she is not going anywhere until she signs the form."

"You are not being accurate. I handcuffed her to the table so nobody got hurt and explained to her about signing the document."

"You told her you would allow her to leave if she signed the form." Mike's voice edged louder as he crept closer to the witness.

"Yes, because all the paperwork would be complete."

"But she wouldn't agree to sign the form."

"No, she was being difficult."

"So, you wouldn't let her out of the handcuffs."

"True."

"Fine," Mike said dismissively, "let's focus on what happened in the room. You held Mrs. Gebbert in handcuffs for over two hours."

"I believe that is true."

"You took all of her personal items away from her, including her cellphone."

"Yes."

"So she couldn't call anyone and she couldn't leave the room unless you let her go."

"Also true."

"She kept denying she took anything."

"And I told her multiple times I saw her take something on the videotape."

"She asked to see a manager."

"Yes, and I told her a manager didn't have authority to let her go, I was in charge."

"So your company's policy empowers a twenty-six-year-old security guard with less than one year experience, while the manager of the store who has worked for the company for over twenty-five years can't override your decisions."

"Yes, because they trained me to handle these situations."

"Of course," Mike said, not hiding his sarcasm. "By the way, you don't have any video of what happened in the room, do you?"

"No, policy is not to have cameras in the room."

"That way it becomes your word against the other person's word."

"I suppose."

"Just so we are clear—you accuse Martha Gebbert of stealing a piece of chocolate. You take her off the sales floor so nobody can see what you are doing. You take her to the basement and chain her to a table. You put a paper in front of her and tell her you won't let her go until she signs the document admitting she committed a crime she denied committing so far."

Lombard thought for a moment and nodded. "Yes, that is true."

"Mrs. Gebbert was in the room for over two hours."

"I think that is true."

"Most of the time she was in the room by herself."

"Yes, but I would come back and check on her."

"You were actually checking to see if she signed the form, but every time you came back, she refused to sign and kept asking to speak with someone else."

"Yes, but I told her I was the only one she could talk to."

"How long would you have let her stay handcuffed until you let her go?"

"I don't know. I let her go when she signed the admission form."

"Sir, isn't the only reason she signed the form was because that was the only way you would release her?"

"I don't know why she did what she did. I think she signed the form because she stole something."

Mike frowned, not sure if he should stop his questioning with Lombard's repeated assertion Mrs. Gebbert stole the chocolate, but recognized if the jury at this point still thought of her as a thief he had little chance of convincing them with further questioning. "I have no more questions for this witness," Mike said as he returned to his chair.

Jack stood immediately to try to obtain some beneficial information from his own witness. He spent a few minutes asking about Lombard's background in high school and the few jobs he held before the department store hired him. He drew out more specifics on his training wanting to create the impression the company trained him well.

"Mr. Lombard, how many people have you stopped for shoplifting since you began to work for the company?"

"I believe I stopped about a hundred fifty shoplifters."

"Sounds like a lot," Jack replied with forced seriousness.

"I don't know if it's a lot. Lots more people take things from the store, but they teach us not to stop anyone unless we see them take something and if we maintain visual contact with them until we detain them. That way we don't make mistakes."

"Interesting. Well, did you ever stop anyone improperly?"

"I don't believe so."

"Has any person other than Mrs. Gebbert brought a lawsuit against the company claiming you detained them improperly?"

"No, this is the first time I ever testified." Lombard smiled at the jury wanting to appear earnest.

"Good. Let's now talk about why you stopped Mrs. Gebbert."

"Like I said, I saw her open the box of chocolates and take a piece of candy. The box of candy costs twelve dollars and once opened the store can't sell it. It may not sound like much, but all the stealing adds up. So many people try to steal things in so many different ways. They are getting quite creative these days. We're just trying to keep up with them."

"Did you follow your training when you stopped Mrs. Gebbert?"

"Absolutely. You saw the materials they hand out. I did exactly what I was supposed to do. She took something and she admitted to taking it. It was that simple."

Jack sat, indicating he had no further questions. Mike was about to stand to follow up on some of the answers the security guard gave when Stan placed a hand on his arm. He glanced at Stan who subtly shook his head.

"No more questions for this witness."

Jeri scanned the courtroom and said, "I think we have given the jurors a lot of testimony in a short period of time. Let's break and then we can hear from our next witness."

Chapter 53

September 11, 2018, 11:00 a.m.
Trial Day 2

WILLIAM RUTLEDGE, AN executive for the department store chain, held his head erect, projecting confidence as he took the stand. An experienced security guard for two national retail chains who moved into management fifteen years earlier, Rutledge looked directly at the jurors, never flinching, waiting for Mike's questions.

It was evident from the beginning of his testimony that Rutledge, wearing a Brooks Brothers suit that did little to mask his history of tailing suspects on the street, was not going to allow Mike to put words into his mouth. In response to Mike's second question, "Are you the Director of Loss Prevention for Wendell's department stores?" he stated, "No, my correct title is the Vice-President of Loss Prevention and Shrink for Wendell's, Inc." Mike knew his questions had to be precise or Rutledge would throw his words back in his face.

"Mr. Rutledge, you drafted your company's shoplifting policy, didn't you?" Mike asked.

"Yes, I did. I spent a lot of time formulating our procedures to make sure they were comprehensive and appropriate."

"You lived and worked in Texas at the time you wrote the policy?"

"Yes, that is where the company has the most stores and also the most problems with shoplifters. I checked with our attorneys to make sure the policy complied with the law."

"Is that really accurate, Mr. Rutledge? You asked for an opinion from your Texas attorneys, but you never made sure the policy complied with the laws of other states."

"Our lawyers reviewed the procedures and told me they were fine and legal in Texas. The laws in other states with respect to how to treat shoplifters are almost the same as Texas."

"Sir, did you ever obtain a lawyer's opinion that your shoplifting policy would be legal in Pennsylvania?"

"Not exactly. Like I said, our Texas lawyers said it should be okay."

"And you, Mr. Rutledge, are not a lawyer, so you can't say your policy would be legal in Pennsylvania."

"I'm not a lawyer, but I am comfortable our policy complies with all applicable laws and regulaiions."

"Your policy compels your security guards to chain suspected shoplifters to a table."

"Yes, to make sure nobody gets hurt."

"But you don't instruct your guards to involve the police."

"No, under the law we don't have to. Our security personnel are all trained on how to deal with shoplifters. Nobody has ever sued us anywhere before." Rutledge waved his hand as though sweeping away Mrs. Gebbert's lawsuit.

Stan handed Mike a stack of papers and Mike moved back to the lectern. "Mr. Rutledge, let's move to a different area of questioning. Your company makes money whenever one of your security guards stops a shoplifter, doesn't it?"

"We are saving money by stopping people from taking items they didn't pay for."

"Not quite what I am asking," Mike said, frowning at Rutledge's response. "You make money because you try to extract a civil fine every time someone signs one of these confession forms." Mike waived a stack of papers over his head.

"Each state allows us to collect a civil penalty in addition to the retail cost of an item when someone steals something."

"You collect three hundred dollars in civil penalties each time a person signs this form. You write it on the form, the person 'will pay to the company three hundred dollars in a civil penalty or additional fines and penalties will be levied,' don't you?"

"Yes, the fines are so the courts don't have to get involved with petty theft and acts as a deterrent so people won't steal again."

Turning to the screen, Mike pointed to a spreadsheet displayed and asked, "In the four hundred fifty stores you operate nationwide your security guards stopped on average a hundred and fifty people per store last year for shoplifting, correct?"

"Yes, I believe you are correct."

"For those stops, you extracted a three hundred dollar civil penalty each time, didn't you?"

"Not for all of them, but the vast majority."

"Multiplying the stores by the stops per store, means your company stopped sixty-seven thousand five hundred people for shoplifting last year."

"Sounds about right. A lot of people steal from our stores."

"If each one paid their three-hundred-dollar civil penalty, your company received approximately twenty and a quarter million dollars in these fines."

"I guess you are correct."

"Sir, your company accused each of these people of shoplifting and one of your employees handcuffed each one to a table and told them they would be released only if they signed your company's confession form."

"Yes, consistent with our policy."

"And no video exists of how your security guards treated any of these people to coerce them into signing these forms because you don't videotape what happens in those rooms in your stores' basements."

"Objection!" Jack was now on his feet. "What happened in those other situations is not relevant here."

Jeri grimaced from her bench. "A little late to be making that objection now. The horse is already out of the barn. The objection is overruled. Mr. Rutledge will answer the question."

Rutledge shifted in the witness stand. "We don't have any video cameras in any of our detention rooms."

"So, stopping people and accusing them of stealing is a profit center for your company?"

Jack jumped to his feet and yelled, "Objection!"

"Overruled."

Although knowing he didn't have to repeat his question, Mike elected to ask the same question slightly differently. "Mr. Rutledge, your company made twenty million dollars accusing people of stealing from your company last year, didn't it?"

"We caught people red-handed. They confessed to it. They pay a penalty. It's fairly simple."

As Rutledge was giving his explanation, Mike returned to his seat. Quiet enveloped the courtroom for a moment as the 20-million-dollar figure screamed from the screen. Stan slowly rose and turned off the projector while Mike announced he had no further questions.

Jack stood to question his witness, asking him to justify his company's policy in his own words. Seeing a friendly face, Rutledge relaxed and turned to the jury to explain. "Theft is a horrible problem in this country. Lots of people go into stores and take merchandise without paying. Some offer a justification by saying it's a victimless crime. I disagree. Stealing adds to the cost of everything.

"We have studied reports indicating theft adds twenty percent to the cost of all products. Violence in our stores and outside of the stores increases because of this. So, theft from a company's point of view is not a victimless crime.

"Secondly, people who steal will lie to cover it up. We train our security guards how to approach suspected shoplifters and minimize the chances the interaction will escalate. When you accuse people of stealing, their response is often to resort to violence.

"This is why we instruct our guards to detain any suspect only after being positive that theft has occurred and then to take them off of the sales floor. This, we found, reduces the chances of an interaction escalating into violence, but also protects our real customers who are innocently shopping. Even with all of the precautions and training sometimes people still become violent. This is why we use handcuffs. When a person is in handcuffs, the chances of violence are reduced to almost zero."

"Why does the company charge a civil penalty?"

"For many reasons. The law allows us to include a civil penalty. The collection of the civil penalty offsets some of the costs we incur to detect and prevent theft. The penalty also deters some people from committing crimes in our stores again. I realize the numbers we went over sound like a lot, but we maintain an excellent record at preventing people from stealing and compared to other companies in our industry we do a top-notch job at informing people we will prosecute theft. I think our system has worked extremely well and has reduced crime, making our stores much safer for the shopping public."

Jack and Rutledge stopped talking and looked at the jury.

Seeing Jack conclude his questioning, Mike stood and asked, "Sir, where in your policy does it say how long one of your guards should allow someone to be handcuffed to a table?"

"It doesn't specifically address that. What our procedures allow is our security guards the freedom to process the paperwork without having to worry about the thief becoming violent."

Mike paused, knowing Rutledge hadn't answered his question and continued. "Mr. Rutledge, if Mrs. Gebbert never signed the confession form, she would still be chained to the table, wouldn't she?"

Rutledge squirmed, unsure how to respond. "I doubt it."

Shaking his head like dealing with a petulant six-year-old, Mike dismissed Rutledge from the witness stand.

Chapter 54

September 11, 2018, 1:30 p.m.
Trial Day 2

AFTER LUNCH, STANDING before the jury, Mike called his security expert as his next witness. Ken Fishbeck worked in security for 25 years before opening a consulting business that assisted all types of companies wanting to fix security related problems. At times, lawyers also retained him to act as an expert witness to discuss the successes or failures of a particular company's security program or how one of its employees handled a security issue in litigation.

Stan had previously retained Fishbeck in a case involving a shooting at a bar. In that case, Fishbeck testified how the bar failed to hire adequate security given the extent of crime in the area of the bar. Although Stan lost the case, Fishbeck did his job competently and Stan suggested that Mike hire him to dissect Wendell's shoplifting policies.

Fishbeck took his seat without any sign of arrogance or nervousness. His charcoal grey sports coat and tie belied a toughness forged from years of dealing with society's dregs. Mike quickly led Fishbeck through his professional accomplishments and briefly touched on the types of cases on which he usually consulted. The jury listened intently, drawn into Fishbeck's world of investigation and interrogation, as Fishbeck described his career in a clipped northeastern intonation.

Mike turned his questioning to the law that governed how retail establishments dealt with shoplifting. Fishbeck took the jury through Pennsylvania's Retail Theft Act, explaining that the statute gave store owners the right to stop and detain suspected shoplifters, but only if they had a reasonable suspicion that a criminal act was being committed. Fishbeck also conceded that a retailer still could enjoy the protections afforded by the statute even if the suspected shoplifter turned out not to have done anything wrong, so long as the person detaining the suspected shoplifter had a reasonable suspicion to stop the person.

When asked to discuss Wendell's policy of handcuffing suspects, Fishbeck became animated and opined to the jury that such a policy was beyond the bounds of the law and was not found in any other shoplifting policy that he had ever reviewed. "Being chained to a table to make someone sign a confession form calls into question every confession that Wendell's has ever gotten."

Another failure of the shoplifting policy that Fishbeck cited was the lack of a camera in the detention room. "If I wasn't doing anything wrong in that room, I certainly would want videotape to back me up. On the other hand, if I wanted my security guards to do something that was improper, I would make sure there wasn't any evidence."

Mike finally asked about Wendell's policy of extracting fines from suspected shoplifters. Fishbeck conceded that under the statute, store owners didn't have to call the police and were authorized to seek civil penalties, but also believed that Wendell's plan was profit driven and the stores stopped people for shoplifting in an attempt to coerce the penalties so that Wendell's profits would increase.

Jack did not want to press Fishbeck much on cross-examination, knowing his own expert would refute Fishbeck's conclusions. Jack knew he wouldn't be able to dissuade the expert from his conclusions so he would use his questions to highlight the conclusions that Wendell's own expert would present to the jury.

Jack started his questioning by emphasizing statistics evidencing the unrelenting growth of theft and then had Fishbeck agree that retailers were easy targets given the array of merchandise, the number of customers in their stores, and the immense areas security guards had to watch.

Fishbeck again conceded that retailers had been given the right to stop and detain suspected shoplifters and that the use of signed confession forms was standard in the retail industry. Jack never challenged Fishbeck's conclusions, but by the time the witness walked off the stand Jack was confident he had blunted the significance of his testimony.

Mike held his head high when he turned to the jury and announced, "Plaintiff has one last witness to call."

Chapter 55

September 11, 2018, 3:15 p.m.
Trial Day 2

THE JURORS QUICKLY took their seats after a break, ready for the final witness for the plaintiff. When they were seated, Mike motioned to Stan who was standing at the entry doors to the courtroom. Stan poked his head outside, signaled, and then returned to his seat next to Mike. The jury waited as the courtroom was cloaked in silence.

Moments later, the doors drew outward and a group of three women entered. Stephanie Regalski and Stacey Gebbert gently held a woman between them by the arm—the person whom the jury had been waiting to see.

Martha had put on a light blue dress that morning and waited for Stephanie to call and tell her when to leave for the courthouse. A friend drove her to town and dropped her in front of the building. Martha sat in a small, secluded room in the rear of the courthouse with Stephanie, sipping water and waiting for her turn to testify.

When they reached the last row of seats for the spectators in the courtroom, Stephanie and Stacey let go of Martha and sat. Martha looked back at them before beginning her walk to the witness box. The two-inch boxed heels she wore made a slight shuffling sound as she passed the jurors.

She took the two steps into the witness box and Kathy, the judge's tipstaff, swore her in. "Do you swear to tell the whole truth and nothing but the truth, so help you god?" Kathy asked.

"I do." Martha sat, her eyes cast down at the weathered hands in her lap and the wedding ring on her finger. Martha clutched her purse and forced herself to exhale. Finally, She looked up.

With a slight quiver in her voice, Martha told the jury her name and where she lived. Other than Mike's questions and Martha's answers there was no sound in the courtroom as the jury strained to hear her answers.

Martha struggled, but got through the preliminary questions without major issue and explained how she had been married to Paul for nineteen years and how they had raised Tanner and Stacey. She painted a picture of a reasonably happy family with well-adjusted children.

Mike wanted to have Martha describe the incident before any meltdown occurred, so he moved quickly into questioning her about that day. She explained that she often shopped at Wendell's because of the varied selection and reasonable prices. She went to the store to hunt for some towels and had picked out a few things that she was considering buying. She aimlessly browsed, not really sure where she was going next.

"I wasn't in a hurry. I didn't have anywhere to go," Martha explained in response to Mike's question, "and I saw a counter with all sorts of candy and chocolates. I love chocolate." She smiled and looked down. "I walked towards the counter with all the pretty chocolate. I saw a box of chocolates on the counter. I assumed they were samples, so I took one and ate it. It was really tasty."

"Martha, was the box of chocolates open?"

"Of course. The lid was off and sitting next to the box. Nothing was covering the chocolates." Mike again played the video of Martha taking the chocolate. The lid clearly was lying next to the box.

"Were any other chocolates missing from the box?"

"I don't think so," Martha admitted. "I think I took the first piece."

"What happened after you ate the sample of chocolate?"

Martha gazed up nervously. "I finished the piece of chocolate and wanted to find a register to pay for the towels I had. Before I did anything, I was stopped by the store security person."

"What did he do?"

"He said he was a security guard and had been watching me on video and asked me if I would come with him. I didn't understand what he meant. I actually thought I had won some prize. He again asked me to come with him."

"Did he tell you why?"

"Yes, he told me because he said that I stole the chocolate. I was shocked. You can see it on the video. I told him that it was a sample and if I was wrong about that, I would pay for the chocolates."

"How did he respond?"

"He laughed and said, 'That's what everyone says after they are caught stealing.'"

"What did you do?"

"He told me I had to go with him so I followed. He took me downstairs and put me in a small room. He took my arm and put a handcuff on it. He attached the handcuffs to a rail on the table. I was horrified. He took my name and address and began to fill out some forms. He took my purse and my cell phone."

"Did he give you any instructions?"

"He put this form in front of me and said that if I signed it, I would be released from the handcuffs. I read the form and said I wouldn't sign it because I hadn't stolen anything. He left the form in front of me and told me to sign it. He then left the room."

"What did you do?"

"I sat in the room for a while. I wasn't going to sign that form. At first, he came back about every twenty minutes. He would come in the room and see if I signed the paper. When he saw I hadn't signed the form, he would just say, "You can leave once you sign the paper. This happened a few times and then he started to wait longer before he came back."

"What did you do?"

"I got nervous and scared. I thought I wasn't going to be able to get out. I wanted to call my husband, but he wouldn't give me back my cellphone. So, when I thought that he wasn't coming back I started screaming. I think I got a little hysterical."

"Did this change anything?"

"Not really." Martha's cadence was slowing down and the judge instructed her to keep her voice audible. "The next time he came back, I asked to speak to a manager or anybody else who would listen. He just said, 'I'm in charge here. You can only speak with me.'"

"How long were you in the room?"

"It was over two hours. He came back into the room probably five times and started to get mad because I hadn't signed the form. He wouldn't let me speak to anybody else and he wouldn't let me out of the handcuffs." Martha twisted the edge of a handkerchief she had pulled out of a pants pocket and was staring past Mike as he tried to keep her focused.

"What did it feel like when you were locked in the room?"

"I'm not sure I can explain. I was in prison, but I hadn't done anything wrong. There wasn't any trial, but they put me in jail anyway. They treated me like a dog and I was begging for that kid to release me. I was crying, but he wouldn't let me out. The room felt like it kept getting smaller. The last time he came in the room, I would have done anything for him to let me out of those handcuffs."

"Martha, after being chained in that room for over two hours, how did you finally get out?"

"I realized I wasn't going to be able to leave until I signed the form. I told him so many times I hadn't stolen anything. He just wouldn't listen. Finally, I got so mad I told him I would sign the form just to be able to leave. Once I signed it, he took the handcuffs off me and said I could leave. I tried to grab the form back from him, but he was too quick. He just opened the door and told me to leave. It was so humiliating."

Mike paused his questioning and looked at the jurors. He knew his case was sunk if they suspected that Martha had stolen the candy but he had no idea what ideas were bouncing around in their heads.

Mindful of Stan's advice to keep their presentation narrow and tailored, Mike took Martha through her injuries expediently. By this time the jury had already listened to her psychologist and had seen the effect the incident had on her kids, so Mike was wary of beating the damages horse until it died. Martha had limited ability to articulate her problems and any attempt to draw out her testimony would be futile.

Instead, Mike asked Martha a few questions about what her life was like presently. Martha told the jury that mainly she liked to read books in a quiet corner of her home. This contrasted sharply with the picture her husband and kids had painted of Martha from before the incident of a vibrant, caring woman who would do anything for her family.

Mike indicated he had no more questions.

At no point during her direct examination did Martha lose her composure, but her ability to keep it together during cross-examination remained in question. Jack stood and shuffled some papers. He didn't look up for nearly thirty seconds before addressing Martha.

"Mrs. Gebbert," Jack began, "on the day in question, you had picked up a few items."

"Yes."

Mike cringed, realizing Martha was about to ignore his instruction to explain all of her answers and not just say 'yes' to the questions Jack asked.

"Let's look at the video. You were walking through the store, aren't you?"

"Yes."

"You pick up some items and then begin walking through the store. You walk through five different departments and past five cash registers without paying for those items that you are carrying, don't you?"

"I wasn't counting," Martha replied. "I was trying to decide if I should buy more things."

"My point is Mrs. Gebbert, if somebody was watching you and saw you carrying all those items, and you walk by all of those registers, it might appear like you were never going to pay for those items."

"I don't know what someone would think. He stopped me before I got to pay for them."

"You then went up to the candy counter and took a piece of candy."

"I did."

"You had no intent of paying for that box of candy, did you?"

"Of course not. They were samples."

"You took the first piece out of the box," Jack continued.

"I believe I did."

"So nobody else before you thought they were samples."

"I don't know what other people were thinking and I don't know how long the box had been on the counter."

"The security guard asked if you had stolen the chocolate."

"He did."

"You never denied stealing the chocolates, did you? In fact, you offered to pay for them."

"Yes."

Mike chastised himself for not objecting to the previous question, because it was actually two questions. Martha had answered the second part of the question, but her answer made it sound like she hadn't denied stealing the chocolates, which she had told Mike many times she had.

Mike offered a little prayer Martha would stop answering "yes" to the questions and start explaining her answers.

"In fact, you didn't say they were samples when he first stopped you, you actually offered to pay for them."

"Yes, I did."

"Mrs. Gebbert," Jack continued, "when Mr. Lombard asked you to go downstairs, you followed compliantly, didn't you?"

"I guess I did. I didn't think I had a choice."

"Ultimately, you signed a form admitting you had stolen property."

Although Martha had signed the form, Mike hoped she did not simply answer "yes" to the question.

With both of her hands tightly gripping her purse, Martha's gaze darted between Jack and Mike.

The courtroom was silent and the jurors all looked at Martha. She lifted her head and looked past the jurors, finding her daughter Stacey and Stephanie looking at her sympathetically.

She returned her attention to Jack and said, "Mr. Rogers, you and I both understand why I signed that form. Not because I stole any-thing—because I didn't. The candy was sitting open on the counter for anybody to take some and so I took some. I signed the form because your guard chained me to a table like a dog for two hours. I begged him to let me out. I screamed and I cried, but nobody listened. Mr. Lombard didn't care. He said the only way I was getting out of the handcuffs was if I signed the form. So I signed it. Not because I stole anything, but because I wanted to leave and see my family."

Martha exhaled deeply and leaned back in the hard wooden seat. She patiently waited for her next question.

Jack felt his face flush. He stared back at Martha, unable to question further. He started to ask another question, but couldn't formulate one. He returned to counsel table and took a sip of water.

Mike smiled at Martha, realizing that Jack had lost his rhythm and was unsure how to proceed. One good answer had thrown Jack off of his game. Mike looked down at his yellow pad so Martha would direct her attention to Jack.

Jack returned to his position in front of the witness, shrugged, and adjusted his jacket. "Mrs. Gebbert," he began, "when was the first time you were treated by any doctor for your injuries?"

"Well, I haven't seen a doctor, I have only seen the psychologist."

"That wasn't my question, but you make a solid point. You haven't seen any medical doctor for your injuries, have you?"

"No, only the psychologist."

"When was the first time you treated with the psychologist?"

"About eight months after this incident, right after we first met with our attorney"

"Eight months?" Jack echoed. "You didn't get any type of treatment for your problems for eight months after this occurred and you have never seen a medical doctor for your problems?"

"Yes."

"And your attorney suggested it?"

"No, he didn't suggest it. My husband suggested I see someone right after we met with him."

"So we are clear, you don't visit with any doctor for your problems for months after this incident. You call Mr. Reigert..." Jack pointed at Mike as if he were on trial. "You meet with him and then the next day you make an appointment with the psychologist."

"I think that is accurate."

"Didn't you go to the psychologist because Mr. Reigert thought it would help your case?"

"No, he thought it would help me."

"So the idea to see a psychologist came from Mr. Reigert."

"I'm not sure, I guess so." Martha glanced around the courtroom confused.

Jack moved closer to the witness. "Nobody ever said you should go to a medical doctor, did they?"

"No."

"So, you have never had any x-rays or MRIs or any other kind of medical test, have you?"

"No."

"So, nothing is wrong with you medically?"

"No, nothing."

"You haven't taken any medication for any of your problems, have you?"

"No."

"What do you do to try to improve?"

"I talk to Dr. Rathman every week. He helps me."

"Other than talking to Dr. Rathman, is there anything else you do to get better?"

"No, he's the one who is helping me."

Jack followed up with one last question. "Mrs. Gebbert, if all you do is talk to your psychologist once a week, isn't it true nothing is really wrong with you?"

Martha's throat tightened and her head spun. She looked at the jurors and then the people sitting in the back of the courtroom, but could not concentrate on anything in particular. She saw her two children and finally responded, "Mr. Rogers, you don't understand, do you? I have been so hurt by what your department store has done to me. I can't explain why, but I can't leave my house. My kids are growing up and I am missing it. My husband now is sleeping with someone else. I cry myself to sleep every night and hope when I wake up I can walk outside and enjoy the sunshine. But every day is the same and every day I sit in my room too scared to do anything. So, Mr. Rogers, I have been hurt real bad and I am so tired."

Jack's shoulders slumped. He looked at his outline, but he had no further questions. He returned to his seat.

Stan leaned over to Mike and whispered, "That's what happens when you ask one too many questions."

Martha now was sitting up straight in the witness box and looking directly at Jack. Mike drew out the moment before dismissing Martha as a witness.

"Mr. Reigert, any more witnesses?" Jeri asked from the judge's bench.

"No, Your Honor," Mike announced. "The plaintiff rests."

Jeri nodded and turned to address the jury. "The plaintiff has rested her case. Now the defendant will put on its witnesses. I understand the defendant believes its case will proceed quickly. I have to meet with the attorneys to discuss the law I will give to you. It appears we can finish testimony tomorrow morning. The attorneys will then give you their closing statements and the case will be yours for deliberation in the afternoon. You are dismissed for today. Counsel, I will meet with you in chambers."

Chapter 56

September 11, 2018, 4:30 p.m.
Trial Day 2

J ERI SAT BEHIND her desk waiting for the lawyers to enter her chambers after gathering their materials and making the necessary arrangements with their clients. Seeing Jack and Mike enter, she was pleased they would be spending time together even if it was to go over her charge to the jury. When the court reporter stuck her head in to see if Jeri wanted their discussions on the record, Jeri waved her away and told her they would memorialize their discussions in the morning before the jury arrived.

Jeri directed her two friends to the curved hard leather seats facing her desk. She smiled, but received nothing back from either of them. "Let's go over my points for charge." She handed them a copy of the instructions she intended to read to the jury once closing arguments were complete. "Take a few minutes to read them. I incorporated both of your requested instructions. I don't think there is a lot of room for disagreement. I took most of this from the Pennsylvania Statute on

Retail Theft and it will inform the jury what standard applies to store owners dealing with theft. We can discuss any objections you have to the charge after you review it."

Not a word was spoken for the next twenty minutes while Mike and Jack digested the fifteen typed pages. Jeri busied herself with papers on her desk, bothered that her two friends did nothing to acknowledge each other.

When both attorneys had completed their review of the proposed jury charge, they waited for Jeri to indicate she was ready for discussion. Finally, she said, "Do either of you have any issues with the proposed jury charge?"

"No, Judge, I mean Jeri," Mike stammered, unable to change gears now that nobody else was watching. "I'm not finding anything objectionable with the charge.

"Good," Jeri replied with a hopeful lilt in her voice. "How about you Jack? Any objections on behalf of the defendant?"

Jack looked up with his face flushed and a drop of perspiration above his lip. He spoke slowly. "For the most part, I don't have any problems with the instructions. I don't have any issue with how you are going to tell the jury about a store's right to detain possible shoplifters and how they don't necessarily have to be right, they only need a reasonable basis for stopping someone. I also don't have any problem with the compensable damages you include if the plaintiff prevails on liability. But you have in here an instruction for punitive damages indicating the jury, if they find the department store liable, may also punish the store and award punitive damages. There is no basis for punitive damages."

Jeri nodded to Mike, requesting him to respond.

"This case is clearly one where a jury could award punitive damages," he began. "Wendell's has a policy instructing its security guards to handcuff people to a table to extract confessions. This is in violation of Pennsylvania's law, which only allows for shoplifting detentions for a reasonable time and in a reasonable manner. This policy is so over the line the jury would be within its rights to punish the company for putting people through this ordeal."

Jeri looked to Jack to counter.

"Wendell's has a policy which its lawyers have reviewed. It is perhaps aggressive, but entirely within the bounds of the law. The Wendell's executive explained the basis for the policy. Handcuffing is done to protect our security guards from violence. The policy is not negligent, let alone so over the line a jury could punish the company for trying to protect its assets."

After pondering the arguments, Jeri responded: "I understand the reasons Wendell's says it developed the policies and the potential public policy reasons for allowing them to have this policy. On the other hand, it is possible this jury will find the policy is so over the line and inconsistent with the mandates of the Act to warrant the imposition of punitive damages. I think the jury needs to weigh in on these issues."

Hearing Jeri's ruling, Jack threw up his hands, sending his copy of the jury charge airborne before landing scattered on the floor. "Damn-it Jeri, you can't let punitive damages go to the jury. You're wrong. This messes with my entire case."

"Jack, there's enough to let the jury decide. Here's what's going to happen. The jury will decide first if the company is liable. If the jury finds liability, the jury will decide compensatory damages and will also decide if punitive damages are warranted. If it decides punitives are appropriate, they will hear further evidence regarding the net worth of the company so it can decide the amount of punitive damages to award."

Jack slapped the front of Jeri's desk in frustration.

Mike chirped at Jack, "Sorry Jack, sometimes when you handle people wrong and try to push them around, there are consequences."

Enraged by the developments in chambers, Jack jumped to his feet and faced Mike. "Fuck you, Mike," he spat out.

Mike remained calm in his chair. "That's it Jack. Go ahead and get pissed when things don't go your way. You can't intimidate me like you tried with Megan."

Jeri, surprised by the sudden outburst in her chambers, deftly moved around to the front of her desk and got in between Jack and Mike. "Stop it, you two. What's going on here?"

Breathing heavily, Jack sat back into his chair. Mike stared straight ahead avoiding eye contact with anybody.

"Go ahead Jack, tell Jeri what happened at her wedding," Mike said, as Jeri returned to her chair. Jack sat staring off distractedly, refusing to respond. Jeri directly asked him what had happened, but Jack didn't budge.

Instead, Mike began to talk. "The night we got to your wedding, Jack talked to me about settling this case. Although he made a healthy offer, my client wanted to have her day in court. He got pissed off when I told him the case wasn't going to settle. Jack waited for Megan outside of the bathroom. He threatened her and was inappropriately aggressive with her."

"Jack, is this true?" Jeri asked.

"Of course not," Jack said. "He's talking nonsense."

Jeri shook her head in exasperation. "Jack, this is serious if what Mike is saying is true. I am thinking about whether I have to report this to the disciplinary board. Let's see how the rest of the trial proceeds and I will decide what I need to do."

"Do whatever you think you have to do, Your Honor," Jack sneered. "My focus is on winning this case and making Mike regret the day they didn't accept the money."

"I am so disappointed with both of you. I thought your friendship would be more important than winning a case. Get out of here and we will finish this trial tomorrow."

Chapter 57

September 11, 2018, 7:15 p.m.
Trial Day 2

I'M GOING TO punch that asshole in the face when I get the chance. He was so smug and lied right to Jeri's face. Locked eyes with her and lied about everything..." Mike's voice trailed off when he realized he was yelling.

Megan ran her fingers through Mike's hair. "You have to forget about Jack," she said. "You have to think about your closing. We've been here for hours and you aren't finished yet. You are so distracted by what he did, he's winning because you can't get anything done. I'm worried about you. I'm worried about the trial. I'm worried for Mrs. Gebbert. You need to focus on finishing the trial so I don't have to worry so much."

"What he did is so wrong and you are able to forget about it?" Mike asked.

"For now, we both have to forget about it."

"This just adds to the list of what I have to forget. My dad showed up for the trial today. He sat in the back and said nothing, but I knew he was there. I'm waiting for him to yell out, 'nice question asshole, you just blew the case for your client.'"

"I'm glad to hear he behaved. Is he going to hear your closing?"

"He said he's coming tomorrow. But with him I never know what to believe. I wouldn't be surprised if he doesn't show up and I don't see him for ten years."

"Good. Then I'm going to get a chance to meet him. I took a day off from work tomorrow."

"Oh great," Mike replied, unable to hide his ambivalence.

"I wanted to see the end of your trial, so I finagled time off. I have to keep an eye on you to make sure you don't do anything stupid. I'm going to sit in the courtroom to make sure your closing is brilliant and nothing Jack does has any effect on you. I don't want to see you end up in jail."

"I don't think I'm going to come to blows with Jack, but it's nice to know you'll be there. That helps."

"Okay buddy, enough. Get up on your feet. You still have a lot of work to finish your closing." Mike stood in front of Megan, ready to practice his argument once again. They were facing a long evening.

Chapter 58

September 12, 2018, 6:30 a.m.
Trial Day 3

THE EARLY MORNING was quiet when Ed Wagner and Jack walked up the concrete steps to the venerable courthouse building. The sun was just peeking over the roof of the building and the street in front was nearly devoid of traffic. They passed the statue of the city's former mayor and entered through the revolving door.

They had spent a long evening first meeting with their expert witnesses to get them prepared and then pulling together the materials they needed for Jack's closing argument. Much of their evidence had already been presented through the questioning of the employees Mike had called on behalf of the plaintiff.

Two hours later, the jury members arrived and were seated. At nine sharp, Jeri asked Jack to call the first witness for the defense. Manuel Cybeg, hired by Wendell's to opine about the appropriateness of its shoplifting policy, confidently took the stand. Despite his large frame, Cybeg maneuvered gracefully into the witness box. He absent-mindedly polished his glasses and waited for Jack's questions.

Cybeg explained to the jury he had started in security twenty-three years before, when he worked as a store detective for a national grocery-store chain. He moved up at the grocery chain until he was head of their security department, creating security programs for the 275 stores the company had nationwide. When he turned forty he left the grocery company and began a consulting business where he advised companies on how to develop security programs and offered specific advice when a company was faced with a difficult security issue. The consulting business had grown markedly over the past five years, coinciding with an uptick in testifying for Fortune 500 companies that were being sued for false imprisonment and other security related issues.

During his brief cross-examination of Cybeg on his expert qualifications, Mike established that Cybeg's credentials and experience were comparable to that of the plaintiff's expert, Kenneth Fishbeck.

Cybeg's substantive testimony was brief, as Cybeg offered his opinion that the company's shoplifting policy was reasonable and consistent with other industry companies. Cybeg reiterated Wendell's talking points that crime was rampant and that Pennsylvania law allowed companies to detain suspected shoppers as long as their suspicion was reasonable, even if the person didn't actually steal anything. Cybeg concluded that Wendell's policy was acceptable under Pennsylvania law.

Mike's cross-examination of Cybeg was also swift. He established that Cybeg could not identify one other company having a policy nearly as aggressive as Wendell's. When asked to name another company which allowed handcuffing, Cybeg offered, "I am not aware of any other company." Mike finished by getting Cybeg to agree that having a video camera in the detention room would have helped to determine exactly what had occurred there and how long Mrs. Gebbert had been handcuffed.

Once Cybeg left the courtroom, after his thirty minutes of questioning, Ed Wagner leaned over to Jack and whispered, "There's five thousand dollars our client just spent on a witness that the jury has already forgotten. At least his testimony cancelled out the testimony of the plaintiff's expert."

Chapter 59

September 12, 2018, 10:30 a.m.
Trial Day 3

JACK ANNOUNCED THAT the defendant's last witness would be Dr. Bernard Lawson. Dr. Lawson met none of the jurors' expectations of how an expert witness was supposed to look: young, short, and dressed casually with black chest hair sticking out of the top of his sweater. Lawson smiled at the jurors as if they were old friends. The doctor had none of the dignified intellectual aura that marked the other expert witnesses. Rather, he was overly muscular, indicating time spent in the gym rather than studying medical treatises.

Listing his qualifications and accomplishments as a medical doctor and as an evaluator of psychiatric illness like he was reading the wine list at an upscale restaurant, Lawson reveled in having a captive audience. Dr. Lawson went into exquisite detail about the papers he had published, the hospitals on which he was on staff, the courts in which he had previously testified, and the number of companies for which he had already consulted. When asked if he had any questions for Lawson on his credentials, Mike passed, not wanting to belabor the point, and also recognizing Lawson's resume was more impressive than Martha Gebbert's psychologist.

On his direct examination, Lawson didn't bother with the question/answer format, but rather gave a narrative recitation of how he came to his opinion Mrs. Gebbert was not suffering from any type of cognitive or psychological problem associated with her detention by Wendell's. Holding Dr. Rathman's office records like they were covered with toxic waste, Lawson testified Mrs. Gebbert had no identifiable problem caused by her detention at the store and no need for any treatment resulting from the conduct of the employees at the store. He went on to opine that Mrs. Gebbert was lonely and needed to talk to Dr. Rathman for human interaction.

When asked if Mrs. Gebbert ever had prior treatment with a psychologist, Lawson took evident glee in stating, "Not only did she have treatment in the past, she went to great lengths not to tell me about it when I asked if she had ever been treated before."

Jack followed up to ask Lawson about the significance of the prior treatment. Lawson spoke at length as to the significance of the treatment. "In fact," he said, "she complained about how her husband wasn't paying attention to her. It's clear they were having marital problems for a long time and this created significant cognitive issues that required additional treatment, which she apparently never got."

Dr. Lawson used a single line in the medical record to conclude that Paul Gebbert's marital infidelities likely began long before the detention, and was due to Martha Gebbert's longstanding inability to have a close relationship with men.

Stacey and Tanner Gebbert sat behind Mike listening to Lawson's diatribe, not fully comprehending the meaning, but certainly appreciating that Lawson was demeaning their mother to a room full of strangers. Unable to sit still while Lawson spoke directly to the jury, Tanner Gebbert stood, pointed at the witness and said, "You don't know my mom. You're paid to say bad things about her."

Jeri banged her gavel on her desk, instructing Mike to control Tanner. Stan stood and turned toward Tanner, putting one hand on his shoulder. He whispered something in his ear causing the boy to smile, placated. Tanner sat back in his chair and nodded at Lawson as if instructing him to continue his testimony.

To conclude his direct examination of the doctor, Jack asked him what conclusions he had drawn from examining Mrs. Gebbert and reviewing her records. Jack stood back while Lawson talked directly to the jurors. "I believe Mrs. Gebbert has longstanding psychological issues which have recently begun to manifest themselves. Given her family history of mental illness, her apparent unhappy home life as evidenced by her husband's infidelities, and her dissatisfaction with the general state of her life, her current mental health has been compromised.

"Based upon my review of her psychological records, my examination of her and the testing I had her undertake, I could not find any connection between what happened at the department store and her current psychological problems."

Jack paused after Dr. Lawson had offered his opinion, noticing the jury still was looking intently at the doctor. He indicated the doctor was available for cross-examination.

Mike leapt to his feet to begin his questioning. "Doctor, based on your testimony that Mrs. Gebbert has 'current psychological problems,' you would agree she presently has psychological issues, don't you?"

"Yes, the testing I undertook indicates she suffers from agoraphobia and fears to go outside."

"This is legitimate, isn't it? She's not faking?"

"No, I believe it is real."

"She didn't have any symptoms before the events at the department store, did she?"

"That's unclear. She had this prior treatment and she hid it from Dr. Rathman. I would think she still needed treatment for the issues she had then. So, I see a link between her problems now and her prior issues."

"Doctor, that was five years ago."

"True."

"And she only had five visits with a psychologist."

"I know. My review of those records suggests that her issues were not resolved and likely continued to worsen because she didn't get further treatment. Plus, since she never told Dr. Rathman about these problems, he never could provide her effective treatment."

"Her entire family said she led a normal life and functioned without issue up to the time she went to Wendell's that day."

"I'm sure they did. Families often have no idea how badly another person in the family may suffer. Mrs. Gebbert clearly was good at hiding things. Nobody in her family knew anything about this prior treatment. I think what happened at the department store may have brought out her problems, but they were coming out at some point."

"She led a normal life before."

"Perhaps."

"And she hasn't led a normal life since."

"That is correct."

"Doctor, she has no symptoms before this event and begins to have symptoms afterwards. Isn't this post-traumatic stress syndrome like Dr. Rathman described?

"No, I disagree with your conclusion. Post-traumatic stress disorder occurs after a major trauma. We find it often in people returning from war or people who have been involved in a major accident with serious bodily injury, but this type of trigger was not present here."

"She was locked in a room and thought she was never going to be released. Isn't this sufficiently traumatic under the definition of post-traumatic stress disorder?"

"No, like I said, this is not the type of stressor that triggers PTSD. I do not think it is a proper diagnosis."

"Doctor, you are being paid today to testify, aren't you?"

"Yes, I am."

"Neither myself, Mrs. Gebbert, nor anyone associated with Mrs. Gebbert is paying you today, are we?"

"No, you aren't paying me."

"Doctor Lawson, you and I have never met before today, have we?"

"No, we haven't."

"You only met Mrs. Gebbert once before this, when you examined her, which took only forty-five minutes."

"Correct."

"You are being paid by Wendell's to testify today, correct?"

"Yes, they are paying for my services."

"You have met with Mr. Rogers, the attorney for Wendell's, many times to prepare your testimony?"

"I have met with him to discuss my testimony, yes."

"He reviewed your expert report before you signed it, didn't he?"

"I wrote my report, but he reviewed it before I finalized it."

"This is not the first time you have testified for Wendell's department store?"

"No, I have testified for Wendell's three times in the past three years."

"You have made nearly fifty thousand dollars testifying for Wendell's in the past three years."

"Yes, that is accurate."

"And you have made another one hundred and fifty thousand dollars testifying for other stores as a hired witness."

"Yes, I have offered my expert services to other stores when they have retained me."

Mike paused and took a sip of water to slow down his questioning, then returned to the spot directly in front of Dr. Lawson. "Dr. Lawson, isn't it possible your conclusions are shaded by the fact you are a hired gun, retained to offer opinions to help Wendell's, because they have paid you a lot of money in the past and you want them to hire you again when they are sued by someone else who is locked in a basement against their will?"

Jack jumped to his feet. "Objection! Your Honor, that is outrageous and I move to strike."

Jeri didn't hesitate before ruling, "The objection is sustained. The question is struck. Mr. Reigert, please ask a less objectionable question."

Mike was ready with his revised question. "Doctor, could the fact Wendell's is paying you to testify today shade your testimony?"

Lawson gripped the sides of the witness box and took a deep breath. He replied, "No counselor. My conclusions are drawn from my years of experience and my review of Mrs. Gebbert's records with her own psychologist. She clearly had underlying issues that were brought to the fore. The event at the store was not sufficient to have triggered them and like I have said, I believe her prior knowledge of her husband's unfaithfulness would have led to the need for psychological treatment."

Resisting every urge to argue with the doctor and rehash how he had arrived at his opinions, Mike stated he was through with his questioning.

Jack breathed a sigh of relief and informed the court the defendant had no further witnesses, resting its case. Jeri turned to the jury and said, "You have heard all of the evidence in this case. You will next hear closing arguments from first Mr. Rogers on behalf of Wendell's department store. Mr. Reigert will then give his closing argument for Mrs. Gebbert. After that I will instruct you what the law is that will apply to your deliberations and then the case will be yours to decide. Let's take an hour recess so you can eat and so the lawyers can ready their closing arguments."

The jurors nodded, indicating they understood. An air of excitement permeated the courtroom as the jurors whispered among themselves.

Chapter 60

September 12, 2018, 1:00 p.m.
Trial Day 3

THE COURTROOM WAS buzzing with activity for the hour before closing arguments. Mike and Stan set up in the hallway to make sure Mike had everything he needed for his closing. Jack and Ed Wagner stayed at their counsel table with Jack finalizing his outline. Mike darted into the courtroom a few times to gather documents from his files. Jack walked into the hallway twice to stretch his legs. Although Mike and Jack walked past each other multiple times during that hour, neither glanced in the other's direction and not a syllable passed between them.

When the jurors returned to the jury box, Jeri informed them the defendant would give its closing argument first. Jack approached the jury rail and took the same position as when he had given his opening. With no notes in his hands and his yellow pad left by the jury rail, Jack paused momentarily and then began. "Theft is a huge problem facing all retailers. The statistics are grim. Certain people come into Wendell's department stores every day with the sole intent to steal–to walk out of the store without ever paying for anything. This hurts everyone and makes the prices of everything higher.

"Pennsylvania law is clear," Jack continued. "It allows stores selling goods to the public to protect their merchandise and stop people they believe are shoplifting. In fact, store employees can stop a person mistakenly, and not be liable, if they have a reasonable suspicion shoplifting had occurred. This is exactly what happened here. The store detective had a reasonable suspicion Mrs. Gebbert stole the chocolate because he saw her break the cellophane and take the first piece out of the box."

Jack locked eyes with one of the jurors. "It doesn't matter if Mrs. Gebbert denies she was stealing. Everyone says once they are caught they were going to pay for the item. What makes what the store detective, Mr. Lombard, did okay is it reasonably appeared Mrs. Gebbert had stolen the chocolate.

"What else doesn't matter? How much the stolen item cost. The piece of candy wasn't a big-ticket item—the box cost twelve dollars. What matters is, it was stolen. The testimony is clear—stolen goods cost companies billions of dollars a year and ultimately you, the consumer, pay that cost.

"Once you have determined that what Mr. Lombard did was appropriate, you can discuss Wendell's policy of how it deals with shoplifters. Wendell's' policy is designed first to get the shoplifter off the sales floor. This protects other customers who are innocently shopping and protects the shoplifter from public humiliation. This is completely reasonable.

"Taking the shoplifter to a private room again protects everyone by reducing the chances of the situation escalating, and the use of handcuffs is appropriate as it once again reduces the chances the shoplifter becomes violent when she realizes she has been caught. This policy was thoroughly thought out, tested, and has been extremely successful in reducing shoplifting at Wendell's and has prevented shoplifting situations from becoming violent."

Jack concluded his liability argument by saying, "Given the sound reasons behind Wendell's' policy, and the reasonable manner in which Mr. Lombard conducted his investigation, when you have to answer the first jury question, 'Was Wendell's department store negligent?' the only appropriate answer is 'no.' And when you answer that Wendell's was not negligent you can return to the courtroom and render your verdict in favor of Wendell's."

Jack wanted to sit down. He also wanted to see the jury unanimously nodding their heads, signaling their agreement with his client's position. The jury, however, stared at him impassively. Sensing the jury's impatience, Jack began a short argument that Mrs. Gebbert wasn't actually hurt by this incident, while also reminding the jury he still believed his client had done nothing wrong.

"Mrs. Gebbert lied to her doctor, lied to our doctor, and lied to you," he said, pointing at a female juror in the second row. "She didn't want you to know she had treated before with a psychologist. Why did she lie? Because she had emotional problems before and she didn't want you know that. She told her first psychologist she had issues with her husband. Clearly those issues weren't resolved.

"Do you think Paul Gebbert only had one affair? No, men who cheat on their wives are usually serial cheaters. Martha Gebbert is clearly hurt by her husband's actions, but she wants to blame the department store for her problems. The doctors told you she is in denial about her husband's infidelities and her longstanding psychological issues."

Jack finished his closing by trying to walk a tightrope. He argued his client hadn't done anything wrong, but if the jury thought it had, they still shouldn't award much because she hadn't been hurt badly.

The final issue Jack had to deal with was the issue of punitive damages. He explained if they found the company liable they would have to decide if punishment for the company was warranted. He emphasized that if they wanted to award punitive damages, they would be called back into the courtroom to hear more evidence and would have to deliberate a second time. He argued they should cheer Wendell's for trying to stop shoplifters aggressively and punishment was the last thing his client deserved.

"Stopping crime is not always pretty. Shoplifters walk in and out of every Wendell's stores every day. Wendell's spends huge amounts training its security guards to try and stop this wave of shoplifters. These people guard the innocent shoppers and protect them against criminals, attempting to keep violence off our sales floors. Wendell's tests its policies to make sure that they work and that innocent people's rights are protected. Everything Wendell's did was reasonable and we ask you to find in favor of Wendell's when you return from your deliberations." Jack took one more look at the jury, turned, and headed back to his counsel table.

Standing and adjusting his tie, Mike felt the same gnawing in the pit of his stomach as before the trial began. He said a silent prayer he would be able to keep his lunch down until he finished his closing.

Mike walked closer to the jurors and with his eyes alert said, "Let's make this as simple as possible—Wendell's department store's policy of chaining a person to a table with no chance of release until the person confesses to a crime—which may never have occurred—is abhorrent and in complete disregard of the laws of Pennsylvania."

The jurors engaged as Mike walked them through his argument that nowhere in civilized society would we tolerate locking people to a table with no hope of release. Mike argued any confession received under those circumstances was absolutely suspect and the jurors had to question the motives of a company endorsing such tactics.

"Think about the millions of dollars this company has made by chaining people to their tables, out of sight and helpless. The store takes away their phones so they can't communicate with anyone and the store never gets the police involved so they can do whatever they want in that room. The policy is wrong and how they utilize the policy is wrong. Only you can stop them from doing this to other people."

Mike turned his attention to the evidence of what Martha did that day. "If you believe what the store is trying to tell you, the worst Martha ever did was take a piece of chocolate. Everyone agrees the box of chocolate was sitting unattended on the counter with the lid off. If the store thought the candy was for sale, shouldn't they have taken it off the counter and put it away so nobody made the same mistake? Don't you also think it is possible the store left the candy on the counter on purpose trying to bait people like Martha into taking a piece so they could arrest them and accuse them of stealing? This is their plan. Once they take people downstairs, they can handcuff them to coerce them into admitting to stealing so they can make money off them"

Speaking directly to the jurors, Mike calmly argued the company never had a legitimate basis to have stopped Martha in the first place. As Mike continued his argument, Stan displayed the images from that day on the screen so the jurors could view the available footage. Once again Mike suggested the evidence supported Martha's claim she believed she was only taking a sample of chocolate and the company never could prove Martha broke the cellophane on the box of chocolates because the videotape didn't support this contention.

Mike attempted to get the jurors to imagine they were being taken downstairs to the detention room. "Picture someone accused of stealing being led down the steps, not knowing why they were being taken far away from the sales floor. This might happen to anyone, because Wendell's doesn't care if you have stolen anything. They realize you will admit to stealing because if you don't, you will be stuck in handcuffs."

Shifting the discussion to Martha's injuries, Mike wanted to take a shot at Jack before discussing them in depth. "Counsel for Wendell's," Mike said while gesturing dismissively in Jack's direction, "suggests Martha's injuries aren't real and even if they are real, Wendell's didn't cause them. The evidence supports neither argument."

Sensing the jury's empathy for Martha's problems, Mike suggested if the jury were to believe Wendell's position on mental illness, then nobody could ever prove they had a mental illness because nothing would ever show up on an x-ray. "If you think Mrs. Gebbert is making this up or in any way faking, go back to the jury room and come back in five minutes with a verdict for Wendell's. She is not faking. Look at her. Look at Tanner and Stacey. They are the real victims here. They have essentially lost their mother."

Mike moved on to the issue of Paul Gebbert's infidelity. "Mr. Rogers and the Wendell's witnesses have suggested Paul Gebbert was unfaithful to his wife before this incident. They presented absolutely no proof of this. They hope he had been unfaithful before so they don't have to accept responsibility for the consequences their illegal policy has caused.

"Apparently Martha had been to a psychologist before this. Come on. It was five years before and she saw the guy five times. There was no diagnosis then. Now she has agoraphobia and post-traumatic stress syndrome. And as Dr. Rathman told you, these came directly from how the department store treated her and nothing else.

"According to everyone in the family, this was a nice, normal, well-adjusted family before this incident and everything started to go bad after Martha returned from Wendell's the day she was chained to the table. All of them have testified Paul became unfaithful after this event and because of this event. It is a sad reality Wendell's wants to hide from."

After 30 minutes of discussing the events of that day and analyzing the effects it had on the entire Gebbert family, Mike moved onto his last and perhaps most crucial area—whether Wendell's should be liable for punitive damages. Mike understood the standard was high and juries were usually loath to award extra damages to a plaintiff just to punish an offender, but also understood certain cases warrant these penalty damages. The jury had to buy into his entire argument to this point to stand any chance for punitive damages.

"Wendell's needs to learn locking people to a table until they confess is abhorrent. They don't think anything is wrong with their policies and will continue to teach its security guards to take people to a separate room and force them to sign a confession by not letting them out of handcuffs. This is repugnant. Tell them to call the police. Tell them to stop following people looking for a reason to detain them. Tell them that trying to profit from a ritualized program of forced confessions must stop."

Mike paused, holding the gaze of one juror before continuing. "You can send them this message by saying loudly and clearly, they should be punished. You can stop this insanity by telling the company they must pay punitive damages."

Mike finished his closing by walking the jurors through their verdict slip as Stan projected a copy of it onto the screen. He suggested the jury find Wendell's negligent and that they find Wendell's negligence caused Mrs. Gebbert's injuries. He recommended they award an appropriate amount to compensate Mrs. Gebbert for her injuries and that they decide punitive damages are appropriate and be willing to hear additional evidence to allow them to decide to what extent they would punish Wendell's.

"Mrs. Gebbert and I are confident you have taken your oaths as jurors seriously and will evaluate the evidence fairly and return a verdict compensating Mrs. Gebbert for all she has endured as a result of Wendell's department stores' illegal policies."

Flushed with relief from completing his role in this trial, Mike sat back in his chair to listen to Jeri tell the jury the law that applied to their deliberations.

Chapter 61

September 12, 2018, 2:30 p.m.
Trial Day 3

JERI WAITED UNTIL all of the jurors settled and each was looking at her. She then began her recitation of the law and instructions on how they were to conduct their deliberations. Mike had sat through a few jury instructions previously and Stan and he had discussed his belief that the charge usually did not have much of an effect on what a jury was going to do. Lawyers argue for hours over the precise language of what the judge will read to the jury, but jurors focus on the overall concept of the charge rather than parsing words. The language in the jury charge was important primarily because the appellate courts might order a new trial if the language was not absolutely correct, but jurors ordinarily did not worry about such arcane details.

Mike understood that jurors want to do what they think is right. They want to follow the law, but often if they believe the right decision is contrary to the law as the judge instructs them, they will follow their gut, and not the court's instructions. Most jurors knew what they wanted to do and the instructions the judge gave had little bearing on their final verdict.

Both sides in this dispute agreed on the applicable law. The requested jury charge submitted by each side asked the judge to charge the jury that a shop owner had the right to stop a suspected shoplifter and detain the shoplifter to determine the identity of the shoplifter, recover any stolen property, and to institute criminal proceedings, so long as the detention was done in a reasonable manner and for a reasonable duration.

The statute did not provide a specific length of time to determine if the detention was for a reasonable duration and provided little guidance to define when a detention was performed in "in a reasonable manner." That meant, Mike believed, the jury would follow its own thinking to determine if Wendell's had a reasonable suspicion to have stopped Mrs. Gebbert and whether its detention was reasonable.

When Jeri completed reading her instructions to the jury, she ordered them to the jury room to begin their deliberations. The jurors rose and solemnly strode from their seats and disappeared underneath the red light bulb that would illuminate when they had completed their deliberations.

Once the jury was safely squirreled away in the jury room, Jeri stood and informally asked the lawyers and parties to remain near the courtroom in case the jury came back with a quick verdict. She indicated if no verdict were forthcoming within an hour they were free to leave the courthouse and her staff would call them when a verdict was reached.

Mike and Stan occupied two seats outside of Jeri's courtroom. Mike fretted, not liking what Jeri had said because he thought Jeri presumed a quick verdict was imminent. A quick verdict, he believed, would likely be a verdict in favor of Wendell's.

Stan placed a hand on Mike's knee and without looking at him, said: "Don't try to read into anything. None of us knows what the jury is going to do. But let's hope they are out for a while—that likely would be much better for us."

As the two sat in silence, Mike's dad exited the courtroom and walked a few steps towards them. He waited until Stan motioned for him to join them.

"Charles," Stan said, "it's good to see you. I saw you in the back of the courtroom." The two men shook hands.

Charles looked at Mike, a glimmer in his eye. "Mike, thank you so much for letting me watch. It was amazing."

"Thanks, Dad," Mike said.

"Also, I met Megan while I was sitting in there. Seems like a really nice woman. She told me that she is sitting in the courtroom sending good thoughts to the jury."

Mike smiled.

Charles continued. "I have a lot I want to say, but I know now is not the time, but Mike I wanted to tell you how impressed I was by everything you did in there." He pointed towards the courtroom. "I never have told you this enough before, but I was so proud watching you in there. You are a real lawyer."

Mike and his dad gazed at each other. Mike put a hand on his dad's arm. Charles spoke first. "I need to leave. I think I would be a basket-case if I had to wait for the verdict. Please let me know what happens."

Charles gave Mike a pat on the shoulder and started to walk down the hall. "I will, Dad. I will," Mike called down the hall.

After Charles left, Stan and Mike sat in the uncomfortable wooden seats trying to kill time, but found nothing to talk about to distract them from thinking about the jury deliberations. There was little left for them to do other than focus on what was happening in the jury room.

Forty-five minutes of painful, stilted conversation and awkward silences had passed since Stan and Mike had relocated to the corridor. It was then that Jack and Ed Wagner eased out of the courtroom, heading toward the bathroom. None of the attorneys had said a word to their opposition since the jury began its deliberations and nobody wanted to offer good wishes to the other side, as was the usual custom after a jury begins to deliberate.

Jack and Ed were about to walk past Stan and Mike without saying a word when Kathy, the tipstaff, peeked out of the courtroom. "Gentlemen, we have a verdict," she announced.

Mike felt the blood drain out of his face and then he felt his uncle's hand on his back. He faintly heard Stan say, "You never know, Mikey."

Mike had no time to process his emotions when Jack turned back to the courtroom and faced Mike, a huge smile on his face. "Oh well, buddy, that didn't take too long. Guess we're going to be able to catch the early flight tonight. Maybe you should have convinced your client to take our money."

Before Mike could formulate a response, Jack and Ed pranced back into the courtroom to await the announcement of the jury's verdict.

Chapter 62

September 12, 2018, 3:30 p.m.
Trial Day 3

MEGAN STOOD IN the back of the courtroom as the lawyers and parties filed in. Mike and Stan shuffled to their table, their eyes downcast. Wagner and Jack waited a few feet away, standing tall, looking at the jurors returning to their seats. Megan closed her eyes tightly as a small prayer passed over her lips.

Once the jurors were seated, Jeri emerged from her chambers and took her seat behind the bench. "Jurors, have you reached a verdict?" she asked, knowing the answer. All eyes were locked on the piece of paper the first juror carried into the courtroom, which was now being delivered to Jeri.

Megan gently tapped her feet on the floor impatiently waiting for Jeri to review the three pages of questions the jury was supposed to answer. Megan did not notice Jeri nod to her tipstaff who declared, "Members of the jury, harken to your verdict."

Jeri read aloud for the courtroom: "Question one: 'Is Wendell's department store negligent?' Answer: 'yes.'"

Megan pumped her fist.

"Question two," Jeri continued, "'Was the negligence of Wendell's department store a substantial factor in causing harm to the plaintiff?' Answer: 'yes.'"

Megan jumped up.

Mike's back was towards Megan. He and his uncle had their arms on each other's back, waiting for the next answer. Megan glanced at Jack and noticed him stoop forward, both hands now leaning on the counsel table for support. Megan looked over at Martha Gebbert in the back of the courtroom and saw her smile.

Jeri continued: "Question three: 'What amount of damages do you award to compensate the plaintiff for the injuries she incurred as a result of the negligence of the defendant?' Answer: 'Eight hundred and seventy-five thousand dollars'."

Megan let out a little whoop, which was joined by muted cheers elsewhere in the courtroom. Jeri slammed down her gavel and the courtroom returned to order. Turning her attention to the jury, Jeri asked, "Is this your verdict?" When she was satisfied it was, she returned to the verdict form. "Turning to the final question: 'Should the defendant pay to the plaintiff punitive damages?' Answer: 'yes.'"

Mike and Stan barely could contain their excitement. Another short phase to the trial so Mike could put on evidence in the punitive damages phase would follow. Jack stood at the other counsel table, the back of his neck burning red. His co-counsel turned away from Jack. Jack was standing alone.

Jeri, sensing the growing commotion in her courtroom, banged her gavel again and announced a thirty-minute break before the punitive damage phase and dismissed the jurors. She apologized to the jurors that they all might be working a little later into the evening.

Noticing Jack was not focused on what she had said, she announced, "I want to meet with counsel who will be trying this phase in my chambers alone. Mr. Rogers and Mr. Reigert please come to my chambers immediately." Jeri shook her head at her court reporter, indicating their conference would be off the record.

Stan shook Mike's hand. "Mikey, you have done great so far, but you need to calm down and focus. You have the testimony you need for the next phase?"

"Yes, Uncle Stan. We're ready."

Mike was beaming as he went to Jeri's chambers; Jack trudged behind. As he passed through the door leading out of the room, he smashed his hand against the doorframe, the loud thump echoing throughout the courtroom.

Chapter 63

September 12, 2018, 3:45 p.m.
Trial Day 3

JERI IMMEDIATELY SENSED Jack was having difficulty accepting the verdict. She instructed both lawyers to sit at her desk, but Jack only stood in the back of the room muttering to himself, his face turning an ever-darker shade of crimson.

"Jack, please come forward and sit down," Jeri said as Jack began to pace. When Jack did not respond, she repeated her instruction, but to no avail. Mike sat in the chair in front of Jeri's desk, elated at the turn of events and enjoying watching Jack's difficulty in accepting what had transpired.

Raising her voice, Jeri again instructed Jack, "Sit down Jack, we must proceed."

"Fuck this. Fuck this jury,"

"Enough, Jack," Jeri yelled back at him. "We may be friends, but you are still in court and you will maintain your professional conduct."

"Fuck this. This is outrageous."

"What is outrageous Jack?"

"Everything–this whole fucking trial."

"You will not speak out or act like that anymore. Accept what the jury has done and deal with it. I don't want to hold you in contempt."

Defeated, Jack slumped into the chair next to Mike, bumping Mike on the way down.

Jeri was relieved Jack had taken a seat and appeared to have regained control of his emotions. She asked her two attorney friends, "How are we going to proceed?"

Jack stared straight ahead, not responding, so Mike began: "We have some interrogatories that the company answered which we want to read and we will call a representative of the company who is in the courtroom to verify some financial details. It won't take long. I think we can put the entire punitive damage case on in about twenty minutes."

"Sounds good," Jeri said. "Any objections Jack?"

"Oh, that sounds great," Jack muttered. "Fucking great."

Ignoring Jack, Jeri continued, "When we go back into the court-room you each can give an opening statement. The plaintiff can put on evidence of net worth. Jack, you can put on evidence for the company if you want to."

"Like you care what I do," Jack said off to the side.

Jeri stared at Jack, hoping to get his attention, but Jack offered no response. "Jack, you need to snap back to reality. You are going back into the courtroom in a few minutes to defend a punitive damage claim."

Jack stood, ignoring Jeri's admonition. He wandered to the back of the room and began muttering and pacing anew.

"Jack Rogers," Jeri bellowed as she stood and walked around her desk, her movement slowed by her protruding midsection. "Get back over here and sit down."

"Not now, mommy," Jack snapped back.

Jeri walked towards Jack and stood face to face with him, staring into his eyes, Jack panting. Mike stood and approached them. "Can we just wrap this up? Jack, nothing good is going to happen until we get back into the courtroom and finish."

"Finish? This case should have been finished months ago. You couldn't even convince your ridiculous client to accept our money. We offered you a sick amount of cash and she said she would rather go to trial. This never should have happened."

Mike extended his hands in a conciliatory gesture, but Jack slapped his hand away hard enough to sting. "You are weak, Mike, and your weakness is going to cost me my partnership."

Mike stepped back. Jack continued his rant. "You are so weak, so fucking weak. I can't believe what you have cost me."

Jeri watched Jack's deterioration, trying to figure out a way to help him regain his equilibrium. As she was pondering, Jack lurched with sudden exigency towards Mike, shoving him backwards, causing him to lose his balance and tumble to the ground. "It's all your fucking fault," he yelled. Mike's head smashed against the corner of the small table in between the two chairs in front of her desk. Jeri screamed when she saw blood spewing from a huge gash near his eye.

"That's what happens when you mess with my stuff," Jack raged as Mike lay dazed on the floor. Sweat emerged on Jack's brow and his face burned with rage. Jeri, stunned, couldn't decide whether to call for help or intercede. She stood alternating looks between Mike on his knees groggily reaching toward his bleeding wound and Jack, still panting, not appearing to have calmed.

Jack took a sudden step toward Mike, raising his hands over his head yelling, "You did this. You stupid asshole, you did this." Seeing Jack still intent on hurting Mike, Jeri got in between them, slowly approaching Jack with her hands extended. "Jack, you need to regain control. Why don't you sit down and we can talk this through?"

Jack stood straight for a moment, suggesting he was willing to relent. A gaping smile jetted across his face before he threw back his head and said, "Sure Jeri, I will do whatever you say, just like always." He turned his back on her. "This was so easy. All Mikey had to do was take the money. His client would have made lots of money. He would have made lots of money and I would have been made partner. But no, that fucking idiot and his client decide they want to go to trial. And look what's happened. I'm not going to get my partnership. Fuck Jeri, I've lost everything and I blame Mike."

Without any warning, Jack again lurched towards Mike. Jeri attempted to intercept him by placing her hands on his chest. He immediately smacked them to the side and pushed Jeri out of his way, his sights set on Mike, who still was kneeling, rubbing his head. Jack's shove caused Jeri to stumble backwards. Her legs caught the edge of her desk and she tumbled over the top, landing hard on her shoulder.

Jack turned towards Mike, who was still kneeling, blood dripping down his forehead. Jack moved in. As he approached, he saw the metal rhinoceros trophy on Jeri's bookcase. He grabbed it, the walnut base secure in his hands.

Jack stood above Mike and raised the rhinoceros over his head. His eyes were wide open and he snarled as he focused on the back of Mike's head.

Jeri screamed, "Jack, stop now or I will stop you."

Jack ignored her, and as he began the downward swing of the statue towards Mike's head, a bang reverberated from behind Jeri's desk. Jack was knocked back a couple of steps, a red mark appearing on his white shirt near to his left shoulder. He immediately returned his sights to Mike, again lifting the rhino high. But before he could drive the statue into Mike's head, a second bang exploded from behind the desk, driving Jack backwards against the bookcase. He slammed into it, causing a bundle of casebooks to fall off and land on top of him as he collapsed to the floor. Blood oozed from bullet wounds in each shoulder.

As Jack slumped to the floor, two uniformed county officers burst into Jeri's chambers, guns drawn, their attention on Jeri, her judge's robe torn and her face swollen, a nasty bruise already forming below her eye. She pointed her gun directly at Jack, a wisp of smoke rising from the tip.

"Judge, put down the weapon," one of the officers ordered. "He's not going anywhere."

Jeri slowly lay the gun down. She limped around her desk and put an arm on Mike's back. "Are you okay, Mike?"

Dazed but regaining his equilibrium, Mike wobbly stood and looked around the room. A lump was forming at his hairline where he had fallen against the table. Alternatively glancing at the gun on the desk and at Jack moaning in pain, he asked, "What just happened?"

Jeri threw a piercing look at Jack. "That gun was the service revolver my dad carried. I probably shouldn't have kept it here. Never thought I would ever use it, but I'm certainly glad it was here. I'm not sure what Jack might have done." As Jeri checked Mike's wounds, the officers apprehended Jack. Jeri also confirmed medics were on the way.

Thirty minutes later, the officers accompanied Jack, strapped to a gurney, as he was wheeled out of Jeri's chambers. Two other medics attended to Mike.

The courtroom was in disarray. Everyone had heard the shots coming from Jeri's chambers and then witnessed the officers' entrance. Another few deputies detained them in the courtroom while Jeri's chambers were secured. Stan and Megan were aware the medics were taking care of Mike, but they were still feeling uncertain as the deputies prevented them from entering Jeri's chambers.

The jury remained upstairs, unaware anything out of the ordinary had happened.

Chapter 64

September 12, 2018, 4:30 p.m.
Trial Day 3

ED WAGNER HUDDLED with his client in the back of the courtroom. In a hushed voice Wagner said, "I'm so sorry about how that trial went. Jack really screwed this one up. He's not going to be at the firm much longer."

The executive didn't smile. "You completely mislead us. You told us no jury would award a lot of money on a case like this. I can't believe how your firm screwed this up. Somehow you better make this right, but I can tell you now there will be no more legal work coming your way."

"I'm sorry to hear that, but I need to get back to chambers. There still is a punitive damage claim. We have more work to do, but I will make sure every minute is on the bill when we send it to you."

Outside of Jeri's chambers, Stan checked with the medics to make sure they had taken care of Mike before he entered. The medics informed Stan they were transporting Mike to Presbyterian Hospital, and he was responsive and stable.

Five minutes later, Jeri called the attorneys into her chambers. She sat behind her desk and touched the bruise on her cheek. She rubbed her shoulder, but she had refused any treatment from the paramedics. Stan and Ed Wagner sat in the chairs Mike and Jack occupied an hour earlier.

The court reporter sat next to Jeri's desk, transcribing everything Jeri said as she recounted what had occurred in her chambers. After completing her summary of the events, she said, "The jury is upstairs and Kathy has confirmed that they are completely unaware of what has happened here. We are lucky to have two experienced and capable attorneys present representing the parties. Despite the unavailability of Mr. Rogers and Mr. Reigert, we can still proceed with the punitive damage portion of this trial and I intend to get the jury back in the box as quickly as we can. They, I am sure, are eager to finish this case."

"Your honor," Wagner said, "on behalf of the defendant, I believe we would be prejudiced if the trial continued at this point. I would request a continuance for at least two weeks so Wendell's can obtain substitute counsel for Mr. Rogers. I am not up to speed on all of the nuances of this case."

"Mr. Wagner," Jeri intoned, "you are counsel of record in this case and you entered your appearance on behalf of Wendell's, didn't you?"

"Yes, Your Honor."

"I see no reason for delay. We will proceed in fifteen minutes and you will represent the defendant against the punitive damage claim."

Wagner's face turned ashen. "I haven't questioned a witness in a courtroom for twenty years."

"Fifteen minutes, Mr. Wagner."

Wagner wiped his hands against his pants and shifted his feet. "Your Honor, I think I may have a solution to this. Would it be okay if Mr.Rotmen and I stepped out into the hallway to discuss a resolution of this case?"

Jeri smiled. "Of course, Mr. Wagner, but please do this expeditiously. We have jurors who want to make it home tonight."

Stan led Wagner into a small room down the hall from Jeri's court-room and motioned for him to sit in a small plastic chair next to a weathered wooden table. Wagner refused and stood in the dank space.

"Okay Ed, you wanted to talk. Looks like we are the relief pitchers in to finish out the game. What do you want to do here?"

Wagner collected himself. "I thought we could resolve this and possibly get out of here."

"I'm not in any hurry to get home, Ed. I'm feeling pretty good about this jury. They liked what we were selling the first time. We are happy to stay a little longer and present your company's financial records to the jury. I think they will find them extremely interesting."

Wagner winced. "Well, if we can't get this resolved, I think we can make a favorable impression with our company witnesses. But let's try. What will it take to resolve this?"

"I don't know Ed, I'd be feeling a little desperate if I were in your shoes. I'm not prepared to tell you what my clients will take, but it's a pretty big number. We already have our client's authority, but I don't feel any need to give you a demand until you at least offer my client something. You'd agree we are in the driver's seat, right?"

"Well," Wagner said, shifting his feet, "I don't have any authority at the moment."

Again, Stan smiled. "I guess you better go talk to someone, but I would suggest you do it quickly, because we are itching to get back into the courtroom."

Five minutes later, Wagner met Stan in the hallway down from Jeri's courtroom. He avoided small talk and said to Stan, "I have half a million to offer to you. Perhaps I can get a little more."

Stan expressed his thoughts without rushing. "Ed, we both know that you are bluffing. Let's cut to the chase. This jury thinks your client is scum and is itching to send them a strong message." Stan glared at Wagner and continued, "Let's be serious here. Neither one of us knows what this jury is going to do, but we are much more willing to find out than you are. Your client's net income was two hundred and twenty-eight million dollars last year. They made over twenty million dollars last year by stopping alleged shoplifters. I don't know what the jury is going to do, but there are some large numbers they are going to hear to help with the decision. Mrs.Gebbert isn't greedy. Get us five million dollars and you can go home."

"That doesn't sound unreasonable. I know my client won't go to five million, but let me see where we can get to."

"We don't have much time before the judge calls us to start. Get your guy in here so we can finish this." Stan stood face-to-face with Wagner.

It took two more minutes before Wagner arrived with the suited executive who had been in the courtroom for the entire trial. Wagner introduced him to Stan, who spoke only to the suit. "I'm sure Ed informed you my client will settle for five million dollars."

The suit nodded.

"I think you and your company are in a whole lot of danger if we go back into the courtroom, don't you?" Stan asked.

The suit wavered, then responded, "Who knows what the jury will do? We can't pay you that amount, but I can offer you one and a half million."

Stan enjoyed watching the suit sweat. Bemused, he took his time before saying, "We both know that number is nowhere close to where it should be, so I am going to ignore it. Our client has been more than reasonable since being stopped by your company and you never wanted to stand up and do the right thing. So here is the final demand. My client will accept three million dollars for the punitive damage portion of the case."

Stan stared unflinchingly into the eyes of the suit and continued, "I want you to speak with Ed alone. I'm sure Ed will tell you how reasonable the demand is. But before I walk out, there is one more condition to the settlement. You will have three minutes to let me know if you accept and if not we tell the judge to get the jury back down here."

After telling his adversaries the parameters of the additional condition, Stan left the room to await their decision.

Five minutes later, Stan and Wagner returned to Jeri's chambers with Wagner's face flushed with relief.

"Are we ready to get back to the trial?" Jeri asked.

Wagner held up his hand and said, "Your Honor, I am pleased to report the parties have reached a settlement on all claims."

Stan jumped in. "In addition to the jury verdict already rendered, Wendell's has agreed to pay three million in punitive damages and has also agreed to change its shoplifting policy and forego the use of handcuffs."

"Congratulations, I'm always happy when the parties can reach a resolution. Mr. Wagner anything else you would like to add?"

"One thing Your Honor–sometimes you think you are the best dancer, but then you realize other people know a lot more about dancing than you do." Wagner started to gyrate his hips, but stopped and walked out of the courtroom.

Stan rushed out to go the hospital. Jeri yelled her congratulations and best wishes to Mike as Stan hustled to the door.

Martha Gebbert gathered her coat and slowly walked out of the courtroom with Stacey and Tanner at either side. She waved at Stephanie Regalski, who mouthed, "Congratulations," while flashing a thumbs-up. "I hope you feel vindicated," Stephanie yelled from across the courtroom. "I think tomorrow is going to be a better day for you."

Epilogue

June 24, 2022

THE SUN SHONE brightly along the hills as Mike and Jeri pushed strollers through the park. Dogs ran in the field and kids played on the nearby swings.

"Soon that boy is going to be running all over the jungle gym," Mike remarked while gesturing toward the toddler in Jeri's stroller.

"Just look at how happy Ethan is," Jeri replied, as she pointed to her husband happily pushing a giggling three-year-old on the nearby swing.

"Things certainly change quickly, don't they?" Mike said wistfully.

"I suppose, but I'm sure there is a reason for everything."

They walked further without talking. Jeri stopped and faced Mike. "Are you ever going to make it to Geneva?"

The baby in his stroller cooed. "I don't know," he said. "I love working with my uncle. Right now, it seems like the work we are doing is more important than the work I would have been doing in Geneva. I can't believe I am saying this, but sometimes we make a difference in people's lives. When we were in school, I thought going to Geneva was the most important thing ever. Now it feels different."

"A lot of things aren't like they seemed in law school. Maybe we were too close to things, but I don't think we knew anything or anybody back then."

"I know. Sometimes change is good. At least now my kids have a chance of getting to know their grandfather."

"I hope so."

Mike leaned on his stroller, faced Jeri, and asked, "Do you ever see Jack?"

"No. Not for a long time. I saw him being walked through the courthouse in cuffs sometime after everything happened. He pled out. That made me glad so neither one of us had to testify. He got out of jail after twenty-two months. Would've been a lot sooner except you aren't supposed to hit a judge."

"I heard he got disbarred."

"That's going to happen under those circumstances. Sometimes you're going to lose a case. You have to learn how to deal with the unexpected. He never figured that out, I guess."

Mike nodded and replied, "I thought the three of us were going to be friends forever. We were all going to be such successes. The future seems so much rosier before it gets here."

"You and I have survived. You are doing well with your uncle. I'm still a judge. A little older and perhaps a little wiser, maybe, but we're doing okay."

"Remember what they told us first year in law school—'Look to your left. Look to your right. One of you won't be here at the end.' I guess that one person was Jack."

Jeri nodded in agreement as she and Mike stood watching the kids on the swings. She slowly put her head on Mike's shoulder. He gently reached up and stroked her hair.